David Dodge was born in B[illegible] August 18, 1910. His career as a writer began [illegible] with his wife Elva that he co[illegible] than the ones they were reading [illegible] a rainy family vacation. He drew on his professional experience as a Certified Public Accountant and wrote his first novel, *Death and Taxes*, featuring San Francisco tax expert and reluctant detective James "Whit" Whitney. It was published in 1941 and he won five dollars from Elva. Three more Whitney novels soon followed. Upon his release from active duty by the Navy in 1945, Dodge left San Francisco and set out for Guatemala by car with his wife and daughter, beginning his second career as a travel writer. The Dodge family's misadventures on the road through Mexico are hilariously documented in *How Green Was My Father*. His Latin American experiences also produced a second mystery series featuring expatriate private investigator Al Colby, who first appeared in *The Long Escape*.

In 1950, the Dodge family relocated to the south of France, which provided the background for his most famous novel, *To Catch a Thief*. With its dramatic suspense and exotic setting, *To Catch a Thief* marked a new literary direction for David Dodge and was his greatest career success, due in no small part to the fact that Alfred Hitchcock turned it into the classic 1955 Paramount film starring Cary Grant and Grace Kelly.

For the remainder of his career, Dodge alternated between mystery and travel writing, continuing the saga of the Dodge family as they bumbled and bargained their way around the world. *The Poor Man's Guide to Europe*, a "tipsheet for nickel-nursers and skinflints" appeared in 1953 and was so successful that it was revised and re-issued annually for the next six years. In 1968, David and Elva settled in San Miguel de Allende, Mexico. Declining health—both his own and Elva's—and slumping book sales increasingly curtailed Dodge's writing activity. Elva died on October 17, 1973. David died less than a year later on August 8, 1974.

Written later in his career, *Carambola* is a classic "chase" novel and reflects Dodge's love of travel and rugged individualism. The narrative boomerangs from the posh climes of Cannes to the treacherous smugglers' trails through the Pyrenees. It is a story of self-discovery, sacrifice, and, ultimately, tragic love.

CARAMBOLA

a novel of pursuit

BRUIN CRIMEWORKS

CARAMBOLA
DAVID
DODGE

CARAMBOLA

Designed and edited by Jonathan Eeds

Cover design by Michelle Policicchio

Original cover art provided by the Viet Hung Gallery, 90 Nguyen Hue Street, Ho Chi Minh City, VN

This book was crafted in the USA but is printed globally

ISBN 978-0-9883062-8-8

Published February, 2016
Bruin Books, LLC
Eugene, Oregon, USA

"This is for Kendal"

In David Dodge's thirty-year career as a fiction writer—fourteen novels were published during his lifetime, a fifteenth appeared posthumously in 2006—he created a wide variety of male protagonists. Accountants, private investigators, jewel thieves, journalists, ship captains, government agents, and con men all featured prominently in stories often set in exotic locations around the world. One prominent characteristic of these men is that they are, for the most part, unencumbered by family ties. They have love interests, certainly, and perhaps marriages in the future, but there are hardly any wives in the stories, no parents, and certainly no children. In fact, in all of Dodge's fiction, parent-child relationships are almost non-existent, with a notable exception exemplified by the characters of Francie Stevens and her mother Maude (portrayed memorably by Grace Kelly and Jessie Royce Landis in Alfred Hitchcock's film adaptation) in *To Catch a Thief*. Unique among Dodge's novels is *Carambola*, in which the father-daughter relationship is a primary motivating factor in the protagonist's actions.

Carambola begins on a beach in Cannes when Andy Holland, an itinerant mining engineer, recognizes one of the contestants in a beauty contest even though he has never seen her before. The nearly eighteen-year-old American girl, who introduces herself as Mike (short for Micaela) Magill, is the spitting image of his ex-wife, Marsha, who had left him in the middle of a Peruvian jungle a little more than eighteen years previously. As a novice engineer engaged in his first contract he—as Marsha puts it—chooses a gravel bar over her. Realizing that the girl in the bikini must be his daughter, Holland soon tracks down Marsha herself, setting off a chain of events that lead him into danger and the threat of death, all for the sake of protecting a daughter that he never knew he had.

When *Carambola* was published in 1961, David Dodge's own daughter Kendal was a twenty-year-old student at Wellesley, living away from her parents for the first time. From the time Kendal was five years old, Dodge and his wife, Elva, had been traveling around the world, settling down for extended stays in Guatemala, Peru, and the South of France where Dodge would gather local color for his international thrillers and practical advice for cost-conscious travelers. (*The Poor Man's Guide to Europe* was on the best-seller list for much of the 1950s.) After five years back in the United States, upon Kendal's graduation from high school, David and Elva began traveling again, but this time leaving her behind in college. No doubt they were feeling a bit insecure about their little girl growing up.

Although in his humorous travel books, Dodge wrote freely about his own wife and daughter, he may have avoided the parent-child relationship in his fiction because his own relationship with his parents was complicated and fraught with loss. David's father George Andrew Dodge was born in San Francisco in 1864 and, by the age of twenty-six, had established himself as a professional architect. In 1893, he married Maude Bennett. The couple set up house in the city and George's business grew. Their first child, daughter Kathryn, was born in 1899. In 1903, he entered into partnership with another San Francisco architect named James Walter Dolliver and they worked together under the firm name Dodge & Dolliver.

It was an exciting and frustrating time to be an architect in San Francisco. The earthquake that struck at 5:12 a.m. on April 18, 1906, and the subsequent fires that raged out of control for the next three days and nights, had an unprecedented impact on the architectural history of the city, destroying historic and new buildings alike. In 1903, Dodge & Dolliver had been hired to design a courthouse for the county of San Mateo in Redwood City, located on the San Francisco Peninsula about twenty-five miles south of the city. The courthouse had just been completed and was ready for occupancy when the earthquake hit, demolishing the entire building except for its domed rotunda. Dodge & Dolliver designed and built Saint John's Presbyterian Church in San Francisco's Presidio Heights neighborhood; the first service was held on Easter Sunday, April 15, 1906. Three days later, during the earthquake, the chimney toppled onto the organ and the stained glass windows fell into the street. The Great Earthquake not only knocked down Dodge & Dolliver buildings, it also created opportunities for new work. The Independent Order of Odd Fellows (I.O.O.F.) of San Francisco hired the firm to design a new Odd Fellows Hall #2 to replace the one that had been destroyed by the earthquake and fire. The building stands today at the corner of Seventh and Market Streets in San Francisco.

At the time of the birth of their youngest child David on August 18, 1910, the Dodge family had relocated across San Francisco Bay to Berkeley. George had moved his growing family, which now included three daughters—Frances and Marion having joined older sister Kathryn—into a large house near the center of town. The new home was within a short walk of the Key Route, the streetcar system that provided Berkeley and Oakland commuters with transportation to the San Francisco ferry, making it convenient for George's daily trip to his office in the city. George was forty-five when his son was born and was at the height of his career as the demand for architects and builders soared in the years following the earthquake. In the 1910s, the Dodge household was a full one, with a nanny named Lizy who lived with the family and accompanied them on vacations to the beach at Santa Cruz, and a dog named "Duke White" that provided David with much-appreciated companionship.

Then tragedy altered the course of the family's life.

On July 31, 1919, just weeks before David's ninth birthday, George Dodge was killed in an automobile accident in the tiny San Joaquin County town of French Camp (near Stockton). The car in which George was a passenger collided with a Southern Pacific train. Witnesses described the driver, Robert Oliphant, a steel salesman from San Francisco, as trying to beat the train to the crossing, ignoring its warning whistles. George was pinned beneath the wreckage and died instantly. Oliphant was seriously injured but survived the crash. At the time of his death, George Dodge had stopped active participation in the Dodge & Dolliver firm in order to take a position as manager of the Building Material Exhibit in San Francisco. Obituaries reported that he "worked indefatigably to make the Exhibit a success and his efforts had just begun to show signs of achievement."

Maude Dodge, now the head of the family as a widowed single mother, let Lizy go and relocated her family to a smaller apartment. Kathryn, just twenty years old, was thrust into the role of bread-winner, working as an assistant manager in a building materials business. The Dodge family's time in Berkeley, however, was soon coming to an end.

Maude Ellingwood Bennett Dodge, known as Monnie, was born in San Francisco in 1873 and was, by all accounts, a terrible mother. She was a passionate, self-centered, and bitter woman. All four of the Dodge children had strained relationships with their mother and found ways to get away from her as soon as possible. The girls married young and badly; David dropped out of school as a teenager and later joined the merchant marine. Following her husband's death, Monnie became involved with an itinerant farm worker named Brian, twenty-five years her junior, and uprooted her family to follow the crops around the state with him. Monnie finally shed Brian after he bilked her out of everything she owned. This experience left Monnie even bitterer and more difficult. From then on, she made the rounds among her married daughters, living with each in turn before eventually winding up in a nursing home in Los Angeles, where she died in 1963.

And David? As the youngest, it took him the longest to break free from his mother. While a daughter, as far as Monnie was concerned, could simply be married off, a son needed an independent source of income. So, at the age of fourteen, David dropped out of high school in Los Angeles and went to work. In 1927, when he was just sixteen, he took a job as a messenger at a bank and began night school classes at the American Institute of Banking. Young David obviously had a head for figures. In just a few short years, after starting as a simple messenger, he had moved up in the bank to a bookkeeper position in charge of the bank's commercial books with responsibility for several thousand accounts involving millions of dollars. He was, however, still living with his mother.

In his early twenties, David finally got his chance to get completely away when he quit the bank to join the merchant marine. In 1931, he took a job with the Grace Steamship Company on their South American run, starting out in the engine-room as a wiper. As the ship made trips back and forth to Chile, he progressed from wiper to oiler to fireman, showing the same ability to move quickly up the ranks that had marked his career at the bank. His time as a sailor was relatively brief (he came ashore sometime in late 1932), but he remained fiercely proud of his maritime experiences, frequently drawing upon them in his fiction.

Although he supported Monnie financially her entire life (and dedicated one of his books, *Shear the Black Sheep*, to her and named one of his most memorable characters—the aforementioned Maude Stevens in *To Catch a Thief*—after her), David Dodge hated his mother. When the Dodges returned to the United States for Kendal to attend high school, they settled first in Burlingame, south of San Francisco. After one year, they abruptly sold their house and moved to the east coast, to Princeton, New Jersey. The reason for the sudden move? “Monnie was there,” David explained to Kendal years later. Living anywhere in California was simply too close to his mother.

In *Carambola*, one of Andy Holland’s primary motivations is to save his daughter from what he views as a potentially disastrous marriage. David Dodge grew up witnessing his mother’s ill-considered relationship with a contemptible man, and was living with the burden of the knowledge of his sisters’ unhappy marriages. Now that his nuclear family was fragmenting and his own daughter was gaining maturity and independence, it is not surprising that he was feeling paternally protective and that the theme of fathers motivated by love for their daughters found its way into his novel. Faced with the uncertainty of his daughter’s future, Dodge’s deceptively simple dedication, “This is for Kendal,” is especially poignant.

Randal S. Brandt
Berkeley, California
January 20, 2016
www.david-dodge.com

This is for

KENDAL

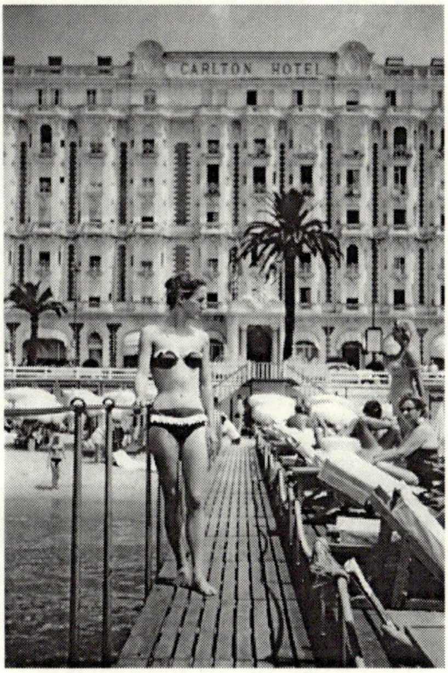

Kendal Dodge, Cannes, circa 1956

CARAMBOLA

I

THE FIRST TIME HOLLAND saw her, which was the first time he suspected her existence, she was giving her name to a hard-working master of ceremonies on a platform raised from the beach in front of Holland's hotel, in Cannes. He had been strolling the Croisette, enjoying a cigar and the sun, not thinking about anything in particular until he looked down from the esplanade above the sand just as the master of ceremonies held a hand microphone to the girl's mouth and jollied her to speak up to the crowd standing around the platform where she was, for the moment, the center of attention. In the sketchy, next-to-nothing, impersonal patches of body covering that were the uniform of her age and sex on any French beach, she would not otherwise have caught his notice.

"A little louder, please. So we can all hear you."

"Mike Magill." She had a low, pleasant voice, unaffected.

"Mike Magill." The master of ceremonies repeated it, consciously wooden-faced, wide-eyed for the crowd's benefit, waiting for the joke to prime itself before he asked, with magnificent innocence, "You *are* a girl, aren't you?"

The laugh broke like surf around the platform. The girl laughed with the crowd.

"Micaela," she said. "Mike is easier."

"Mike it is then, Mike. Tell the pretty people how old you are."

"Seventeen, nearly eighteen."

"Nationality?"

"I'm American."

"Ah, you Americans." The master of ceremonies heaved a sigh of protest into the microphone. "You're never satisfied. First Miss Atlantic City, then Miss America, then Miss Universe, now you expect to conquer France." He waited for his laugh. "Measurements?"

"I don't know. I've never measured."

It brought still another ripple of amusement from the crowd. She had everybody in it with her, and the master of ceremonies too. He made his own judgment of the candidates as they came up to the microphone, deciding on the moment how far he could go with each one, which wisecracks to use, whether to be fatherly or suggestive or ribald for the crowd's benefit. With this one, he was fatherly. He was an old hand at beauty contests.

"All right," he said. "We'll pass the measurements. Step over here, please. Occupation?"

"I'm a student. University of Barcelona."

"Lucky Barcelona. Now turn around, please. That's it."

It went on that way, the man with the microphone using it and the urgings of his banter to move her about on the platform—turn, face the photographers' cameras, face away from them, smile for the judges, laugh with the crowd. Once when she laughed she looked directly, fleetingly up at Holland where he stood with a broken cigar forgotten between his fingers until it burned him, both hands gripped tight on the guardrail of the esplanade, thinking in bewilderment, stunned, incredulous. Seventeen years. Nearly eighteen. It had to be more than a coincidence. It couldn't be only coincidence. There wasn't that much coincidence.

She wasn't particularly pretty; just nice-looking, very brown from the sun, with the good appearance of good teeth, good bones, good health, regular features. At least half a dozen of the other girls had figures more likely to appeal to a judge's eyes. Hers was one he remembered well: the hips too narrow by accepted standards of womanliness, the flanks too lean, shoulders too wide, breasts still to reach fullness, the long colt legs. Her hair was another part of it—black hair, almost blue-black, thick and glossy and straight, he was certain, as straight as a string, if she were to let it grow and hang instead of wearing it as she did, done in a coil at the base of her neck. Indian hair. It couldn't all be coincidence. Not the hair, and the body, and her age, and the trick of throwing her head back when she laughed.

He watched her, intent on the way the near-naked form moved when she left the platform and disappeared into a kind of tent where the other girls waited their turns. Another candidate, a smoothly tanned, consciously enticing girl with hair the color of champagne, came up the steps of the platform to identify herself for the microphone. Two dozen cameras focused on her leopard-skin bikini, and several of the beach boys whistled. She smiled, pirouetting on spike heels. The tone of the M.C.'s wisecracks changed subtly.

No longer held by a concentration of attention, Holland became conscious that he was himself being observed. It was hard to overlook one head turned the wrong way among all the others. His watcher was a tall stilt of a boy, a good three or four inches over six feet, as American as the Star-Spangled Banner. It was hard to miss Americans, even when they wore only swimming trunks in a crowd of other swimming trunks on a Mediterranean beach. It was their size, the cut of their hair, the way they carried themselves; an intangible something else that a fellow countryman could catch. This one looked away when Holland's glance shifted to him, but not before Holland had seen his glower. He was a few years older than the girl and big-boned for all his leanness. Holland registered Boy Friend and thought, I'd better be careful about staring.

To dissimulate his interest he paid equal attention to the girl's successor on the platform and to other candidates, as provocative or more provocative, who followed. The beauty contest was an annual event on the Cannes beach. It followed the spring film festival, when the stars, producers, directors and others whose names made headlines had taken their prizes and their famous faces and figures back to Paris, Rome, Hollywood, London, Tokyo, wherever else they had come from, leaving nothing behind of the yearly rookery but the press photographers and the hopefuls. The photographers always hung on for another day or two, persuading the prettiest of the hopefuls to enter their own prize contest. It was never any trouble to find a variety of contestants among a variety of nationalities. The film festival and its possibilities attracted all kinds, including girls who had staked everything they owned on a wardrobe and the fare to get there, hoping to catch the right eye; a director's eye, a famous producer's eye if they were lucky, any eye rather than none. The winners of the beauty contest got their pictures in the French newspapers wearing a loop of movie film to supplement the sketchiness of their costumes, and usually a number of propositions in a number of languages which they were free to understand or not as they liked. The girl who called herself Mike Magill did not seem the type to win either prize or proposition.

Against Holland's expectations, she came in third in the judging. The champagne-haired girl in leopard skin was first, an almost equally spectacular redhead second. Something about the colt legs in contrast, the unaffectedness that had won her the crowd, influenced the judges against prettier entries. Third place never seemed to be in question, although there was close balloting for first and second. The master of ceremonies won a final laugh and a scattering of applause from the crowd when he made the award: ". . . to the pretty American who has never measured, Mademoiselle—it *is* mademoiselle, is it not, mademoiselle?—Mademoiselle Mike

Magill! Third prize!"

Hands clapped, cameras flashed, girls who had won nothing tried to smile while congratulating the winners. The crowd broke up and began to disperse.

He could not follow the girl, as he had made up his mind to do before the judges were finished. She was taken over by the tall boy who had glowered. He had a car, a scruffy Fiat with a doctored muffler that made a tremendous racket when they drove away. Holland, inconspicuous in the melting crowd, careful to keep his back turned, eavesdropped briefly before they were gone.

The boy was still glowering.

"—bunch of quail-hunters looking over the shooting," he was saying. "You should have seen this one guy drooling at you. His eyes stuck out like doorknobs."

"But that's what it's all for, silly. Grow up. Besides, when did you ever turn your back on a bikini?"

"That's not the point. Sure, I look at the girls. I whistle at them, too. But when I'm old enough to be your father and you catch me licking my lips in public over a bunch of undressed twerps your age—"

"Who are you calling an undressed twerp?"

"You. Third prize."

She laughed, without rancor, with enjoyment. The noisy Fiat roared away up the Croisette. Holland found that his palms were sweating, and wiped them. His finger was blistered where the cigar had burned it.

The hotel in back of the beach had a famous name. It was more popularly known as La Belle Poitrine because of the two swelling towers that capped its otherwise uninspired roof. Its director was an old friend of Holland's who knew everybody and everything of importance to be known on the Côte d'Azur, some things that should not have been known. He raised an eyebrow at Holland's urgent request for information about the girl.

"Third prize? What was the matter with the other two?"

"Nothing was the matter with the other two, except that they don't interest me."

"I have disagreed with the judges myself, from time to time."

"I don't disagree with the judges. I just want the girl's address, if you can give it to me."

"I must trust you to be discreet about where you got it, mon cher. The hotel, you understand—"

"There's nothing to be discreet about! I only want to know where she lives to talk to her." Holland's neck was red and he knew it. "Stop being so bloody French!"

The hotel director shrugged and said no more. He was himself always discreet.

Because La Belle Poitrine sponsored the contest to get its own recognizable profile into the newspaper photos along with the bust measurements of the contestants, it was no trouble for him to turn up the address, a respectable middle-class pension up on the Californie hill. A tactful telephone call, one hotelier to another, developed the further information that Madame, the girl's mother, was in residence with the daughter. They had been at the pension for more than a week, less than two weeks. They were not regular guests. No husband or father appeared in the record.

The last information made Holland's next step easier than it might have been, although he was still unsure what the step should be even after a taxi had put him down at the pension on the hillside. It was a plain, undistinguished place surrounded by gardens; flowers, shrubs, trees and, in Provençal style, a patch of vegetables—rows of leeks, lettuces, radishes, cabbages, carrots. A grapevine grew in espalier against a wall, a pair of rabbits nibbled alfalfa in a hutch, chickens scratched in a run. The miniature farm was out of keeping with the colorful gardens of the villas that surrounded it, but it had their same fine view of the Mediterranean and the flamboyant city on its shore; the long sweep of beach and esplanade and boulevard looped from white casino at one end of the bight of roadstead to pink casino, yacht harbor and the anchoring rock of Old Town at the other. When he had given his card to the concierge Holland waited in the garden, not for the view but because he felt less uncertain of himself in the open than he would have under a roof.

He doubted that the girl would have returned from the beach—there had been no sign or sound of the noisy Fiat—but he did not know that the mother was not also away, or that "mother" meant what it said, or even that, given the fact of a blood relationship, the whole thing—body, hair, trick of laughter, all of it—was not in fact the coincidence that he did not believe, and that he would not within the next few minutes find himself stumbling through an apology to some cold-eyed stranger fully aware that there were men of his age who would stoop to subterfuge to make the acquaintance of a pretty child. Even worse if he were well received as one of them. And then, when his courage had almost gone and he was ready to turn and run before it could happen, the concierge came down the garden path to return his card.

"Madame does not wish to receive you," he said.

"If the hour is inconvenient, I can come back later."

The concierge made a dismissing gesture. His hand was a peasant's, calloused and strong; the hand of a man who tended his own garden, fed his own rabbits and chickens, lived without subtlety and spoke without subtlety. "Madame does not wish to receive you at any time, now or later. Madame wishes you to go quickly away and not return. I am at madame's orders. Please leave." Then, when Holland still stood immobilized by the shock of certain knowledge that it had not been a coincidence after all, that it was no stranger turning him away but the woman who had been his wife, mother of the daughter whose existence he had not even suspected until, that morning—his daughter, the concierge took him by the elbow and began to urge him toward the gate at the foot of the garden.

"Please," Holland said. "Stop. You don't understand."

"I understand that madame does not wish to see you."

The concierge's firm grip kept him off balance, awkwardly propelled, unable even to set his heels in the loose gravel of the path. He had a choice of ignominious physical ejection from the garden or the resistance to it he chose. Without malice, even without anger, unless the impatience he felt for the man's interference at such an important moment in his life could be called anger, he reached with his free hand for a lock on the thumb at his elbow, bent it back upon itself until the concierge groaned, turned into and against the turning thumb and struck sharply with the edge of his palm at the side of the thick peasant neck as the concierge's knees sagged under the pressure he could not resist. He was a big man, heavy with flesh and country muscle. The blow dropped him on all fours in the path, stunning him without finishing him. He rested that way for a moment, shaking his head to clear it, still formidable; more formidable than before because now he would be ready to strike back on his own grounds and within his rights against an interloper. Still without malice, Holland lifted his hand for the calculated rabbit punch that would end it, but held the blow when Marsha's voice said, urgently, "No, Andy!" He looked up to see her coming to him, recognizing her immediately and unmistakably at a distance after all that time. Seventeen years, nearly eighteen, their daughter had said, accurate to the season. It hadn't been a coincidence.

She carried herself as she had always carried herself—erect, straight-bodied, sure-footed. Her face was still young, still attractive in its way of good bones, good teeth, good health, regular features. Her figure was fuller than he remembered it, but the fullness was an improvement. The almost pretty girl had become a handsome woman; not beautiful, but handsome enough for a second look even in France. It was the promise of what was to come that he had seen and recognized in her child; in his child, springing into existence out of nowhere after seventeen, nearly eighteen years.

She said, "You weren't so insistent the last time I told you I didn't want to see you again."

"I didn't know then what I know now. Why wasn't I ever told?"

She did not pretend to misunderstand. Neither did she answer the question. To the concierge, climbing warily to his feet, she said, "You're all right?"

"Yes, madame." The concierge flexed his thumb. "If madame will go back into the house and leave us, she will not be troubled further."

"I've changed my mind. I'll talk to him. Thank you just the same."

The concierge was neither relieved nor disappointed. He nursed his thumb for another moment while he looked Holland over, measuring him against another occasion, then turned away and went back up the path to the house, rubbing his neck. Halfway there he saw a weed in his lettuce rows and stopped to pull it before going on. Weeds in his garden were of more concern to him than his guests' visitors.

"Why wasn't I told?" Holland asked again, when the man had gone.

"It isn't that easy to answer, Andy. I wasn't expecting this. Give me a little time."

Time, he thought, hating her. A little time. Before he could think of an expression for his resentment and protest, she said, "How did you find out?"

"I saw her on the beach. She looks the way you did, with my hair. Her age worked out, too."

"Did you speak to her?"

"I had to make sure first."

"Thank you for that."

"Why?"

"It's part of the explanation you asked for."

He was not a cruel man. But he was angry, and made angrier by her cool acceptance of the situation. If she regretted anything, or recognized that she had done him a wrong, she did not show it. He had to sting her, somehow. He said, "You're sure I'm not being unreasonable? After all, I'm only her father."

Still cool, she said, "Let's sit down. There's a bench over there, by the rabbits."

They sat down. The rabbits nibbled alfalfa noisily, the chickens scratched and talked to themselves in their run. The garden was peaceful, pleasant, breeze-cool in the Mediterranean sun, half the world and a generation away from where they had last sat together.

"Iquitos," she said, after a while. She sat straight-backed, her hands in her lap, looking off at the sea. "Think back to Iquitos, if you can. Do you remember what it was like?"

"I remember," he said.

~§~

Iquitos. Sweaty, steamy, jungle-trapped Iquitos, bush-bound on the upper reaches of the Amazon. The Peruvian montaña had been no place to take a bride. But Holland was himself inexperienced, had never been in jungle before, didn't know what they were getting into. They had been married for only weeks. At first it had been a novel honeymoon, a tropical lark for a young mining engineer with his first important contract, a young wife on her first adventure.

"I'm not asking you to be understanding, at this late date," she said. "But try to remember that I'd never before been more than a few hundred miles from San Francisco in my life. I didn't know a word of the language. There was no one to talk to even if I could have carried on a conversation, the Indian girl you hired for me cheated me with complete contempt for anything I could do about it, that awful, unending, inescapable sticky heat was—is, even now, in my mind—indescribable. Do you remember the place that called itself a guesthouse, where you left me?"

"I didn't leave you," he said, remembering. "You left me."

"Where you left me! Alone, except for an Indian girl who was a cheat, whom I couldn't talk to!"

"Go on."

"The guesthouse. It crawled with vermin all day and hummed with mosquitoes all night. I couldn't eat. I couldn't sleep. I couldn't communicate. There was nothing to do, no place to go, nothing. Not even a road to get away by, just jungle all around; the river on one side, the mountains on the other, the plane from Lima overhead three times a week like a—a mockery. I'd lie awake nights, scratching mosquito bites and listening to the cockroaches scuttling under my bed, hating everything and everybody, as miserable as any woman could ever be—or so I was sure, until I found out that I was pregnant." She sighed at the memory. "I began having morning sickness, along with everything else."

"It was a mistake to take you there. Having taken you there, it was a mistake to leave you alone. I admit both errors. There are women who could have survived them."

"I wasn't that kind of a woman, obviously. You didn't marry me because I was a frontier type. I had a month of insomnia, solitude, homesickness, heat rash, mosquitoes, a dishonest maid and, finally, pregnancy and nausea. I hadn't heard a word from you in weeks—"

"I explained why, as soon as I was able to. I was in jail, a bamboo hut with a corrugated iron roof and a bucket for furniture. Mail privileges didn't go along with it."

"You could have come for me when you got out of jail."

"I explained that, too. It was impossible."

"Why was it impossible? You were released. What was to stop you?"

Lack of communication, he thought. That's what beat us, more than anything else.

It had been just too hard to explain, even to the people who wanted explanation most. He had killed a man, a worker on that first job; caught him pilfering, shot him in greenhorn panic when the man, himself panicked, had ineffectively attacked. The killing had been senseless, unnecessary, legally justifiable, morally indefensible. The man had left a wife and four children, naked brown rickety monsters who lived with their ugly mother in a grass hut on a raft tethered in a backwater of the Alta Ucayali. He had tried to explain to the woman first, then to the other workers, who put down their tools and sat passively on their heels around the sweatbox of the bamboo jail all the time he was in it, waiting; afterward to Marsha, when he had been freed. Not to have completed the contract would have meant a man's life wasted without meaning, thrown utterly away, and the killing had very nearly wrecked the whole operation at its most critical development. He had pulled it out in time, even won himself a bonus, but the cost in sweat, unremitting effort and backbreaking recovery of lost ground had been more than the reward was worth. He hadn't realized until too late that it would cost him Marsha as well.

"I can't add anything to what I wrote you at the time," he said. "Except that I didn't realize then that I was choosing between you and the job. You might have let me know that you were pregnant."

"Would it have made a difference?"

He thought about it. "Probably not, at that stage. But you could still have let me know."

"I didn't want you to know. I wanted you to choose me over your job for myself, not because I was carrying your child. I hated you for abandoning me in that hell-hole of heat and mosquitoes—please, *listen!* You asked me for an explanation. I'm trying to make you see how it was. I hated you for that—

because you didn't come to me, because you wouldn't send for me—"

"You wouldn't have lasted any longer if I had. The project was even more primitive than Iquitos, a bush camp on a gravel bar."

"But we would have been together! Anything was better than being abandoned. I needed you! I needed to know that I was more important to you than a—a gravel bar. When I found out I wasn't, when you chose it instead of me—"

"I didn't, consciously. You know that."

"I didn't know it. I don't believe that I know it now. However it was, that was the end."

"Except for the letter you left me."

"I'm sorry about the letter. I wish I could say more than that."

"I'd have come after you if you had been a little less forceful."

"Poor Andy." She put her hand briefly on his, the lightest of touches. "Poor us. We had a pretty good start, too. I'm sorry it had to end the way it did."

"Then what?"

"Then?" She lifted her good shoulders and let them drop. "I went back to California, got a job, divorced you for desertion, cruelty and the rest, had the baby, met Harry while I was still on the rebound, took up where I had left off."

"Harry is your husband?"

"Yes."

"Still?"

She turned her head to look at him quickly, intently. He noticed for the first time the dark shadows under her eyes and signs of strain in her face, close up, that he had not seen before.

"Why do you ask that?"

"He doesn't seem to be around. I made inquiries before I came here."

"He's in—"

On the instant of answering, a new thought stopped her. Even after so many years he could read her reactions. She needed time to think about something she had not thought about until then. He could not guess what it was, except that it had nothing to do with Iquitos.

"Let me answer the other question first," she said. "You asked why you never heard about Micaela."

"I still want to know."

"I didn't let you know because I didn't want her to know. She thinks Harry is her father."

"That's not fair, to her or to me."

"Isn't it? She loves him. He's the only father she's ever known. She's had the security of belonging to both of us all her life; emotional anchorage. Your existence would have an emotional question mark. I couldn't allow it, for her sake."

"What about mine?"

"Until a few minutes ago you didn't know she existed. You can't have suffered very much."

"And now that I know she exists?"

"I don't know." She answered him thoughtfully, with honesty. "I just don't know. Tell me something about yourself first."

"Why should I?"

"Because I'm not going to say any more until you do."

"What do you want to hear?"

"Biography. Accomplishments. Attachments. Did you ever marry again?"

"No. No attachments to amount to anything. I've moved around too much to settle in anywhere."

"Still mining?"

"Still engineering. There's a difference."

"You look prosperous."

"I am."

"And heavily sunburned."

"I've been in Saudi Arabia. Two years."

"What are you doing here?"

"My contract ran out. I wanted a change from the desert. This is a good place to make connections."

"Cannes? Not the kind of connections you need, surely."

He explained. There were more contacts to be made on the Côte d'Azur than the obvious ones. Wealth was always there; wealth that poured out of Middle Eastern oil wells, African diamond pipes, Ruhr coalpits, South American copper mines. The yachts, the casinos, other occupations of the playground ate up money in quantities, and for every spender there had to be a producer, if not millions of them. He was one of the producers. A good mining engineer could write his own contract in Cannes, if he didn't care where he worked and was in no hurry to get there. The South of France was a pleasant place not to be in a hurry.

Under her probing questions he gave her a rough sketch of his life. He felt vaguely on the defensive before he could turn the probe aside.

"I still don't understand why you never married again," she said. "You say you're well off, you're at an age to be attractive to most women, younger women in particular, and you're better-looking than you used to be when I thought you were good-looking. Why?"

"Most women wouldn't like the life. You're not unique."

"I know that. But other women haven't had a chance to find out what I did." She added unsubtly, "Or have they?"

"Not for any length of time. I told you, I've had no attachments to amount to anything. You've got the biography you asked for. Let's go back. What and when are you going to tell my daughter about her father?"

She thought about it for a while, looking off at the sea.

"Micaela will be eighteen in a few weeks," she said at last, obliquely. "It's a kind of maturity. I'd want her to go on believing in Harry until her birthday, at least."

"Will you tell her then?"

"Perhaps."

"There's nothing to stop me from telling her if you don't."

"She wouldn't believe it if I denied it. You're a stranger. I'm her mother."

"I could prove that you were married to me when she was conceived."

"Perhaps. You couldn't prove that I hadn't been unfaithful to you, though. With Harry."

His feeling of frustration grew. He said, "Blood tests."

"They only prove who couldn't have been a father, not who was. No, Andy. The only way she'll ever know the truth, and believe it, is when I tell her. If I tell her."

"All right." He gave in, baffled. "What are you bargaining for? Let's get it out in the open."

"Yes," she agreed. "Let's."

She left him. Still baffled, uncertain again, he watched her go up the path, straight-backed, sure-footed. She had always carried herself superbly, like a soldier on parade. Martia, he had thought of her when he first knew her. The name went with the good shoulders, the lean flanks, the fine long legs. Micaela had the same soldierly carriage. No one could possibly mistake mother and daughter, seeing them together. There was nothing of him about her except the hair.

He ran his hand irritably over his skull and the short hair that would grow long, black and straight as a string if he let it. Indian hair. He wondered if she had been as confident about blood tests as she seemed, and, again, why the issue was being made.

She came back with a photograph. It was a glossy press shot, a good one, of a man, hatless and carrying a briefcase, standing on the embarkation steps of a plane. He wore glasses that sharply magnified his eyes. He was balding, slight, stoop-shouldered, past his best years and unremarkable.

"Your husband?"

"My husband. I hope you'll be meeting each other soon. I want you to be able to recognize him."

He returned the photograph without comment.

"I never regretted Harry for a moment," she said steadily. "You were my fling with youth, romance and the tropic moon. He was kindness, devotion, security. I needed those things, after Iquitos. I was badly scarred. When I was carrying Micaela and couldn't keep a job any longer, Harry paid the bills, told me not to worry, held my hand during the labor pains. He asked me to marry him before he even knew if the baby was legitimate or illegitimate. I couldn't say no to that."

"Why are you telling me?"

"I want you to understand how much I owe him, so you'll be able to understand the rest."

"Get on with the bargaining."

"Harry was—is—a manufacturers' agent and importer. In Spain. We've lived in Barcelona for five, nearly six years. Do you know Spain?

"Fairly well. Barcelona quite well."

"Then you could know what it's like to do business there. You have to have a contact, and you have to pay for it. It's impossible to accomplish anything any other way. For five years Harry had a working partnership with a man in the customs service who saw to it that his applications for import licenses went to the head of the list instead of the foot. It made the difference between a going business and none."

She had sat down and was looking off at the sea again, her fingers tight on the photograph she held in her lap. She sat as erect and straight-backed as ever, but there was something in her voice, an insecurity, that belied her appearance.

She said, "I won't try to describe the man because I couldn't be fair to him. I'll only say that I found him unattractive—vain, overbearing, arrogant. I—we had to be pleasant to him because it was important to Harry. I entertained him in our home, introduced him to friends, made the usual gestures one does. He thought, or chose to believe, that the gestures meant more than they did." She shuddered, violently and uncontrollably, without any change of expression. "He made suggestions. When I didn't respond to them, he raped me; in my own home, on my own bed. Harry arrived in time to hear him trying to persuade me not to tell of the rape because if I did my husband would be out of business. Harry shot him. He cursed me, not Harry, while he died."

A truss of alfalfa had dropped to the ground from the rabbit hutch. She stooped from the bench to pick it up and feed it to the rabbits through the wire mesh of the cage. Watching her, still with the impact of the confession in his mind but unable not to observe the grace of her body and movements, he thought he could understand the urge to ravish, as well as the cursing. It would be the need to humble her, and the consciousness of failure even after the violation.

He waited for her to go on.

She said, unexpectedly, "Do you think of yourself as a murderer?"

"When I think of it at all, yes."

"Because you killed a man in a moment of panic?"

"Panic isn't an excuse for killing, any more than anger. Anyone who keeps a gun within reach does so because he expects to use it. I've never carried a weapon since it happened to me."

"You don't need a weapon. I saw what you did to Gaston with your hands. Harry isn't like you. He's small and frail and nearsighted. He kept the gun in the house to protect us, his family, and he used it against a—a criminal. You can't call it murder. Nobody in fairness could call it murder."

He said carefully, "I haven't called it anything. I don't even know why you told me about it. Does it have something to do with Micaela?"

"You'll see the connection in a minute." Her voice changed and was cool once more, remote. "Does the name Vilasar mean anything to you?"

"No."

"The Marqués de Vilasar. Carlos. He drives racing cars, when he doesn't crash them. He made headlines when he went out of control into the crowd at Le Mans."

He shook his head.

She persisted.

"The Mille Miglia. The Monte Carlo Rally. The Cross Continental. He turned over in the Cross Continental and spent five weeks in the hospital."

"I don't follow auto races."

"He's more than just a driver of fast cars. You've got to understand Carlos, too. His family is important in Madrid and Barcelona. He has influence where influence is valuable, and he's been helpful to us. When it—happened—we called him right away, to know what to do. Micaela was at the University—ordinarily we'd see her only on weekends and holidays—and we agreed among us to keep it from her as best we could; if we could, as much as we could. She knows how Harry does business with the customs-house, and it's cruel enough for a child of her age to have to accept the fact of bribery as a normal part of living without learning that her father has shot his business associate for raping her mother."

"By 'father,' you mean your husband."

"I'm not choosing words to spare your feelings, Andy. It's the way she thinks of him. It's the way she'll go on thinking of him if anything happens to him, or if she finds out the truth."

"How did you keep it from her? How long do you expect to be able to keep it from her?"

"I don't know how long I'll be able to keep it from her. Long enough, I hope. Nobody outside of Spain ever sees a Spanish newspaper. In the beginning it was simple enough. We got her out of school and out of Barcelona the same day. Harry wouldn't run—or, I should say, he and Carlos agreed that it wouldn't help him to run because even if he got out of Spain he could be extradited, and it would weigh against him to be tried as a fugitive. Carlos brought us, Micaela and me, here on his father's yacht while Harry went into hiding in Barcelona. Micaela knows he's in trouble with the police, because we couldn't just bundle her up like a baby and rush her off to France without some kind of an explanation, but she thinks it's because of the bribery; one of the minor complications of corruption, something to be settled by reaching the right person with the right amount of money. In the meantime Harry's staying out of sight, as she believes, until Carlos pulls the right strings to straighten out the difficulty. Of course Harry's money and business and everything else we own in Spain have been impounded, and the police want me as a witness. We can't go back to Barcelona until it *is* straightened out, and Carlos is our lifeline—between Micaela and her father, between Harry and me, everything that holds us together and can bring us back together. Do you begin to see?"

"Dimly. Carlos is in love with her?"

"He wants to marry her. He says he loves her. I think he believes it himself, but he says the same thing with the same sincerity about a new racing car. She's American, imported, exotic, something other Spaniards don't have; a Cadillac. Next year he'll want a Ferrari. And I—I've cheated him, Andy! I've cheated them both! I've promised her to him—in exchange for Harry!"

She had never cried easily, he remembered. The straight back and the soldierly carriage went with a stiff upper lip. She was not going to cry now, either; not while she was bargaining. But her eyes were overbright.

He said, "Tell me more about Carlos."

"He's what Spain would call an hidalgo; somebody, the son of somebody; well bred, well raised, well educated. He has money, a title, charm, good looks, everything, except—" She made a small gesture of helplessness. "It's hard to say, to someone who doesn't know him. I'm not even sure that I know him well enough myself to say it in justice. But behind the charm, the good looks, the exquisite manners he's—to me—the same man as the—as Harry's business partner. I don't mean necessarily in terms of physical violence, but in the smash-and-grab mentality; I want it, therefore it's right that I should have it. Coming here from Barcelona, on the yacht, he told me that he wanted to marry Micaela, and quite baldly what it could mean to Harry. He explained that he wasn't himself sufficiently important to accomplish much in Harry's favor, but that his papa and the uncles—his words—could do a great deal if they chose to. The one thing that would make it necessary for them to choose, make it essential for them to use their influence on Harry's side, would be if he were one of them, one of the clan. Carlos' father-in-law, for example."

"He sounds straightforward enough."

"Oh, he is; as straightforward as smash-and-grab. And there's something about unashamed egocentricity that appeals to girls like Micaela. She's half in love with him already. I can push her toward him, or I can push her away. He knows that. When he asked me for her, I explained that American mothers don't arrange their daughters' marriages; that when a girl comes of age she's supposed to choose for herself. But I told him that when she was old enough to speak for herself, within a few weeks, I would encourage her to say yes; that I—I was on his side—so he would tell his family, you see, and they would have to do something. And now he's going to ask her, the minute she's eighteen, and before that time I've got to tell her—I've got to try to explain not why she *shouldn't* marry him but what it might mean to her father, the man she thinks of as her father, if—if—"

He said, "What's the worst that could happen to your husband if the shooting were to be judged on its merits?"

She still held tightly to the photograph in her lap, as if she drew something from it she needed to go on. She said, "Do you know what a garrote is?"

"I thought garrotes went out with the Inquisition."

"Some of that survives in Spain, too. You're tied to a chair with a thick post at your back and a hood over your head so that no one can see your face when the executioner puts the collar around your throat and tightens the screw. It doesn't break your neck like a rope, or lop off your head like a guillotine, or convert you to ashes like burning at the stake. It only strangles you. Your body remains nicely in one piece for resurrection on Judgment Day, and if you scream a little before they shut off your breath—"

"Stop it," he said. "You don't have to put it around your own throat. Would they give him that for shooting a rapist?"

"I don't know." Her fingers were very tight on the photograph. "I don't *know*. That's why it's so horrible. I don't even know that what I've done was necessary. Sometimes I can convince myself that it isn't possible, even in Spain; that a trial would be no more than a formality. But then sometimes I wake up early in the morning, just at dawn, the time they put people to death, and I can see Harry sitting with his back to the post, the hood coming down over his face—"

"Stop it."

"I can't stop it, Andy! I can't stop my thoughts! I can't stop remembering why he did it! Even if they were only to send him to prison, he wouldn't survive it long. He's nearly sixty, and not strong. I can't deny him Carlos' help, I can't sell his daughter—your daughter!—to buy it. I've got nowhere to turn!" In naked, unashamed appeal she faced him, begging. "Say you'll help us! You've got to help us! It had to be more than a coincidence that you came along when we needed you most!"

He looked at the rabbits in their cage, moodily, thinking, *It's never a coincidence.* The whole orderly unwinding of the universe would have been disrupted if he had not been there to recognize his daughter on the beach that morning.

He said, "Assuming that you're unjust in your analysis of Carlos' character, as you say you may be, what do you have against him aside from the fact that he's an egocentric playboy with a weakness for fast cars? You say that she's half in love with him and that he loves her, or thinks he does. Are you so sure that you know better than both of them?"

"How much does a seventeen-year-old child know about love and marriage and having babies? And what kind of love does a man have for a girl he's ready to leave a widow any weekend for the sport of risking his life—not for the need for it, not even to win prizes, only for the sport?"

He said nothing. She said, "I don't want my daughter, our daughter, to marry the wrong man before she's old enough to recognize the right one."

"As you did, and survived it."

"As I did, and survived it with scars. But it was my own free choice to make. I wasn't sold into it, or forced into it, or trapped into it by circumstance. All I ask for Micaela is the same chance, to make her own mistakes."

He watched the rabbits for another while, thinking.

"Does your husband know the situation, aside from his own part in it?"

"No."

"Why not?"

"I don't know how to get in touch with him without going back to Barcelona. That would be worse than useless. They'd watch me until I led them to him."

"What do you think I might do?"

"Go there for me. You speak the language, you know your way around, and nobody will have any reason to suspect a connection between you and Harry. I'll tell you how to find him. Explain things to him, then get him out of Spain—buy him out, bribe him out, smuggle him out, anything, only get him out of the country before Carlos Vilasar can give him to your daughter on a silver platter for a wedding present—and I'll tell her what you want her to know: who you are, what you've done and why. You couldn't begin better with her than by having her gratitude."

"She might not think she had reason to be grateful to me."

"I'll make her see it. When I'm free to talk to her as a mother—Andy, please! Don't punish me!" She put out her hand to him. "Say you'll go!"

"Gratitude isn't much for what you ask." He ignored the hand. She let it drop again in her lap.

"I forgot. We were bargaining, weren't we? What more do you want? Money?"

He thought, rephrasing it, *What more do I want that I haven't got, that you could give me?* and answered himself, uselessly, "What I might have wanted, once, is the seventeen years."

"I can't give those back to you. You know that."

"I know. You asked what I wanted."

"What do you want that you can have?"

"I'm not sure. I'm not sure that you have anything to give me, except more information."

"Ask me."

"For one thing, if she's as devoted as you say she is to the man she believes to be her father, and knows he's in trouble with the Spanish police, even for a small thing like bribery of a public official, what was she doing down on the beach this morning exchanging happy wisecracks with the master of ceremonies of a beauty contest?"

"The beauty contest wasn't her idea. Larry entered her in it as a joke, and she took him up on it. As for what you call happy wisecracks—"

"Wait a minute. Larry?"

"An American boy she met on the beach. He has a car. He takes her around when Carlos isn't here. That's all."

"All right. Go on."

"The wisecracks, as you call them, were happy because she's happy. Carlos gave her his word that she could stop worrying about her father. She had been worrying, she isn't any more. It's that simple."

"What is Carlos' plan of action?"

"He hasn't formed one yet. It's not the kind of thing that goes by a timetable. He's in Barcelona now, talking with his family. He'll know more when he gets back."

"When will that be?"

"I'm not sure. Sometime before her birthday. He's planning a party for her aboard the yacht."

"A father should know the date on which his daughter was born, shouldn't he?"

She flushed. "Next month. The fourth."

"I'd like to meet her before then. I won't give anything away prematurely."

"I'll arrange it."

"And Carlos."

"Why him?"

"You're asking me to step in between two people I don't know who think they're in love. You'd hardly be justified in trusting me to do the job if I didn't want to form my own judgment of the need for it."

"You don't trust my judgment, then."

Choosing his words, he said, "You don't trust it yourself, and I have no reason to," neither expecting nor receiving a reply. She stood up, bending to smooth her skirt against the long line of her legs, so that he could not see her face for a moment.

Later, walking together down the path through the neat rows of leeks and lettuces and cabbages, it was implicit between them that he would make no independent overtures to his daughter before she arranged the meeting. But he said, "If you need money, you could reasonably expect me to help support her while your husband is unable to."

"We don't need money. Harry isn't poor."

"You said his money was impounded."

"Only what was in Spain. We're all right here."

"Then why pick the kind of pension that raises its own vegetables and keeps its own hens? Do you like this kind of thing?"

She didn't answer until they were at the bottom of the garden, ready to part. Then she said, thoughtfully, "No, I don't, really. But I didn't come here for that—" her gesture took in the bright parasol-flowered beach of the playground below them, looped between casino and casino "—and I wouldn't feel right down there with all those pretty people, having fun, until—until—not now. It would be a kind of betrayal. Of Harry, of Micaela, of myself, of everything. Do you understand what I'm trying to say?"

"You were always able to express yourself, when I knew you. Why did you pick that name, of all names?"

There was that still between them, that when either spoke of their daughter their minds met immediately. She said, "You remember it?"

"The Indian maid who cheated. I shouldn't have thought you'd want a reminder of Iquitos."

"It wasn't a reminder of Iquitos. It was a reminder of a honeymoon."

It was his turn to have nothing to say. She finished, "We had a good beginning. I wanted to remember that part, not the end of it. Thank you for coming back when we needed you, Andy."

He said something then, something awkward, he could not afterward remember what it was, and walked away, down the hill toward the pretty city by the blue sea, back to the pretty people with uncomplicated lives who only needed him for the money he knew how to get out of the ground for them, thinking, reassuring himself, I haven't gone back. I haven't promised anything. I haven't signed a contract. I'm a free agent, as free as I ever was . . . But he did not feel free.

II

THE SOLID FACT of a seventeen-year-old daughter in unexpected but indisputable existence preoccupied his mind for the rest of the day, into the night and for another day and night without bringing him to any conclusion except that he wasn't sleeping well. On the morning following the second restless night he had a long and frustrating talk on La Belle Poitrine's beach with a Turk, a man not yet as enormously wealthy as he would be, who held an option on most of the bauxite deposits in Anatolia.

The Turk was more than willing to discuss bauxite development but kept having his attention distracted by the hopefuls; still on hand, still prettily hoping. None of them, or at most very few, could afford to stay on at the playground at La Belle Poitrine's high rates, but the strip of sand in front of the hotel was open to all and a pretty girl could be seen and noticed there by hotel guests who, like the Turk, were not blind to pretty girls. They were the geisha of the Mediterranean; all young, all enticingly on display. Some were accompanied by mothers or women who served them as mothers; sharp-eyed duennas who sat in respectable black under parasols on the esplanade and knitted, on the lookout against unprofitable entanglements. Not every attractive girl on the beach was one of the geisha, but those who were could not be mistaken. Several of them, as entrancing as naiads in the inconsequentialities of their universal beachwear, sunned themselves on the sand near Holland and the Turk. One was the girl with champagne hair who had won the beauty contest.

The Turk could not keep his eyes from the leopard-skin bikini. He was embarrassed by his inability to concentrate on bauxite, and because his thoughts wandered from the subject Holland's own thoughts wandered in their own way. He had an engineer's visual memory, trained to reconstruct blueprints and scale drawings. In any of the geisha he could make himself see Micaela again, laughing on the platform; the trick of her head when she laughed, the sun-glint on her hair that was his hair, the trim drum-major's body. He felt impatience with himself for having agreed, even tacitly, not to speak to her before Marsha permitted it. It was a concession that need not continue.

He suspended negotiations with the Turk, found his robe and went up to the hotel to telephone. A message from Marsha was waiting for him, and when he called her back the concession was no longer necessary. The Vilasar boat was back in the yacht harbor. Marsha had invited Carlos to be her guest, with Micaela, at a gala dinner at the pink casino. The opportuneity would be a good one for an old friend of the family to appear unexpectedly and be introduced.

"You could have done business with Harry somewhere," she said. "I'll make it vague."

"Don't make it so vague that I'll have to explain how I recognized her more or less in the nude because she looked like you. She may have noticed me staring at her on the beach."

The telephone line hummed vacantly for a moment before Marsha said coolly, "Is your memory really that good?"

"It's the kind of memory I have."

"How do you visualize me? In color, or black and white."

"I wasn't trying to be suggestive."

"You managed it."

"I'm sorry. I don't often take you out of the files for intimate private viewings, if it's an embarrassment to you." Then, because she irritated him by taking offense at what was a wholly innocent remark, he added, "On the other hand, when I do take you out you'd be startled by the vividness with which—" and heard the chill click of the receiver cutting him off. It had been only gentlemanly to give her cause for taking offense, even if after the fact. But he was still irritated.

Because he was also nervous about the meeting to come, he armored himself with brandy as the time approached for it; a couple of drinks with the Turk, who was Moslem but not too Moslem for cognac; another with the director of the hotel.

The director's name was Barot. He was a strapping handsome man in his middle years who, because of his position, the nature of the clientele to which La Belle Poitrine catered and the added handicap of a pronounced personal charm, had to be perpetually on watch for man-traps. Much expert talent had been wasted on him by the geisha and others. It was a matter of principle with him never to hire a feminine employee who was not fifty years old and ugly, never to enter a feminine guest's room unaccompanied by another member of his staff, always to keep a barricade of photos of his pretty wife and three good-looking children on his desk. Another protection was to distract poaching huntresses by putting up a decoy whenever possible.

Over the brandy he said, "But you can't go to a gala alone!"

"Why can't I?" Holland asked. He had dressed for the evening in white jacket and cummerbund, and only one event in Cannes still demanded evening clothes in midweek. A less acute man than Barot would have known that his guest was dining at the pink casino. Only Barot could have known that he was without a dinner companion.

"The only unaccompanied men there will be the gigolos," he said. "You'll be misunderstood."

"I don't mind being misunderstood."

"By the guests, it means nothing, I agree. By the personnel, that is something else. Believe me, mon cher. As a suspected interloper on the tips you will find collar buttons in your soup and soup in your collar. Let me provide you with a companion."

"No, thanks."

"A nice girl. Agreeable company, nothing more. She will cost you only the price of her dinner. Give me an hour."

"No, thanks."

"Thirty minutes, then. She will have to dress, for a gala."

"I'll take my chances with the personnel," Holland said. "Thanks just the same."

He passed time on the bar terrace with a fourth brandy after Barot was called away. It was still too early for the gala to have got fully in swing, and he wanted to give the cognac a chance to net the butterflies that danced in his stomach.

What did a father say when presented to his daughter for the first time? Kitchy-koo, probably, or the equivalent, in most cases. But you couldn't very well use baby talk with a poised seventeen-year-old, nearly eighteen, who won prizes in international beauty contests. You said, Enchanted, or, How do you do, or, So much pleasure, or, It pleases me very much, or, You are like the moon—some other formula according to the language she spoke. Her formula would be English, of course—How do you do; or would it, after five years of Spain? It was damnable to know so little about her. Whatever happened he must be calm, cool and quite casual about it all, not in his awkwardness knocking over a glass of brandy and water as he almost did then, surprised, struggling to rise from the chair that had him trapped on the bar terrace, mentally cursing the chair, the brandy, Barot and the circumstances that left him no audible expression but the conventional one, Enchanted, in this case, on being introduced to the spectacular girl whom he had seen before only in leopard skin, now wearing under an inconsequential wrap an evening gown that was as effective a display and offer of her golden-skinned prettiness, in its way, as the bikini had been in its own. She could not have been more than nineteen or twenty.

"Allow me to present you, mon cher." Barot tactfully left it to Holland to supply the girl with whatever name he chose, or none. "Mademoiselle Solière."

"Odile, if you prefer, m'sieur," the girl said politely. "M'sieur Barot says that you have asked for my company at the gala. I am delighted to accept."

"I am delighted that you are free to accept," Holland said. "I'll remember you for this, Barot. Never fear."

"It is always a pleasure to be of service to a friend." Barot bowed, hiding a grin. "Amuse yourselves."

~§~

The gala was well under way when they arrived. The pink casino's business was gambling; one of the attractions supported by that business was the twice-weekly gala dinner, to which gamblers and non-gamblers alike came. The food and wines were always superb, handsome white-toothed gigolos were available to ladies whose escorts did not choose to dance, the music was good. Above all, the galas were a display; of style, of beauty, of jewelry, of new liaisons. Holland was aware that he and the girl on his arm had been noted for one of them as soon as they came in. The geisha were known and recognized wherever they went, as their companions were inevitably a subject for speculation. But it amused him rather than otherwise until he saw Marsha and her party across the well of the dance floor.

There were four at the table: Marsha, Micaela, a dark compact man who had to be Vilasar, and Larry, of the noisy Fiat and the glower. Larry was sitting in a position to have seen their entrance, and had seen it, from the stiff carefulness with which he was not looking their way. Micaela watched them, frankly curious, with the arrested attention of someone who has just heard a whisper to distract her from a table conversation.

Kitchy-koo, Holland thought blackly. Meet your father. He gapes at girls in bathing suits and takes nineteen-year-olds to gambling casinos.

He followed Odile and the maître d'hôtel to a table, maneuvering to have his own chair placed where he could see and be seen from across the floor. Retreat was out of the question.

Odile was superb. Aware as he was that it was her function to please and charm him, he was pleased and charmed nevertheless. She had a pink, pretty mouth, softly mobile, ready with a smile, laughter, a pout of sympathy, whatever his mood and conversation called for. Her eyelashes were too long and dark to be real, but her eyes were faithfully attentive when he talked. He found himself talking a great deal, about himself. When he stopped talking about himself she always asked the right questions to prime him again. When he tried to turn the conversation over to her, she was more skillful at conversation-turning than he, and a better listener. When he asked her to dance, she danced extremely well, with just the right hint of invitation in the movements of her body to say that she enjoyed being in his arms; *his* arms. Her whole attentive golden being was a flattery to his ego, and his ego, for all that he was preoccupied with another interest, was gratified. Taking her back to their table after the dance he told himself, wryly, Careful. Foolishness begins at forty.

"Why are you frowning, m'sieur?" She was as perceptive as ever of his mood.

"Am I? I'm sorry. I was trying to remember where I had seen someone before."

"The dark-haired girl at the table across the floor?"

"How did you guess?"

"There was no other reason for us to dance with my back to her so often. She was in the Miss Festival contest. She won third prize."

"You're acute. But it's the other woman I was really wondering about. Could they be mother and daughter, do you think?"

"They look very much alike," Odile said, and added, in subtle flattery of his taste, "They are both very attractive."

"You're very attractive yourself, Odile."

"Thank you."

"By that I mean to say, if I were at all vulnerable I would not be looking beyond my own table. This is something else. Will you excuse me for a minute?"

"Certainly. But are you so certain that you are not vulnerable, m'sieur?"

He was already on his way and did not stop to answer the challenge. It rankled him, a banderilla standing between his shoulders, as he went to meet his daughter. Distracted by it, he did not have time to be nervous.

A break in the music permitted him to go quickly to the other table, before the orchestra could pick up a new theme and the gigolos new partners. The right note of doubt was in his voice when he bent over her chair to say, "Marsha?"; the right surprise in her response: "Andy! Andy Holland!" After that it went easily enough; the how-long-has-it-been, what-are-you-doing-here exchange, introductions, at last Micaela's hand in his own, her smile and greeting as if she really were interested in his well-being, not just using a formula like Enchanted or one of the others but warmly, engagingly, because he was a friend of her mother's and therefore her own friend for all his unmistakable geisha companion and what Larry had said about quail-hunters. He used the opportunity to say that he had seen her in the competition and been struck by her resemblance to her mother, and while it did not explain Odile away it helped counteract Larry. He saw it in the look that passed between them, hers saying: You see? No friend of my mother's could be one of those. If it was ingenuousness, it was the kind of ingenuousness that made him feel a swell of pride in her, and in himself for having fathered her.

The two men were on their feet for the introduction; Larry towering in a dinner jacket that was adequately cut to hide his big wrists but didn't seem to, somehow; Carlos impeccable, a bit too impeccable in the carefully tailored Spanish way, in white tie and tails. Both had good handshakes, both said the right things on meeting an old friend of Micaela's mother. Later, when he had gone back to his table and the dinner had been served, it was natural enough for Marsha to send a waiter with an invitation for coffee and a liqueur. Everything went smoothly, much too smoothly. It made him think of a well-rehearsed play. He still did not know Marsha's purpose in staging it.

As soon as he could take her into the conversational privacy of the dance floor, he asked, "Why Larry? What's he got to do with it?"

"He makes a fourth."

"I would have made a fourth."

"With your pretty friend?"

"She was an accident. I didn't plan on bringing her.'"

"I'm just as glad you did."

"Why?"

"She makes a sixth."

"Stop being cryptic. I want to know what this is all for."

"You will soon enough. Dance, now."

She would not say more.

He was neither an expert dancer nor a particularly poor one, only indifferent. He did not care much for the doubtful pleasure of taking a woman in his arms, usually a comparative stranger and often in his experience someone with whom he did not have even a common fluency of language, to pace off patterns to music while carrying on a less than spontaneous conversation. But he had forgotten how flawless Marsha was on the dance floor. She had always been skillful enough to make him feel skillful himself, and pleased with what he was sure was their appearance together. That night she wore wine red, a long off-the-shoulder gown that flattered her good figure and carriage. She danced in the same way that she walked and stood; erect, straight-backed, sure-footed, without misstep, responsive to the domination of his lead and command but without surrender of herself. It hadn't always been like that. His memory, stimulated by the false intimacy of their embrace, was more than purely visual. He remembered other embraces, long forgotten, on and off the dance floor, and phrases of music, and odors.

He said, "It's the same perfume."

"What?"

"You're wearing the same perfume that you used to. In my honor?"

"I've never changed it."

"Never?"

"I've experimented, of course. I always went back."

"Does it still come packaged in—" he thought briefly—"green and white, with diagonal stripes?"

"You do have a photographic memory, don't you?"

They were both uncomfortable for a moment, remembering.

"I'll send you a bottle, if I may. For old times."

"My husband might not approve."

"Damn your husband!"

He said it with more heat than he had intended. She answered seriously, "Don't lose sight of the object of the bargain." Then, for the first time in all his experience, she unexpectedly failed to follow his lead, so that he stumbled and, recovering, found that she had made them reverse their positions, that he was facing as she had been facing a moment before.

"Now!" she directed him. "Look at your daughter."

Micaela was dancing with Larry. One of them had just said something comical, because both were laughing; she with her face pushed into his shirt front to smother the laugh, he grinning, his shoulders hunched to bring himself down nearer to her size, his arm awkward around her by reason of his height. His bow tie was crooked. They looked out of place, almost disrespectful among the less conspicuously mismatched dancers around them. None of the gigolos was ever permitted to top six feet, except by the use of built-up heels for an exceptional guest.

"They seem to be having a good enough time," he said. "What else do you want me to see?"

"Carlos. Over there."

Carlos and Odile were perfectly paired; in the dance, on the floor, as girl and man. Marsha's phrase about pretty people came immediately to his mind. They were pretty; each of them, and together. Carlos was talking, Odile attentive, the eyelashes and the expressive pink mouth reflecting her absorption in what he was saying. There was just the right hint of invitation in the movement of her body to say that she liked being in his arms; *his* arms.

"Two pretty people," Holland said. "What more?"

"Oh, much more." Marsha's voice was as sterile of feeling as the polite prose of a society column. "The Marqués de Vilasar, seen with friend in the fashionable whirl at Cannes. The Marqués, well-known racing enthusiast and yachtsman, will shortly announce his forthcoming marriage to Miss Micaela Magill, daughter of Mr. and Mrs. Harry Magill of Barcelona. A rumor that the father of the young marquesa-to-be is wanted by the Spanish police for killing the violator of her mother's virtue—"

"Stop it," he said.

"I'll stop it when you promise to go to Spain. Andy, please!" Her voice was charged with emotion now.

"Can't you see, she isn't for him? She's meant for Larry—"

"I thought Larry was only a kid she picked up on the beach."

"Another Larry, not him necessarily, someone like him, a

boy of her own kind when she's ready, but not now, and not Carlos, ever. Don't make me beg you! Promise!"

"You still haven't given me a chance to judge for myself. You're blackmailing me, before I've even talked to her."

"But can't you *see*—"

"No. I told you. I'll make my own judgments."

She did not argue further. Moments later she said, "Take me back to my table, please."

"Answer a couple of questions first. Has Carlos developed a plan of action?"

"It's mostly one of inaction, for Harry. He's to stay where he is, out of sight, while the family arranges things. When the time comes he'll give himself up and go before friendly judges. If they sentence him at all it will be to a short jail term, and his money and business will be released before he goes to prison."

"Suppose young Vilasar, believing that he is acceptable as a son-in-law, is allowed to go ahead with the plan. What is to prevent you and your husband from simply double-crossing him afterward, by persuading Micaela that she isn't for him after all? You've cheated him once. Why not twice?"

"You don't think much of my moral sense, do you?"

"It isn't important what I think. The question is a practical one."

"Practically, I suppose it could be done. But as long as Harry remains in Spain, the Vilasar influence could be used against him as well as on his side. He might even be brought up for retrial. I don't know enough about the legal system."

"So that in any event a double-cross would be highly dangerous?"

"Yes."

"And it comes down to a matter of getting him out of Spain before Micaela is persuaded to say no."

"Yes."

"Even though he may have to fight extradition afterward."

"He has to be found before they can extradite him. I know that much. If he abandons what we have in Spain, simply lets go of everything and disappears, the Spanish government isn't going to search the world for him. We won't stay in France long enough to be found here."

"You're sure he can be persuaded to give up everything like that—a business, money, whatever property you own?"

"He won't have to be persuaded, once he knows the facts. He's Micaela's—"

She caught herself before she said the word. He took her back to her table.

Afterward he danced again with Odile and at long last with Micaela, taking her awkwardly into the embrace he tried not to make a hug, his first welcome to her, an embrace that was all wrong for dancing, so that she gave him a quick searching look and said, smiling, "Mr. *Hol*-land!" in exaggerated protest, turning it into a joke. Then she was making casual conversation to cover his embarrassment, and he thought, startled, Oh, God, she's putting me at my ease, old roué that I am. He could not keep back a grunt of laughter at the situation, and felt easier.

"What's funny?" She was eager to be friendly.

"Nothing, really. I was just thinking that the last time I danced with your mother you hadn't even been thought of as a possibility. May I call you Micaela?"

"If you want to. Most people call me Mike. My father does."

"Then I will. How is he, these days?"

"Didn't my mother tell you?"

"She told me where he is, and why. We didn't discuss his health."

"I don't really know much about his health except that it's usually good when he keeps his feet dry and remembers to take his vitamins. We—if my mother explained—"

"She did."

"Well, we can't very well get in touch with him when we don't know where he is, and of course he doesn't know where we are, either. I'd give anything to be able to send him a message."

"Anything?"

"Within reason, naturally." She looked up at him innocently, her eyes mischievous. "Were you about to offer a suggestion?"

"Only that Carlos appears to be the type of young man who would be more than willing to take a message to your father if you looked at him the way you just looked at me."

"Oh, he would," she said, and laughed. "But we've all agreed that it would be far too risky for Dad if any of his friends try to find him before—before—well, until the police aren't watching them. Carlos hopes that will be soon. Did Mother tell you?"

"Yes. That would be the message you would want to send?"

"That's the most important part of it, so he'll be patient and not do anything reckless before it's safe for him. He's as cross as a bear when he's cooped up. Then I'd want him to know where we are, and that we're well, and to remind him to keep his feet dry, and to take his vitamins, although I don't suppose he has any vitamins to take, poor dear. He had to run like a rabbit. Do you know Spain, Mr. Holland?"

"I've been there a number of times."

"I love it. I love the people, the way they think, the silly old traditions, their ridiculous ideas of honor, the absolutely inane way they do things—everything about them, when they don't make me furious. Can you understand that?"

"I've felt the same way about the Arabs, from time to time. There's a lot of Arab blood in Spain."

From that point their conversation drifted aimlessly and stopped. She danced as Marsha danced, not quite so flawlessly but very well, with the same feeling for rhythm and her partner's lead. Her enjoyment of the dance was as ingenuous and uncomplicated as the rest of her. She would have sung to the music except that she did not know the words, and could only hum along with "La Vie en Rose."

Hungry for any kind of communion, he said, "Do you get as much pleasure out of dancing with just anyone, or am I better than I think I am?"

She laughed again, lifting her head in the trick he knew, Marsha of twenty years gone but for the hair and eyes and the deep brown of the Indian skin that was his other contribution to her genes.

"I'd be happy dancing with a broom tonight, Mr. Holland. Please don't let it hurt your feelings, but when you've been promised a father for your birthday after not being quite sure if you were going to *have* a father—" An impulsive pressure of her fingers on his hand holding hers finished it. "But you really are a very good dancer, and quite handsome."

"Thank you. You must be very grateful to Carlos."

"Oh, we are. He's been a wonderful friend."

"I meant you, not you and your mother. Would he be a little more than just a friend?"

She looked up at him again, smiled, and said nothing.

It was sweetly done. The smile said, We're friends; I accept you. The silence said, nicely, Let's change the subject.

He changed the subject, still without having come any closer to judgment.

A small thing, almost an irrelevancy, brought him to it. An intermission in the dance music and a dull performance by an adagio team gave Larry and Carlos an opportunity to discover mutual interest in racing cars. Larry held a job with Pan American Airways, in Nice: ". . . selling tickets, meeting VIP's, pitching pub rel, opening the mail," as he explained it. "Utility outfielder, kind of. On my own time, they let me use the shop at the field. I've got an old Jaguar out there now, reboring it."

"Did you ever drive a Pegaso?" Carlos asked. He spoke good, academic, only faintly accented English, even better French with Odile and the waiters.

"They're out of my class," Larry said. "The kind I drive, I put together myself."

"We should have a race sometime."

Larry shook his head.

"You're out of my class, too. I saw you drive the Mille Miglia."

"I did not do so well there."

"You finished."

"But that is nothing, to finish. Anyone can finish, unless he has bad luck."

Larry shrugged, noncommittal. Carlos said, "You do not agree?"

"I'd put it the other way. Sometimes you need good luck to finish."

"As in my case?"

"I didn't say it."

"But you think it. Please, my friend." Carlos was earnest although unoffended. "Do not fence with me. When you criticize my driving, you give me the right to ask why."

"I'll tell you why, then. You were shot with luck to finish the Mille Miglia. You take too many chances."

There was a short uncomfortable silence. Marsha broke it with a question.

"Is it possible to drive a racing car without taking chances?"

"Certainly," Larry said.

"Of course not," Carlos answered in the same moment, and made a gesture of courtesy toward his opponent. "But you first. Please."

"Well," Larry said, frowning. "Let's define it, first. There's always an element of calculated risk in everything. When you send a plane up you accept a calculated risk that it may come down in a place and a way that you aren't prepared for. Not much of a risk with today's planes, but some. You accept the same kind of a risk every time you get into an elevator, or a taxi, or a bathtub. There's a mathematical possibility that you'll get hurt. It's not taking a chance, or at least not taking an avoidable chance. It's part of living. You've got no choice. A chance—"

"But taking a chance is part of living!" Carlos said urgently. "Excuse me. That is the whole point. The uncalculated risks are the adventures. They stir the blood. In motor racing they come when you see a chance to pass on a curve. You do not know what lies around the curve, but the opportunity is open to you. If you go through, you are ahead. If you fail to go through—"

"You're dead," Larry said. "Or, what's worse, two other guys are dead and you've still got all four wheels down. That's what I mean. Three people died in the last Mille Miglia from that kind of driving. You were lucky."

"But then you would never win a race!"

"Fangio won plenty of races in his time."

"Fangio was a businessman, not a sportsman! He drove for the prize money."

"What do you drive for?"

"The race! The excitement! The chances!"

Larry shook his head. "That's not racing. That's Russian roulette."

Carlos struck his forehead in a dramatic gesture of Latin despair, turning his look of appeal to the others at the table. Micaela said thoughtfully, "It seems to me—" and was checked by his further gesture, made without thought, in good temper, infinitely dismissing, an hidalgo's gesture that said, How a matter for men to discuss seems to you is of no consequence, woman. Be quiet.

"Mr. Holland," he invited. "I appeal to you for moral support. Have you never taken a blind curve?"

Only he at the table was unaware of what had happened. Micaela sat with her mouth still half open for the next word. Larry had turned dark red and was frowning at his knuckles. Odile flicked one quick glance at Micaela before the compass needle of her attention swung back to its delicate balance between Holland and the marqués. Marsha watched Holland, waiting for his reaction.

She's sure of it already, he thought, reluctant even then to concede that she had beaten him in the bargaining. She hadn't, really. If you could bring yourself to think as the Moslems did, the cue line and his answer to it had been ordained since the beginning of time. It was not her victory but Kismet's. No random happenings, no coincidences, no choices to be made, only the working out of a pattern. Insha'Allah.

He said, in answer to the question, "I'm on Larry's side. I have to be. I'm an engineer. The only acceptable risks in my trade are the inescapable ones."

Carlos shrugged, gracefully conceding. The argument was ended.

"Speaking nonprofessionally," Holland went on, "since you ask me, I'm inalterably opposed to blind curves and the people who take them. I wouldn't have given you a chance to finish the Mille Miglia, or begin it. I'd have ruled you out of the race before you started."

Carlos continued to smile, but with his facial muscles only. His training was too strong for him not to smile. When the resumption of dance music by the orchestra at that moment gave him a chance to escape from the embarrassment of the pillory he was in, he stood up, bowing formally to Odile.

"You will give me the pleasure, mademoiselle."

It was a statement, not a request. The hidalgo had spoken, the woman had only to obey. Obeying, Odile had half risen to her feet before Holland, unhurried, said, "I'm afraid not."

It froze Carlos, his hand extended to the chair. Holland let it hang there for a long painful moment, until Carlos' smile became a grimace he held to by an effort of will, waiting for an explanation.

Not to have given him one would have been as flatly insulting as a slap in the face, and the same kind of provocation. Holland considered the utility of it. But he could not punish Carlos physically for being an hidalgo even if the hidalgo were willing to descend to personal combat, an improbability, and the alternative would be something medieval like sabers, or racing cars coming together head on. He's too well armored even to know why I'm doing it to him, he thought, and, relenting, said, "I have to ask Mademoiselle Solière to leave with me now. Perhaps you may have the pleasure on another occasion."

Carlos inclined his head as if his neck hurt. His eyes were black with rage and humiliation. Micaela, springing to her feet, said, "You always have me to dance with even when you don't want to, Carlitos mio," and took his hand to lead him to the refuge of the dance floor.

It bothered Holland unreasonably; not so much that she had shown sympathy for Carlos' embarrassment—he would have been disappointed in her if she had not—but because she had taken sides against him, her defender. He began to feel the first bite of personal antipathy to the Marqués de Vilasar, and felt better about the decision that had been thrust upon him.

Marsha, forcing the advantage she had won, said, "Must you leave so soon? I thought we might all go to the gambling rooms together."

"I'm afraid I'm not much of a gambler, either. I want to get an early start for Barcelona in the morning—if Pan American will cooperate."

"I can get you out in the afternoon," Larry said. He still studied his knuckles, uncomfortable because of his part in Carlos' humbling. "There's no morning plane."

"The afternoon will do. Where and how will I find your

husband, Marsha?"

Martia Victoria, he thought, watching her take from her bag the calling card she had ready and waiting for him, sure of his capitulation. On it she had written three words: *Candelas—Barrio Chino.*

"What does it mean?"

"Candelas is a man's name, a nickname. You'll have to ask for him in the Barrio. He won't be easy to find. When you do find him, you can trust him. He'll know where Harry is."

"What message shall I deliver?"

"Tell Harry his wife and daughter send him all their love, and whatever else he wants to know about us."

Her statement of affection disturbed him even more unreasonably than Micaela's siding with Carlos had done. He said an abrupt good night and took Odile away, not waiting to make his excuses to Micaela.

Odile surprised him, for a moment, by asking to be taken back to La Belle Poitrine. It had not occurred to him that she could afford to live at the hotel, and it was no part of the geisha function to be forward about the continuation of an evening into a night without encouragement. But the concierge handed her her own key when he gave Holland his, and they said good night and good-by in the elevator.

"Thank you for an enjoyable evening, m'sieur." She gave him her hand. It was slim, delicate and golden like the rest of her, with pink nails that matched her pretty pink mouth. "Bon voyage. Perhaps we will have another evening together when you return."

"I hope so."

"Tell me, please. Why were you so cruel to the marqués?"

"I didn't approve of his attitude."

"Toward the girl?"

"Toward women in general. He would have been the same with you, with his hostess, with anyone. I found it insulting."

"But then you are not invulnerable after all, are you?" She smiled, mocking him. He liked Odile a great deal when she was not working at her trade. He said, "I didn't mean it to sound like a boast when I said it. I'm sorry if it did."

"I didn't think you were boasting."

"But you didn't think I knew what I was talking about."

"Not even that." The elevator had stopped at her floor, where its white-gloved operator was holding the door for her. "I only asked how you could be so certain of your invulnerability, since you do not permit it to be tested."

"But I do permit it to be tested. You were a test, tonight. If you will let me say so—"

"I am sure you would be gallant if I did." She smiled again, a nice smile, to show that she liked him, too, for all that his vulnerability was not for her. "I could even believe it, if the evening had been your own idea instead of M'sieur Barot's."

"I'm sorry. I didn't think you knew that."

"It is not hard for a woman to tell when she is being pursued and when she is not. Good night, m'sieur. Thank you again."

She left him feeling mildly rebuked, as if he were a schoolboy who had not lived up to the promise of a first date. He had to remind himself that he was old enough to be her father before he could turn his mind to the business of packing a bag for Barcelona.

III

HIS CHIEF RECOLLECTION of Barcelona was the Ramblas. That great thoroughfare, more than a street, more than an avenue, more even than a central artery tying the old seaport of the Greeks and Phoenicians to the twentieth century at Plaza de Cataluña, had not changed in the ten years since he had seen it. He doubted that the Ramblas would change much in fifty years, and hoped never to see the change begin. Not enough boulevards with the same personality survived in Europe for the pleasure of pedestrians. What would have been on the Champs-Élysées a hurtle of wheeled traffic was, on the Ramblas, a tree-shaded paseo closed even to bicycles. Those, and cars, carts, taxis, trucks and trolley cars, fought, honked and squeezed their way up and down the paseo's equivalent of flanking walkways, in violation of all sensible principles of traffic control, and nobody, not even the sweating police who worked to keep the bottlenecks open and the traffic moving, would have had it changed. The paseo belonged to foot-goers, including those who got down from truck or traffic stand on Sundays to take their girls or their wives or their families for a stroll under the plane trees. There was always plenty to do and see on the paseo, any day; bright-colored birds screaming from the racked cages of their peddlers, bright flowers glowing in masses from ranked stalls, racks of cheap bright magazines and comic books and souvenir postcards inviting purchase in rows of newspaper kiosks. On the Ramblas you could have your shoes shined, buy a lottery ticket, get into a fight over the relative skills of Dominguín and Ordoñez in the bull ring, arrange an assignation, dictate a letter, conspire against the government or pass in a few steps to the Barrio Chino, once the worst waterfront slum on the Mediterranean, and for a stranger the most hostile. That much at least had changed. The slum was no longer particularly hostile, except to police, guardias civiles and other authorities it did not recognize.

He walked the Ramblas for an hour or more, savoring its flavor again after the years. Early evening had come before he was free to stroll, and the gas lamps under the plane trees would be coming on before long. He always took pleasure in seeing the lamplighter work his way up one side of the paseo and down the other, the soft glow of the lamps after he had passed. At night on the Ramblas it was easy to forget the hard blaze of neon in the plaza where the paseo ended, and the Barrio Chino itself was always comfortably dark. The Barrio was a good place to look for a man with the odd nickname of Candelas, as it was to find an enemy he came to as a friend.

He was a reasonable man. He knew it to be true because he could recognize his own unreasonableness. It was simply not just to resent the existence of someone whom he had never known, who had done him no wrong, who had in fact carried his burden of parenthood for nearly twenty years in raising a child as attractive in every way as Micaela while holding the loyalty of a woman like Marsha. Yet he was resentful as well as jealous—that Magill had taken his place, that Micaela loved him, that Marsha was loyal to him; above all, with supreme unreasonableness, that it had been Magill who had avenged her rape. He did not know how he would have behaved in her husband's place, except that he would not have used a gun. He was through with guns forever. But hand in hand with the fundamental right to physical possession of the body of a wife went the other right, to defend against and revenge the violation of the first, and by exercising it Magill had closed a door between Holland and the mother of his daughter, a door of which he was jealous logically and resentful illogically. If the Barcelona venture had not been forced upon him, he knew he would have had to come anyway. He had to find and know Magill to be able to hate him with reason.

The lamplighter had finished his rounds. Holland left the paseo for the shadows of the Barrio Chino as he would have gone into the darknesses of a mine, prepared to feel his way as necessary.

The hunt took a good part of the night. Knowing as little as he did about the man he hunted, he could do no better than ask questions in bars and bodegas. His appearance and accent, both obviously foreign, were a help. Because he was neither Spanish nor Catalan he would be neither a spy for the police nor running from them, therefore safe to listen to even if not to talk to. Nobody who heard the name admitted knowledge of the man. Some did recognize it, he was certain. Several people asked him what it was he wanted of whatever-he-called-himself, the man he was looking for. He answered always, "Nothing that will do him harm," but got no further response or information or help from anyone until, well after midnight, he entered a small bodega, barely big enough for the three oversized wine barrels it contained and a single table, around which half a dozen fishermen sat playing cards.

They were drinking red wine from a painted glass porrón, passing it around the table from hand to hand as regularly as the cards fell, each man reaching to his left to take the needle-nosed pitcher, tip a thin stream of wine from it into his mouth while he looked at his cards, swallow once or twice as the stream poured, tip it up again and pass the porrón to his right without a glance to spare for it or a drop of wine spilled before the porrón was empty and ready for refill by the player nearest the barrels. They were all fairly drunk, including the man who ran the place. When Holland asked his question and made his answer to the question that followed, the wine-seller gave a boozy laugh.

"Candlelight you will find in the Calle de las Hermanitas," he said. "How much of it depends on how far your money gets you with the Little Sisters. They sell other things more cheaply than information."

The card game stopped immediately. So did the round of the porrón, and conversation at the table. The card players sat silent, still looking at their cards.

"Many thanks," Holland said. "Can I pay for a porrón?"

"You pay for nothing here," the wine-seller answered uncordially. "You heard nothing, you bought nothing. All I said was the name of a street."

"A glass, then."

"Nothing. Good night."

"Good night."

Holland left.

He heard the argument start the moment he reached the street. They would all be down on the wine-seller as a blabbermouth to begin with, but Catalan argumentativeness would take half of them over to his side before long, and then the argument would continue until they had all drunk themselves stupid and forgotten what they were fighting about. Not a wasted drop would be spilled from the porrón during the whole thing.

Finding the Calle de las Hermanitas was no more than a matter of asking the way, the last time from a woman in the shadows whom he did not recognize for what she was until she suggested another street as a better one to patronize.

"The Little Sisters are not for you, guapo," she told him. She was gypsy, with the Andaluz accent and too much cheap perfume to hide her gypsy dislike for soap and water. "They'll give you a package to carry home with you. Come with me and I'll take care of you like a real sister." She sniggered softly, squeezing his arm.

"Tell me where to find the street."

"What do you care which street you visit, guapo? Mine is prettier."

"I'm looking for Candelas."

Her voice changed. "What's your business with that one?"

"Nothing that will do him harm."

"That's not enough to know. Who are you?"

He stepped aside, to walk around her, but she moved the block of her unwashed, over-scented body in front of him. In the narrow street he could not pass her without shoving her out of the way.

"You'll never find him without opening up first," she promised. "Don't waste your time or mine. Who sent you? What do you call yourself?"

"He doesn't know me. I'm a friend of a friend."

"What have you got that says so?"

The card that Marsha had given him had only the three words written on it in her handwriting, but it was his only letter of introduction. He gave it to the woman. She strutted with a whore's vulgarity of hip movement into the dim light of a street lamp to look at it, then shrugged, stepped out of the light again and whistled sharply up at the dim windows of the building above her. In a moment a basket on a cord came down out of the darkness, stopping with a jerk at waist level. She put the card in it and tugged the cord. The basket went on back up into the dark.

"This is Las Hermanitas, guapo," she said. "Candelas will see you or not as he decides for himself. You pay me now for having whistled, and because my feet hurt."

He gave her a hundred pesetas, then another fifty when she wheedled for more with a gypsy's inevitable greed. She went back to the doorway where they had first spoken, and left it with a man a few minutes later. He did not see her again.

He lit a cigar and waited. Somewhere nearby a radio or

phonograph was grinding out the strongly accented beat of a sardana. The streetlight burned dimly over his head. He moved out of its glow into shadow, seeking inconspicuousness, then, reconsidering, back under the light again. If he was under observation it would be best to be seen for what he was. His clothes and haircut were unmistakable.

Ten minutes went by, a quarter of an hour. In that interval he was solicited three times by women of the Barrio. The fourth passer-by was a man who turned the corner with his head down, did not look up, but, passing, said, "Come along, then," and took him by the arm. The grip was strong, compelling. He dropped the cigar and chopped instinctively at the wrist of the gripping hand, feeling its muscular thickness and strength. The blow did not free him. He was already swinging a more effective chop into the angle of the man's neck before he thought to divert it. It went into the bone of a rocklike shoulder, hurting his hand. He cursed, partly at the hurt, partly because he had been taken unprepared, but let the man bear him along out of light into shadow and the covering darkness of an entryway.

"Candelas," the man said from somewhere below Holland's chin. He was short, very broad, and spoke in a gently musical voice that did not go with his powerful grip and bearlike shape. "You and that puro stand out like a boil on the nose. If you come again, smoke cigarettes and look the whores over before you turn them down or they'll have the cops on you for loitering. Through here and up the stairs."

The building they went into was old and stank of mold. They climbed four flights of shadowy stairs with the squat man leading the way, his wide body almost blocking the narrow stairway. On the last landing he unlocked a door with a key, standing aside to let Holland go ahead of him before he followed, closing and relocking the door again behind them.

In the poor light of the single dingy room that was his bolting hole, Harry Magill looked as his photograph had shown him: slight, balding, past his best years, unremarkable. His face was stubbled with a growth of gray beard, and he was not wearing the strong glasses. In one hand he held Marsha's card, in the other an old-fashioned reading lens. Without his glasses he clearly had trouble seeing Holland except as a shape of indeterminate size and outline. Squinting through the fog of his nearsightedness he said crossly, "Where did you get this? Who are you?"

"Your wife gave it to me. My name is Andy Holland."

"Holland?" Magill searched his memory, puzzled at first but only briefly. He said again, in a different voice, "Oh. Holland."

Good, he thought with sour pleasure. We're off to a fair start. He resents me as much as I do him.

He said, "Your wife and my daughter send you their love. They're both well. Your wife wants you to get out of Spain. I came here to see that you do."

"Your daughter!" Magill had heard nothing after the shocking statement of claim. "*Your* daughter!"

"My daughter. Micaela."

"You have the shameful taste to say that to me, who raised her, the child you deserted before she was even born?"

"I didn't desert her. I didn't know she existed until a few days ago."

"You deserted her mother when her mother was carrying her."

"I did nothing of the kind. Her mother left me."

"And you were too big a fool and coward to go bring her back when she needed you!"

Candelas said warningly, "Fight in castellano if you have to fight, and keep your voices down. You're making too much noise in the wrong language for a respectable neighborhood."

"Shut up, animal," Magill snapped. He used the familiar imperative, master to barking dog, and paid no other attention.

"Whatever I was, I'm still her father," Holland said. "Biologically, by law and in responsibility to her. That's why I'm here. You've got to leave the country, now, before Carlos Vilasar has a chance to clear you with the police."

"If there's any chance that he can clear me, I'd certainly be stupid to come out of the hole before he does."

"You're going to."

Magill bristled.

Antagonism and obstinacy radiated from him, an aura of stubborn resistance to the ultimatum even before he knew why it was being delivered. Holland explained, making no effort to be persuasive. He wanted no part of Harry Magill as an ally in a common cause. He would have preferred to take him from Spain by force and against his will, if that were possible. Magill, listening, squinted to see his visitor's face, narrowing his eyes and leaning forward to peer, trying to penetrate behind the words into the mind of the man who spoke them. Afterward he sat for a long while toying with the reading lens, studying Marsha's card through it, then the skin on the back of his hand and the fabric of his shirtsleeve. The shirt needed laundering.

"Lost my glasses getting away," he said irrelevantly. "The police would have netted me running in blind circles if it hadn't been for the animal here, and Carlos. He's been a good friend."

Holland made no comment.

"You get a little panicky the first time you kill a man," Magill said. "Or do you know about that? How is Mike?"

"Still in the dark about you. She's looking forward to having you back again soon. If Carlos manages to arrange it in time for her birthday, she'll be as grateful to him as you are. Between the two of you he's practically elected into the family."

"With Marsha dissenting."

"And me."

"I wish I could see what you look like," Magill said irritably. "I'd like to know the kind of man who has the arrogance to talk as you do, as if you were a police-court judge imposing conditions on the family life of people you don't even know."

"Your wife begged me to come here. It was her idea in the beginning, not mine. I had to be persuaded."

"And what won you over?"

"A wave of the hand. A simple gesture your good friend Carlos made to my daughter, that said 'Shut up' in the same contemptuous way you just said 'Shut up' to your animal. Do you still want to talk about arrogance?"

Magill squinted through his fog for another moment, his head thrust forward, before he said, "Candelas."

"Patrón?" The squat man was cutting vegetables into a pot that boiled on a charcoal brazier. He looked up from his work without interrupting it.

"How long have we been locked up together in this room?"

"Twenty-two days."

"But we still speak?"

"We exchange filthinesses from time to time." Candelas grinned at Holland. His teeth were strong and yellow, like horse teeth. "And we keep our voices down. We are always caballeros."

"I can't see a yard in front of me," Magill said. "I can't look out the window. I can't move around the room without bumping into things. Until he got me the reading glass I couldn't even pass the time with a newspaper. I could only sit and wait, and grumble, and snarl, not even knowing how long it was going to last. Don't confuse ill-temper and frustration with something they are not."

"Let's go back to Carlos," Holland said. "If you don't get out of here yourself, he'll get you out. There's still another alternative you might want to consider."

"What's that?"

"I could turn you in to the police."

"I recognize the threat, but not the reason for it. What would it accomplish?"

"Good friend Carlos wouldn't have his birthday present to give to my daughter. There'd be no need for her to be grateful."

"Whether the police take me or not, he'd still be able to pull strings. As a matter of fact I'd make an even better present if he gave me back to her out of prison." As an afterthought, Magill added, "Unless you arranged to have me garroted first, of course."

"I don't particularly care about what happens to you, one way or the other. I'm thinking about my daughter."

Magill sneered.

"Your daughter," he mocked. "You keep saying it as if it meant something. Your daughter! All you did was start a process of growth, like so much yeast in a pan of dough. Do you seriously believe that that single contribution could give you the right to make Marsha and me reject Carlos for Mike, if we thought he was right for her?"

It was too close to what he had thought, even wished for. He said nothing. Magill finished contemptuously, "You use the word 'father' carelessly. You should learn more what it means first. Candelas."

"Patrón?"

"Come over here. We have to talk together, the three of us."

The squat man wiped the knife he had been using, then his broad hands, on his shirt front, and pushed the knife into a sheath he wore down the back of his neck.

Magill said to Holland, "I don't know how much thought you've given to how it will have to be done, but he can be useful. You'd better know his qualifications before we go any further. Tell him why you are called what you are called, animal."

Candelas laughed, a musical laugh of gentle descending chords in the bass register.

"It's been so long, I forget what saint the priest sprinkled me for," he said. "You understand, it takes every man a certain number of years to find himself, what he is good for. Years ago, before I worked for others, I was an importer on my own; at one time or another from Andorra over the mule paths, by boat from France, from Portugal across the Guadiara with coffee wrapped in oiled silk under my shirt so it wouldn't get wet when I swam the river. When I was just beginning there was a profit to be made in the spread between the price of a candela in Andorra and the price of same candela, untaxed, in Lerida or Zaragoza—"

Holland, puzzled, said, "Candle?" It was the primary meaning of the word.

"Spark plug," Magill said.

"—but nobody had made anything out of the racket because they were so heavy, my God, how they were heavy! It took a mule to carry a payload, but mules are too stupid to run in the right direction when a customs guard snaps a cap at them, if they run at all. What the business needed was somebody as strong as a mule and enough smarter to know which way to run. I was young and strong in those days; strong as a bull and twice as dumb. I used to take a hundred kilos on my back—figure it, in the Pyrenees at two thousand meters of altitude, an all-night carry for a lousy thousand pesetas, and brag about my business, my monopoly. The Candelas King. I wore no man's collar but my own, me. Until one day another importer, a baron he was but a pal for all of that, said, 'Well, Candelas, you with the strong back and the weak head, carry a hundred kilos of my stuff for me, I'll pay you two thousand pesetas.' He handled lámparas for the radio, the same size and package as my candelas but weighing two or three for one and selling for four times as much. Even I could see that the boss I was working for was too stupid to be in business, so I got another boss. But the name stuck."

He laughed again, in real enjoyment.

Holland said, "What did you import from France by boat?"

"Cognac, perfume, coffee, silk, champagne."

"What went in the other direction?"

"A little absinthe, cigarettes. Anything to make a load."

"Political refugees?"

"I shipped a passenger now and then."

"Do you still have the connections to ship another passenger?"

"How hot?"

"This one." Holland nodded at Magill.

Candelas scowled. "He isn't going to France. He's safer here."

"No," Magill said.

"Patrón, the cops will take you the minute you poke your nose out of the Barrio! They know you're here! You couldn't have got any farther. Stay under cover at least for another few weeks, until the heat has had a chance to cool—"

"No," Magill said again. "There are things you don't understand."

"One thing I do understand, by God!" Candelas turned on Holland, a bear ready to lunge. "Until you came here, he was all right! If I thought—"

"Shut up," Magill said. "You haven't been asked to think. How long before you can get me aboard a boat for France?"

Candelas glared at Holland for another minute before he answered, sullen under the rebuke.

"I don't know. It's been a long time. I'd have to work the waterfront for a night or two, find out who is still around. It will cost money."

"How much?" Holland asked.

"I don't know. Twenty, thirty thousand pesetas."

"I haven't got it," Magill said. "I haven't got a thousand. I haven't got a thing but the clothes I'm wearing."

Holland took an envelope from his pocket.

"There's fifty thousand pesetas. If you need more, you can have more."

"From whom?" Magill did not touch the envelope. "You?"

"That's not your problem. It's money. You need it."

"If it's yours, I'll take it as a loan. Not otherwise."

"You'll take it any way I want to give it to you," Holland said furiously. "Who in hell do you think you are, to lay down rules in your position?" But he recognized his own anger as a danger at least as great as Magill's obstinacy, and mastered it. "Call it a loan if you like. What about glasses? You'll need to see where you're going."

"Marsha has my prescription."

"I'll wire her to send it along."

"You'd do better to go to France yourself, have the glasses made and bring them back with you. A pair and a spare."

"Why?"

"Because every oculist in Barcelona will have been put on the watch for a man with my vision, and it's too risky to assume that the post office and customs-house won't have been alerted as well if they come in by mail. The only other way would be for Marsha to bring them herself, and the police would be hovering over her like hawks all the time she was here. I don't want her here."

"What you want and what you don't want isn't controlling," Holland said. "But I agree that I'd better go after them. We'll need the time anyway, for your man to find a boat."

In that way, bristling, they worked out a plan and a schedule. In the planning they forgot the cause for their hostility if not the hostility itself, so that at the end, when Magill said without thought, "Give Mike a kiss from her father when you see her," Holland was able to recognize the slip for what it was, a slip rather than a challenge, and did not take it up.

"What shall I tell Marsha?" he asked instead.

"That I'm in good shape, or will be as soon as I can see again. Tell her—tell her—" Magill made a vague gesture. "What is there to tell her? She must know what it will mean. There'll be no coming back afterward, so if there's anything that ought to be arranged for first—Mike's school credit, maybe. I don't know. Talk to her about it. She knows more about those things than I do. I wouldn't want Mike to lose credit for a year of college."

It stayed with Holland, and disturbed him, while he was feeling his way back down the dark, mold-smelling stairs to the street. Damn Magill, he thought, that he had been able to give consideration to something like that, an unimportant year at an unimportant university, while preparing to risk his liberty and very possibly more than liberty so that a child—not even his own, a stepchild—should not be allowed to become a woman too soon. Damn Magill and the advantage he held, that he had been her father for seventeen stolen years. Damn Magill for having had them, and damn Marsha for stealing them, damn everyone and everything else that stood between him and his daughter; *his* daughter, for all Magill's sneer about yeast in a pan of dough. When it came to a showdown—

"Hold up here," Candelas said.

He had insisted on going with Holland to the street. There was no need for it, no friendliness in the gesture. Now he blocked the way in the dark entryway with his thick body, and spoke softly in his melodious voice.

"What do you call yourself?"

"Dutchman," Holland said. It was easier than spelling out an unfamiliar name that would be corrupted anyway.

"Then listen to me, Dutchman. I don't have your language, as you have mine, so I don't know what it was that you and the patrón were scrapping about when you first came. But I know you were scrapping, and I think you are not someone he would miss a lot if you were run over by a herd of bulls. Tell me the truth, because I am too stupid to swallow a lie."

"We have no reason to like each other."

"But you have a common interest?"

"Yes."

"In saving his neck?"

"Not even in saving his neck. In seeing that he leaves Spain, with or without neck."

"Why, in simple words? I am also too stupid for subtleties."

"Ask him."

"He'll tell me to shut up and mind my own business. That's why I'm asking you."

Holland shrugged.

"Very well." The pitch of the gently musical voice deepened. "Since you won't talk, listen further. Except for a lie he once told without the need to lie, I would be doing ten years on the rock pile now. I owe him those years. You know the game of billiards?"

"I have played it."

"Then you will understand a carambola. From whatever part of the table the ball is stroked, regardless of the force of the stroke and the skill or aim or intention of its player, it is going to lose something of either its motion or its direction when it touches another ball. Both are affected by the contact, not just one. This flea bin we're in, it isn't much, but if you hadn't come butting into the game the patrón could have sat it out here until he cooled off. Now you say he has to go to France, he says he has to go to France, all right; we start ducking cops again, on your say-so. But so you will know, Dutchman. If they take him, if he goes to the garrote for that pig he killed, you get yours too." Candelas thrust his big square hands into the dim light from the entryway. "From these. Anything else that happens to him happens to you the same way. It doesn't even have to be your fault. Do you understand me?"

“I understand you.”

“Go with God, then.” Candelas stepped aside, unblocking the way.

“Until soon,” Holland said.

IV

HIS PLANE TOUCHED DOWN at Nice around one-thirty. Half an hour later, having cleared through nominal customs and immigration controls, he had claimed his bag and was waiting his turn for a taxi outside the airport terminal when a scuffed, unmistakably noisy Fiat boomed out of one of the parking lots to pass within a few feet of where he stood. Larry, at the wheel, saw him at the same time he saw Larry, and pulled up to ask if he was going to Cannes. He accepted the lift with thanks.

The back seat of the Fiat held room for his bag among an assortment of skin-diving apparatus—a pair of orange-painted oxygen packs, face masks, underwater hunting equipment, the rest. During the first part of the drive they talked about skin-diving, then about racing cars, then diving again. Larry was careful to avoid conversational turns that might lead to anything else. Holland was beginning to suspect him of tactfulness exceptional even for a master of what he referred to as pub rel before the talk turned to anything that could not be called carefully neutral.

"You saw Mike's father in Barcelona, sir?"

"We talked last night."

"How is he?"

"All right, for his circumstances."

"Circumstances?"

"They're a bit confining."

"I know what it's all about, sir, if you'd like to be a little less stiff-lipped about what you let the younger generation hear," Larry said. "Mike told me."

"Knock off the 'sir' routine and I could forget that there is a younger generation. How much did she tell you?"

"I know that her father is hiding from the police on a bribery charge, and that Vilasar is pulling strings to have the charge dismissed. If there's more to it than that, I'd like to hear about it."

"Why? What's your interest?"

They were coming off the stretch of fast double highway that skirts the Baie des Anges between the airport and the race track beyond Cros de Cagnes, funneling with other traffic into the old road through the narrow streets of Antibes and Juan-les-Pins. Larry had let the car wind up to seventy-five or eighty on the straightaway and was cutting speed for the bottleneck ahead, intent on the business of adapting from one driving pattern to another. He drove with care and concentration, and did not answer the question until they were locked into the traffic stream behind a bus doing thirty-five.

"I guess you could say I like Mike and feel sorry for her," he said thoughtfully. "Not because of her father being in trouble, exactly. More on account of being seventeen."

"Tell me what's wrong with being seventeen."

"Why? What's your interest?"

"I'm an old friend of the family. I've known her parents since before she was born."

"Well, I'm a new friend of the family. Mike's a good kid, but she's still only a kid. She's just reached the point where she ought to have five or ten years of living ahead of her, and I don't mean stiff-shirt dinners at a casino, either." Larry moved his head to indicate the diving equipment behind them. "That kind of thing. Fun. Uncomplicated. I'm taking her down the Esterel this afternoon to show her the bottom of a couple of calanques, and then we'll go to the movies tonight and hold hands, and afterward I'll kiss her good night and she can kid herself that I've fallen for her, which isn't true but could be if we had more time and less Vilasar. Nothing serious, just the kind of summer thing you get over before next summer and the next guy, the way you get over him for the guy that will come afterward, and so on until you've grown up and have enough sense to know which end is up and what you want in the way of a guy for keeps."

"Which she presumably isn't going to have a chance to do."

"Mike? She's going to be a Spanish marquesa before she's old enough to vote. Hadn't you heard?"

"I hadn't heard that it was official."

"It's understood between the contracting parties; Mrs. Magill and the marqués."

"You're doing Mrs. Magill an injustice."

"I hope I am. I don't think so."

"You're doing Micaela an injustice by implying that she'd accept that kind of a contract."

"Well, while you're throwing injustices around, who are you to say so? You've seen Mike twice in your life and talked to her once. Staring at a girl in a bikini doesn't make you an authority on what goes on inside her head."

"I told you, I'm an old friend of the family. I knew her mother years ago, when she was only a year or two older than Mike herself. I know her father, her background, her heredity, what went into her thinking processes. I have a basis for judgment of what goes on inside her head, as I had a basis for recognizing her in the bikini the first time I saw her. She's her parents all over again."

"There's no analogy," Larry insisted. "Mental processes aren't hereditary. What you recognized were only the inheritable physical characteristics—the body, the face, the hair—"

He stopped talking, abruptly, on the word.

The interruption was as unexpected as Candelas' strong

grip had been under the street lamp. It caught Holland wholly unprepared, this time without even a physical reflex to act for him while his mind refused to. He could only sit, blanked out, waiting for something to come to him; some casual remark that would pass it over, bridge the gap, change the subject; while Larry, tight-lipped, found an opening in the traffic, shifted down, accelerated, swung wide of the bus and around it in a burst of noisy power and then, still accelerating and with open road ahead of him, braked, pulled to the side of the road and stopped. The bus whished on by, its driver saluting them with a shake of the head and the classic gesture that says, in France, Completely crazy.

"The hair," Larry repeated. He was looking straight ahead through the windshield, his big hands loose on the wheel.

Holland sighed. The gap was beyond bridging.

"She has an album full of photos of her father," Larry said. "What hair he has isn't like hers. Neither is her mother's."

"That's not enough for a conclusion."

"No. But you are; you standing on the esplanade, staring at her with your mouth open, looking at a ghost; you sitting across from her at the table the other night, both of you like Indians; same skin, same hair, same eyes. You and her mother dancing, fitted together like the two halves of a broken plate." Larry turned his head at last, deliberately. "You tell me the rest, Mr. Holland. Or that it's all in my mind, and that I'm adding one more injustice to the others. I don't like to drive when I've got other things than driving to think about."

"It's not an injustice."

Larry put the car into gear. It moved back into the stream of traffic, locked in behind a truck doing thirty-five.

Minutes later Holland said, "I guess you had better know a little more than you do. Her mother and I were married. Before she met Magill."

"Mike doesn't know?"

"Her mother doesn't want her to know."

"Why—if it's any of my business?"

"That much of it isn't."

Larry shrugged, accepting the rebuff.

"You asked for it," Holland said. "Take her skin-diving, take her to the movies afterward, give her a good night kiss and forget the rest of it." It occurred to him then to ask, "Where's Carlos, to be letting his girl go out with you?"

"He took off for Barcelona the day after you did, in a hurry. Mike said he had unexpected news about her—Mr. Magill."

"You'd better practice saying 'father' to her without stumbling. When she finds out who I am, I don't want it to be by a slip of the tongue."

"I'll be careful."

They did not talk again until they were in Cannes, where Holland asked to be let off at the railroad station. He said, "I've got to run down to Marseille. Tell Mike and her mother that Magill's in good shape except for having lost his glasses, and ask Mrs. Magill to have a pair, two pairs, made up from his prescription right away. I'll call her tomorrow, in the morning. Tell Mike–" He could not think what it was he wanted to tell Mike. "Never mind. I'll tell her myself when I see her."

"Tell me one thing, whether it's my business or not. Are you going to let her marry Vilasar?"

"No. That much you're welcome to know. Thanks for the ride."

"The pleasure was mine," Larry said.

Holland's business in Marseille was with the American consul-general there, a man he had known and been friendly with in Africa. He learned what he wanted to learn in a few minutes, and had time left over to call on the Peruvian consul as well. The decision to do so was made on the spur of the moment; at least he had no conscious memory of having thought about it before he happened to see the brass plate of the Peruvian consulate in the same building with the American. He was back in Cannes that same evening. In the morning he telephoned Marsha quite early, made an appointment to see her in the pension garden where the rabbits and hens would be their only audience, then was deliberately late for the rendezvous so that she would be there ahead of him. He was even less sure of himself than he had been before their first meeting, and did not want to be kept waiting with diminishing courage for what he had to tell her.

She was in the garden when he arrived; composed and handsome, sitting in her straight-backed way on the bench by the rabbit hutch. Even there, in a housecoat, among leeks and carrots and lettuces, she somehow managed to look military; Martia Victoria in the cabbage patch, all flags flying under a mimosa in full bloom that shed bright yellow pollen on her hair in a brief riffle of morning breeze. He felt like an invader approaching a fortress, wary of its defenses but determined to attack.

They exchanged good mornings. He said awkwardly, unnecessarily, "I'm sorry I couldn't come yesterday."

"Larry explained that you had to go to Marseille. Was it something to do with Harry?"

"He hasn't any identification papers or proof of nationality. He's going to need a passport as soon as he gets here, and all the protection we can give him against extradition. The consul-general is a friend of mine."

"I'd forgotten that you were so conscientious."

"A job's no good if it collapses after you've done your part of it. Did you order the glasses?"

"They'll be delivered at your hotel this evening."

She made a gesture of invitation for him to sit beside her, which he declined with a shake of his head. Puzzled, she said, "Is everything all right?"

"Everything is as you ordered it."

"How are you going to get him out?"

"By boat. It won't be any great trouble."

"You make it all sound quite cut and dried."

"That's good engineering. The more cut and dried it is, the better. No risks."

He was finding it increasingly difficult to look at her, and occupied himself by pulling a handful of carrots to feed to the rabbits. Over his shoulder he said, "What made Carlos take off for Barcelona again in such a hurry?"

"He recognizes you as an enemy. He doesn't know why you're an enemy, but he's afraid of you. When he heard that you had gone, he had to follow you to see what damage you might do to his plans for Harry."

"He's perceptive."

"So am I."

"What does that mean?"

"You're keeping something from me."

"What makes you so sure?"

"Please, Andy. You were never devious. What is it?"

So because a siege well launched is the most effective siege, he stuffed what was left of the carrot tops into the wire mesh of the rabbit hutch and turned to pick her off the bench, bodily, by the elbows, so that she came up against him standing, her hands locked against his chest. In that position she could do nothing against him when he kissed her but push, vainly, outraged but helpless, because he was stronger than she. He held her that way for a long time, waiting for the least weakening, the smallest sign of surrender. It never came. She was still fighting him to the best of her limited ability when he let her go.

Her face was scarlet. Her voice shook when she said, "What was that for?"

"It seemed like the least devious way to go about it."

"Kissing another man's wife against her will is certainly forthright."

"You were my wife before you were his. You still are."

It made no impression. Her outrage was too deep for anything else to penetrate.

"That's not why I went to Marseille," he said. "But I did see the Peruvian consul. He confirmed what I never had reason to confirm before. We're still married."

It was beginning to penetrate. He could see it in her eyes, in the quick recession of indignant blood from her face. She said, less shakily, "You're joking!"

"No. Better sit down while you hear the rest of it, Mrs. Holland."

The name reached her as nothing else had. She said helplessly, "Oh, my God! Then what—" and abruptly sat down. He did not sit beside her, but explained to the rabbits as intermediaries.

"You never divorced me. You couldn't, except in Peru. You became a Peruvian resident when we went to Iquitos, and Peruvian law doesn't permit a married woman to change her residence without permission from her husband, in writing. No court in the world would hold a California divorce valid when you were never legally in the state, never even legally in the United States, to get one. What that does to your marriage to Magill I don't know. You'll have to ask a lawyer. But you're still my wife, before you're his."

He watched the slow drift of pollen from the mimosa, waiting.

After a while she said, "Why do you tell me?"

"I've only been certain of it since yesterday."

"I don't mean that. Why do you tell me at all?"

"It's something to think about."

"Why must I think about it? Why couldn't you have kept it to yourself, let us go on the way we were? It would have been kinder."

"I thought we both ought to think about it. Together."

"We can't go back. You know that. Even if it weren't for

Harry."

"I don't know that! I don't concede it! I haven't suggested it, but why couldn't we? It's not out of the question."

"It's been too long. We've grown apart. We've lived different lives."

"We could grow together again. We've plenty of time ahead of us. I'm only forty-one; you're thirty-seven or thirty-eight, not even tied, unless it's by bigamy, to a man twenty years older than you. You don't love him—"

"Even if that were true, and it's not true, I don't love you. I don't even know you. You're a stranger."

The siege was going badly. Her defenses were too strong, his attack countered before he had got it under way. In desperation, he said, "Was I any less of a stranger when we'd been to a couple of college football games and decided in the middle of one of them that we wanted to sleep together?"

"We were in love. We wanted to sleep together. Both of us. It's no longer true."

Against the cold wall of that rejection he could carry no further offense. Both of them were wondering how to end it without further hurt to either when a window of the pension banged open and Micaela, in pajamas, called across the garden in one breath, "Mr. Holland, don't go away, please, I want to talk to you, I'll be down as soon as I've brushed my teeth, good morning, Mother dear." As suddenly, the window was empty.

"Better go straighten your lipstick before she sees you," Holland said.

"Give me your handkerchief first."

She was scrubbing at his mouth when he told her, around the handkerchief, "Something you should know. Larry guessed her parentage, or guessed at it, and I had to tell him the truth to keep him from conjecturing about us. He won't talk, as long as he's been asked not to, but you were wrong if you really thought you could keep her from accepting the truth about me. It would be as easy as asking her where she got her hair and eyes."

"You don't know her faith in her parents."

"Would you be willing to let me test it?"

"You promised not to."

She gave him back his handkerchief. He said, "I promised nothing, except that Magill can keep her until she's eighteen and Carlos de Vilasar isn't going to get her. That's all you've bought from me, Mrs. Holland."

Her straight back was as straight and unyielding as ever when she left him. He hated her, and in that moment felt a closer identification with the unknown man who had ravished her than with the husband who had shot her rapist. He would have enjoyed beating her.

Micaela still wore pajamas when she came down to the garden, a shapeless robe slung haphazardly over them and, on her feet, mules that had once been feathered. The tanned skin of her stomach showed through a gap in the carelessly buttoned pajama top, and the beginning of a smooth swell of breast, very white in contrast.

She said, "Where is my mother?"

"She went into the house for something."

"Larry said you had a message for me from my father."

"He's taking his vitamins, keeping his feet dry and said I was to give you a kiss."

She looked at him gravely, studying him. They were his own eyes, looking back at him from Marsha's face, but without friendliness. Even at the casino, when he had made the mistake on the dance floor, she had been friendly.

"Like the kiss you gave my mother?" she asked at last.

"I'm sorry you saw that."

"You should be more careful where you grab people."

"I hope you saw that it was one-sided. She didn't participate."

"I saw that, too. Are you a gentlemanly cad, Mr. Holland?"

"I'm only trying to explain the caddishness."

"Please do."

But I fathered you on her, he thought crazily. You can't stand there in living testimony of what we were to each other and ask by what right a kiss. He said, "I thought of myself as your mother's suitor, once, before your father came along. A man never gets over feeling that a woman he loved might sometimes wish she hadn't chosen the other man. I tried to prove it. I was wrong. That's all there was to it."

"Very gentlemanly." She smiled, unexpectedly, and they were friends again. "To tell you the truth, I don't understand why more men don't try to kiss Mother than do. Isn't she sexy? I mean, she's so beautiful and so obviously not, oh, available is the only word I can think of. Unattainable is better. She must be an awful challenge to men like—well—you know. A certain kind."

Whether she believed his explanation or not, she had accepted it; twice, now, she had helped him save his face when she might have slapped it instead. In his limited experience with seventeen-year-olds they had not always been so mature, nor so gracious. He wondered what she would do if he took her in his arms and said, I love you, child. The temptation was strong.

He said, "I'm going back to Barcelona tomorrow, to take your father his glasses. Is there anything else I can deliver? A message?"

She took a thick envelope from the pocket of her robe. It was addressed, in the neat, angular handwriting taught by Spanish schools, to *My Dearest Dad, c/o Mr. Holland*. He put it in his own pocket without comment.

"It's a blow-by-blow report," she said. "Except for one or two things I don't understand myself. Why were you so mean to Carlos the other night?"

"Mean?"

"Just plain mean. About racing and the rest, when he wanted to dance with your girl."

"I thought I explained that we had to leave."

"You didn't have to leave at just that moment, or in that way. Were you jealous?"

"Yes," he said. "I was jealous."

"You needn't have been. Carlos isn't like that at all. It's just that he's so attractive and, oh, glamorous, women just can't help being interested, the way some men are interested in Mother, for the same reason. It doesn't mean that he's interested in them. He's—he's well, maybe you'll understand why you needn't have been jealous when I say that we're practically engaged to be married, although that sounds kind of smug of me, doesn't it, when he hasn't really asked me yet?"

"Not a bit. Congratulations, and I apologize for the jealousy as well as the meanness. Wouldn't this be a good moment to deliver your father's commission?"

She laughed, in the way she had that had been Marsha's way, once; her head back, her brown throat swelling with amusement. "You *are* a determined man, aren't you? All right. I won't struggle."

She lifted her face, her eyes closed; smiling, inviting, teasing. Yellow pollen from the mimosa flecked her dark hair like gold dust.

He met the temptation by kissing her twice, once on either cheek. Her eyes opened, still with laughter in them. She said, "Oh, that's far too respectful for Dad," and kissed him back, an inexpert honest kiss that tasted of toothpaste and that somehow, when she had gone and he was walking back down the hill, got mixed up with the other kiss he had given, or imposed on, her mother, so that later in his mind they were not two different kisses but one, and Marsha, the young Marsha he had loved and married, had kissed him back instead of fighting him. At least that was how he was able to remember it when he did not remind himself that she had fought him, without a sign of surrender.

He called Larry from La Belle Poitrine to arrange for a seat on the next day's plane, then went down to the beach for lunch and a swim. His Turkish friend was there, surrounded by a number of the geisha who had established contact and were clustered around him on the sand. The Turk was a big man, roly-poly, who habitually wore a tarboosh, partly as a gesture, partly to protect a bald spot from sunburn. In it, with a half-dozen nearly naked girls in varying shades of suntan gathered around his beach chair, he looked like a sultan in the middle of his harem. Odile was not part of the group, nor to be seen on the beach.

The Turk spoke bad French badly, and was in a bad mood. In response to Holland's purely conversational inquiry he said, grumbling, "Merde alors, if you really want to know, it goes like the devil. Yesterday I lose the little blonde thing, last night I lose five thousand francs at the casino, today I have indigestion. How goes the business in Spain?"

"I'll be done with it in another day or two. Which little blonde thing, and how did you lose her?"

"The honey-color, with the hair like moonbeams. You know? Only the day before yesterday we are getting along beautiful, she and me. I invite her to the casino, to bring me luck and whatever comes afterward, insha'Allah. She says yes, with much pleasure, everything is nice between us except that she does not keep the rendezvous. Not even a message. Yesterday I ask her—I have to telephone because she does not come to the beach—why? She says, cool like a melon, she is not yet twenty-one; they will not admit her to the gambling rooms. Such regret. Hah."

"It's true enough. They'd ask to see her carte d'identité at the door."

"What is there about a carte d'identité that a few francs will not bring up to date?" The Turk was honestly indignant. "Besides, not even to send a note is a rudeness beyond explanation. No, no, she is no longer available. She does not even present herself again on the block, like these others." He waved a hand, indicating the harem. "Between one day and the next, she has found a friend."

"You still have plenty of others."

"Not like that one." He sighed. "I do not approve of this place. It is immoral. I tell you what, how would you like to go to Anatolia, two weeks, three weeks, whatever it takes to look over the ground, all the expenses will be mine, then talk contract?"

"I'd want a day or two to think about it. I still have to finish up in Spain."

"Take your time, take your time. I am not yet gnawed by loneliness." The Turk patted the oiled back of one of the girls lying at his feet. "Turn over, little one. You are beginning to char on this side."

Later in the day, Barot raised his expressive eyebrows in protest at Holland's suggestion that he might reveal the identity of Odile's friend.

"Mon cher, you know I could not tell you the name. If it were yourself, would I give your apartment number to the first person to ask for it? Besides, the implication is ungentlemanly. Mademoiselle Solière has always paid her own bills. They are quite modest."

"It could be that someone has told you within the last day or two not to worry too much if the bills suddenly became less modest. Would it be a fair guess?"

Barot considered the question before conceding cautiously, "I would not deny that her credit is somewhat better than it might have been two days ago."

"With you? Or generally?"

"Let us say, at this point, as far as Cartier's and Maggy Rouff. I do not know if it goes any further."

"If I tell you the name myself, will you affirm it?"

"Certainly not! I will merely not deny it with the same

vehemence as I would if you were wholly wrong."

"The Marqués of Vilasar."

Barot shrugged, spreading his hands. "Voilà."

"That's all," Holland said. "I'll be leaving again in the morning."

It was in keeping with the hidalgo character. For Carlos to have made an attempt upon the virtue of the girl he meant to marry was unthinkable. To purchase one of the geisha while the marriage impended was something else entirely. Holland did not believe that Odile meant anything to the Marqués beyond the fact that she was pretty and accessible. But she was also Holland's, or had seemed to be, and the connection was obvious. Having humiliated Carlos publicly, he was himself to be humiliated privately. The speed with which Carlos had moved, within hours after the insult, was the only surprise.

To confirm what hardly needed confirmation, he telephoned Odile and was told by a maid—so soon a maid, solid evidence of arrival—that mademoiselle would prefer not to speak to him. It was unequivocal, honest and without need of excuse.

He said, "Tell mademoiselle that I called only to say good-by and wish her good luck. I'm going to Spain again tomorrow. I don't know when I'll be back."

The maid's hand muffled the telephone mouthpiece. A moment later Odile's soft voice said, "Why are you returning to Spain, m'sieur?"

"Business."

"Has your business something to do with the marqués?"

"Quite a lot to do with the marqués."

There was a silence. Then, "Could I see you before you go? Privately?"

"Certainly. Where? And when?"

"Now, if it is not an inconvenience. In my room."

She gave him the number, which did not coincide with

his remembrance of the floor on which she had left the elevator the night he brought her home from the gala. Since then, along with the maid, she had acquired a top-floor suite and a terrace overlooking the whole sweep of playground from casino to casino; the Croisette, the beach, the wooded islands offshore, the flanking mountains of the Esterel above and beyond the reaching masts of the yacht harbor. She had come into her kingdom at last, and she was afraid of losing it.

She said, "You know what has happened since the night of the gala, do you not, m'sieur?"

"Yes."

"Do you know why it happened?"

"I suspect that the marqués misinterpreted the nature of our friendship."

"It was a very fortunate misinterpretation, for me."

"There's no reason why it shouldn't continue to be. If there's anything I can do to make him believe I'm insanely jealous, I'll be happy to. Would you like me to create a public scene?"

She was, as always, alluring. She wore allure as she wore the pink of her nails and lips, the champagne tint of her hair, the honey-gold of her skin. Everything about her was exactly right, in the way of a geisha. He had never seen her unpoised or unsure of herself, and it disturbed him, in a way, that she had to appeal to him for even negative help. It was like having a golden kitten confess inadequacy of self. In his experience kittens, the golden kind, were never inadequate. They always landed on their feet, and they never wanted for laps.

"A scene isn't necessary. But I should like the marqués to go on believing that you would like me for your friend."

"It shouldn't be hard to convince him of that. I do."

He thought she took rather too long, for a geisha, to say anything more. They were not supposed to permit awkward silences to develop. Before it became uncomfortable she smiled and said, "It is as gallant a compliment as I would have expected from you. I do not think you take very many women into your friendship," and gave him the rose petals of her fingertips. "Good-by, m'sieur. Once again, bon voyage."

"And to you, Odile, wherever you go. May I see you when I come back?"

"That depends on when you come back—and the plans of the marqués, of course."

"Of course."

~§~

The next day, with minutes on his hands at the airport while he waited for the Barcelona plane to be called, he sent her a sheaf of pink roses. He wrote *My own idea this time* on one of his cards, then, thinking of Vilasar, added *Wait for me.* It had the right touch of arrogance for an hidalgo. With Barot's espionage system as good as it was, the marqués would know what was on the card soon enough even if Odile didn't show it to him.

He was frowning over another card, unable to compose a message to go with flowers to the pension on the Californie hill, when Marsha found him.

Her hair was wind-blown, unusual for her. She said breathlessly, "I went by your hotel but they told me you had just left, and when I called Larry he said I'd have time to catch you here if I hurried. Did you get the glasses?"

By the airport clock, only a few minutes remained before his call. He said, "You didn't come all the way from Cannes to ask me a question like that, Marsha. What is it? We don't have much time."

She sighed.

"I'm no good at deviousness, either. But I could wish for more time and less bluntness. There's something I've got to know, Andy."

"What?"

"It's difficult."

"I'm sorry. We have only about two minutes."

"Do you really believe—do you really want to—go back?"

He knew that she was not speaking of his return to Barcelona. And because there was no time left for equivocation, with her or with himself, he said, honestly, "Yes. I do. More than anything."

"But *why?* Why me again, after all these years? You could have any of a thousand women; all younger than I, prettier, unattached, without complications. If it's only Micaela—"

"It isn't only Micaela. It's her, it's you, it's me, it's the three of us. I need more time than I've got for it, but I'll try to explain. If I can." He took her arm, leading her away from the flower stand into a corner where they were out of the way, cut off, free of the bustle that went on around them in the busy airport.

"That first day," he said, and groped for words to follow because he had not thought it out clearly even for himself, "—that first day, when I found you, you said that Iquitos had scarred you. For a long time I didn't recognize my own scars for what they were, but Iquitos was a bad beating for me, too. I made a wrong turn there. I chose what you called a gravel bar when I could have had you and Micaela, as it turned out, and I'm just beginning to see that there never was anything in the gravel bar but gravel."

He stopped her when she would have interrupted. "Let me keep the floor for a minute. Yesterday someone said something curious to me about friendships. It doesn't matter what it was, but it set me to thinking; in particular, about a question you yourself asked: Why had I never found anyone else? I'm not sure that I know the answer even now, but I do know that I don't want to look for anyone else. I want to go back to where I turned wrong and turn right. You said we had a good start; I want to carry it to a good end, instead of nowhere. I want another chance with my wife and daughter. I'll never be a whole man until I get it. Now you know."

"What about Harry?" Her expression was unreadable.

"He's had you for eighteen years. It's my turn."

"And if I won't leave him, if Micaela won't reject him for you, what then?"

A loudspeaker over their heads hissed for a moment, then blared the announcement of the Barcelona flight; first in French, afterward in English. The announcement ended with a call for passengers to go to the international loading gate and a request for no smoking. The loudspeaker cut off with a snap.

"I don't know," he said. "I haven't thought that far ahead. I need more time. It's all happened in the last day or two."

"You're going to have time, Andy." She took his hands, to keep him for another moment. Her own were cold. "You'll have time on the plane, and afterward. You'll think: Suppose, just suppose, that Harry Magill has bad luck; suppose something were to happen so he never got back to them—no, let me talk now, please; you'll have to think this way, even without wanting to! You'll think, *There would be no choice to make!* They'd have to come back to me. I'd get them on the rebound, as he got them from me. But it's not true, Andy! You'll never have us that way!"

Her voice had risen, enough to invite a curious glance or two from travelers moving past them toward the loading gates.

He said, "We have grown apart, haven't we?"

"I'm not accusing you! I'm telling you that it will occur to you, because it has to occur to you! I'm being honest. When I came here, I was going to cheat you—it would have been easy for me—I could have done it—like this—"

She had to go up on her toes to bring her mouth to his, at first still holding to his hands so he could not take her, then releasing them so that he could, taking him with her arms around his neck; body against body, mouth to mouth, the fortress surrendered, the siege won, all defenses capitulated. Theirs was only one of half a dozen farewell kisses going on around them while the loudspeaker buzzed and blared again, repeating the announcement of the plane's departure, but theirs was different from the others; in intensity, in duration, in the fierceness with which they clung to each other, so that even in their out-of-the-way corner they were noticed, and a passing G.I., an American on his way to somewhere from somewhere, unkissed, let out a respectful wolf-whistle that still failed to separate them. Only the need to breathe did it, and even then he did not let her go, nor did she try to escape. Still in his arms, still with her own arms around his neck, her head turned against his chest and the nostalgic familiar perfume of her hair in his nostrils, she said quickly, breathlessly, "I was going to let you think what you wanted to think. You would have believed that you had won, that all you had to do was bring him safely back to take us away from him. It would have been his protection against you. But I can't cheat any more, Andy. You've got to know. We—"

"Don't say it!" He tried to stop her by pushing her face into the cloth of his coat. "Even if it's so, don't say it!"

She would not be stopped.

"—we'll never leave him. We're too important to him, and he to us. We can't ever love you in his place. If you don't bring him back to us, we'll hate you forever. Now let me go."

With that promise she left him, turning quickly from him when he released her. He watched her walk away, erect and military and handsome as ever, her heels clicking like an officer's jackboots on the blue tiles of the waiting room. He was still watching the door through which she had disappeared when the loudspeaker said impatiently, "Mr. 'Olland'. Mr. Andrew 'Olland. Please report to the international loading gate. Thank you," and clicked off.

The routine of passport clearance, boarding the plane, stowing his coat and belting himself into a seat occupied his mind until the plane was moving. After that he could hold his attention on the whistling run to takeoff and the steep slanting climb; first above the red-roofed Italianate villas and gardened hills of Nice, then out over the shading turquoise greens of the Baie des Anges and at last into level flight at cloud height without clouds, the plane hanging between blue sky and the blue water of the open Mediterranean. Only then, when he had freed himself from the seat belt and reluctantly abandoned his wish for the companionship of a cigar—CIGARETTES ONLY, PLEASE! hung like a wagged finger over the window in which he caught a dim reflection of his face and thought to wipe her lipstick once again from his mouth—did the thought come, as inescapably as she had promised that it would: Suppose something does happen to Harry Magill. You killed a man for the gravel bar.

The flight to Barcelona seemed much shorter than before.

V

MAGILL'S FIRST USE of the glasses was to look at Holland through them. His eyes, magnified by the strong lenses, were owlish. He made a thorough inspection, head to toe; not critical, but deliberate. When it was done, he said, "You're not as formidable as I would have expected," and turned his look of inspection first to Candelas, who lifted his hand in mock greeting, then to the room that had been their confinement for so long.

There was daylight in the room, hazed by smoke from the brazier on which Candelas had been cooking, the vapor of hot cheap olive oil. In daylight the room seemed even smaller than it had when Holland first saw it, and dingier. The walls were discolored with leaks from old piping. A pair of cots, unmade, a couple of chairs, a table, the brazier, the message basket on its string and a washbowl with a single tap that dripped made up most of the furnishings, except for clutter.

"I haven't been missing as much as I thought," Magill said. He took off the glasses and tried the second pair before giving it to Candelas to keep as a spare, then motioned Holland to a chair. "Sit down. It puts us at a better level. How's Mike?"

"She's all right. She sent you this."

He gave Magill the envelope. Magill looked at its unbroken seal, then shrewdly at him. "It must have been a temptation. Or did you steam it open?"

"Read your mail. The more she's told you, the less I'll have to."

There were three pages to the letter, covered on both sides with the neat angular handwriting. Holland went to the window and stood looking into the street while Magill read. He had caught a glimpse of the double row of childish naughts -and-crosses at the end of the last page, and his jealousy chewed at his stomach like a gripe. He did not turn around until Magill said, "What's the rest of it? Did you talk to Marsha about the school credit?"

"We had more important things to talk about. Vilasar suspects that he's being sabotaged, without knowing how or why. He's pulling strings harder than ever."

"I know. He got word to me the day after you were here to sit tight and take no chances."

"How did he find you?"

"The same way you did, probably. You can buy anything in Barcelona, if you have the money. He has more than enough to turn up a hideout in the Barrio Chino."

"More than the police?"

"More than the police are willing to spend. I'm just another murderer to them. They have more time than money for those."

"What will happen when he discovers that you've turned down his help for mine?"

Magill shook his head, stuffing Micaela's letter carefully back into its envelope before putting the envelope away in the pocket of his dirty shirt. "I don't know."

"He could be dangerous?"

"Carlos *is* dangerous, when you get in his way. Don't misjudge him because he keeps his nails clean. You might be one of those who failed to jump out of his way when you should have."

"I wasn't worried for myself."

"Your concern for me is heartwarming. But I doubt very

much that a man who hopes to marry another man's daughter would be much of a threat to his potential father-in-law."

"When he finds out that you don't have a daughter for him to marry and never have had, your doubts could be resolved in a hurry," Holland said. "In the meantime, let's get down to business. What about the boat?"

Magill's sallow face took on a little color. He set his lips and said nothing.

Candelas said, "It's all set. We go out with the fishing fleet any morning, at first light."

"Where from?"

"The port. Barceloneta. Muelle de las Baleares."

"Where to?"

"For fifteen thousand pesetas each, anywhere we like on the French coast as far north as Sète. For another five thousand apiece, as far as Marseille. I've put up half the money for three passages to Sète."

"Three?"

"You. Me. Him. Three."

"Why me?"

"I told you. Anything that happens to him happens to you."

"I hadn't planned on going with you, but it doesn't matter. How soon can we leave? Tomorrow?"

"I told you. Any morning at first light."

Holland shook his head.

"Not any morning. A particular morning, arranged and agreed upon. Your man has got to know that we'll be coming and be ready for us. We've got to know that he'll be there."

"He'll be there." Candelas reached into his hip pocket to bring out a fistful of money, or half-money. The wad of bills had been cut cleanly in two. "He wants this stuff too much not to be there. He can't spend his half by itself."

"It's not enough insurance. Tell me where to find him and I'll talk to him myself."

“He’ll be there,” Candelas said again. “I know my own racket.”

Impatient, Holland turned to Magill. He said, “Tell your animal to do what he’s—” and was knocked sprawling out of his chair by a tremendous blow on the side of the head. Going to the floor, his ears ringing, he remembered the vegetable slicer in the sheath at the back of Candelas’ neck, and stayed down long enough to get his hands on the chair before he came up; not to club with, because it was too light to be effective against anyone as solidly put together as Candelas, but because chair legs were the best kind of defense against the knife until his head cleared. But Candelas only stood ready against counterattack; still with the cut bills in his hand, not ignoring the meaning or the threat of the chair but neither reaching for the back of his neck nor giving any other sign of combativeness.

“Only the man who pays me calls me animal,” he said. “We will get along better now that you know it. Put the chair down. You haven’t given me cause to cut you.”

“I may, in time,” Holland said. He could feel the tightness of his lips over his teeth, the rigidity of the tendons in his forearms and fingers. He relaxed them with a conscious effort as he put the chair down. Patient now, knowing that impatience would win nothing except further opposition, he said to Magill, “We can’t afford to do it his way. It leaves too much open to accident. We’ve got to set up a blueprint and follow it, to be safe.”

“That was a useful box on the ear,” Magill said. “I like the way you talk since you got up off the floor. Give him the name, animal.”

“The boat is taken care of,” Candelas answered stubbornly. “You two draw your blueprints to get us out of here and as far as Barceloneta without being picked up. I’ll handle my end.”

“Give him the name,” Magill said again, still mild.

"Patrón, listen to a dumbhead just once. The boat is taken care of. Any morning you want to go, we go. It's as easy as walking aboard a ferry."

"Give him the name," Magil said again, still mild. "It's his money we're spending, and you knocked him down. He's got to have his way now, or he'll think we don't appreciate all he's doing for us. We can't have that."

Candelas shoved the money into his pocket, wadding it well down before he said grudgingly, "Vicente. His boat's the *Montserrat.*"

"How well do you trust him?"

"He'd sell his mother for a profit."

"How do you know he won't sell us?"

"We're not worth forty-five thousand pesetas to the cops. There's no profit in it for him."

"When will I find him at the Muelle de las Baleares?"

"Now until tomorrow at first light."

"And tomorrow?"

"The same. Any day. Every day. I told you, a dozen times. He'll be there."

He was there, sleeping, when Holland found the *Montserrat* moored with the rest of the fishing fleet inside the protection of the Barceloneta mole. Most of the port was asleep with him. Noon was mid-siesta for the fishermen. They had already put in a full working shift since dawn; working ship, hauling nets, discharging the catch, washing down boats and gear. Now, having eaten a meal and drunk their midday wine, they lay around in the shade of sail or deckhouse and dozed, waiting for the cool of the afternoon, when the nets already spread along the wharf would be dry and ready for mending. A dozen of the men would sit together on the same net like old ladies at a knitting bee, stretching the meshes for repair with the hook of a bare big toe and reeling off gossip as fast as they reeled off cord from their mending shuttles. News spread like the smell of fish guts when the nets were being mended on the wharves; news, it might be, of the payment, or half-payment; for three unticketed passages between Barcelona and Sète. It all had to be taken into consideration in drawing up the blueprint.

Vicente identified himself as captain of his boat by coming immediately awake when the regular rock of the *Montserrat* at its mooring lines changed under Holland's weight on the gangplank. Two other sleeping men did not stir. Vicente, warily getting to his feet, was a stocky, gray-haired man; not as broad or as heavy as Candelas but with the same Catalan solidity of bone and gristle. He had an open, strong Catalan face, deeply grooved from nostril to mouth corner, and crafty eyes that did not go with the face's honesty. He said nothing, waiting for Holland to identify himself.

Holland said, "From Candelas."

"What do you have that says so?"

"Another fifteen thousand pesetas."

Vicente moved his head toward the stern of the boat, where the sea breeze would blow their talk out over the water instead of toward the sleeping men. They went aft.

"So now it's Marseille," Vicente said. "Good. I can do business there myself. When do you want to go?"

"As soon as possible. Tomorrow."

The fisherman thought about it, briefly, before he said, "It would be better to wait another day."

"Candelas said you were ready to go any morning."

"For Sète, yes. Sète is nothing. For Marseille, I'll have to take on extra fuel. Everybody in Barcelona will know about it, and that we're going farther than the rest of the fleet, if I have to load up between now and tomorrow morning. Give me another day and a night, I'll shop it around. No questions, no gossip."

"What about them?" Holland nodded at the sleeping crew.

"They're what I'm talking about. I need the extra time to give them a day off."

"Will they give trouble when they find out where we're going?"

Vicente showed his teeth in a buck-toothed grin.

"For forty-five thousand pesetas I can handle all the trouble those two will ever give," he said. "For sixty thousand, I might even slip them a duro or two. Let's see the rest of the money."

"Not here."

"In the cabin. And none of that louse Candelas' knifework on the bills, either. I need cash for fuel."

Holland gave him the money. He would rather not have done so at that point, but saw no help for it. A landing short of Marseille would expose Magill to unnecessary risk, and a blueprint which permitted the existence of any risks but the inescapable was worse than no blueprint at all. When he and Vicente had arrived at agreement on a time for the *Montserrat's* passengers to board her, and other details, he went back to the Barrio Chino to whistle down the message basket in the Calle de las Hermanitas.

Candelas lowered it. Magill was visible at the window with him, peering owl-eyed into the street. Holland printed his note in bold capitals: STAY OUT OF SIGHT WHILE YOU'RE WEARING YOUR GLASSES. BE READY TO GO AN HOUR BEFORE FIRST LIGHT, DAY AFTER TOMORROW. Still painstaking, he added: CONFIRM UNDERSTANDING. ANY QUESTIONS?

The note come back with: CONFIRM, NO QUESTIONS scribbled across its face.

It was late afternoon before everything had been arranged that could be arranged. Walking back through the narrow streets of the Barrio toward the Ramblas and his hotel, Holland felt let down. It had all gone too easily, as far as it had gone. A bodega, promising the stimulation of coffee and alcohol, drew him in.

The only other patron in the place was a woman of the

Barrio. She drank coffee and brandy, like himself, and while she gave him no more than a single quick glance of appraisal when he came in, her body, conspicuously jut-breasted and round-buttocked in a tight, too short dress, was an implicit invitation. He knew within minutes how long he could take for his coffee before the invitation would become explicit, and told her silently, in his mind, I don't need what you offer. I've got a wife and daughter.

His sense of depression deepened with the realization that he was thinking of them as his in fact, not merely by operation of the quirks of law and biology that made him husband and father; that he was denying in his mind both Marsha's promise and Magill's existence, as if Magill were out of the way, vanished, disposed of and forgotten. He left the bodega without finishing his drink and walked the Ramblas for hours, up and down with the crowd that passed under the plane trees between port and plaza; not part of it, not conscious of the cages of colored birds, the flower stands, the lottery ticket vendors calling their promises of luck, the clumps of bullfight aficionados refighting yesterday's mano a mano, not even of the mellow street lamps after the lamplighter had made his rounds, much later, while he was still walking, still worrying the same bone of thought: Suppose something were to happen to Harry Magill.

He had to think about it. Marsha had been right. He couldn't help but think about it. It didn't have to happen by his fault, or even be something he could conceivably prevent. Candelas' promise had been unqualified. And even if he survived Candelas, Marsha and Micaela could never be brought to believe that it was not his fault in some way because he had wanted it to happen. He could not believe that himself. Only a Moslem's article of faith was strong enough to let a man live and die with the conviction that it didn't matter what you wanted or didn't want; that it was all written out for you from the beginning of time; insha'Allah. Moslems did not make good engineers, nor engineers Moslems.

He spent the following morning in part at the American consulate, in part at the office of a lawyer recommended by the consulate. The lawyer was an old man with shrewd bagged eyes and liver spots speckling his face and the backs of his hands like freckles. He had a lawyer's reluctance to answer hypothetical questions.

"It would depend on a number of things," he said. "The provocation, the premeditation, the circumstances of the killing. Generally speaking, murderers are not sentenced to the garrote unless their crime involves an attack on the rights of property at the same time as the taking of human life; for example, a thief who kills while robbing a home. The two values together are sacred in my country, although not necessarily so separately."

"This would be a crime passionnel, not involving property."

"The punishment, again, would depend on circumstances. I have stated a general rule. It is not absolute, and I am not a trial judge."

"Short of the garrote, what might the sentence be?"

"From acquittal to life imprisonment. I am sorry to be of so little help to you, señor, but you do not give me enough information on which to base an opinion. What would be the nationality of this hypothetical murderer?"

"North American."

"It would weigh against him. A few months ago it would have been in his favor. A few months from now it might again be in his favor."

"Why?"

"Because we Spaniards are proud, señor; with or without reason we are proud, as we are extreme. We are either very poor or very rich, very honorable or very corrupt, very kind or very cruel, very generous or very mean, but always proud of it. Your government has just lent my government four hundred million dollars on terms which humiliate us by telling us how the money shall be spent. The terms are fair and will be of benefit to Spain in the end, but humiliating. You, your hypothetical North American, must be punished for that, as well as for his crime."

"Could the right lawyer get him off?"

"You confuse our legal system with your own."

"In what way?"

"Spain does not suffer the weaknesses of trial by jury. The judges who hear evidence and pass sentence on a criminal are swayed only by their own prejudices in the application of thc law, not by the eloquence of a special pleader paid, or retained if you prefer the word, for his eloquence."

"Could money get him off?"

"Not legally."

"Could influence get him off?"

"Not legally."

"But money and influence on his side would be of help to him?"

"Money and influence are always valuable allies, in Spain."

"If I were to give you a set of facts, could you tell me with any degree of surety the punishment a murderer might expect if tried and convicted on the basis of those facts?"

The old man put the tips of his liver-spotted fingers together and looked meditative.

"There are hypothetical cases and hypothetical cases," he said. "Some are less hypothetical than others. If you are asking me now what the statute books say, I can give you an answer. But I suspect that you are a practical man. Shall I answer you accordingly, as if your case were not hypothetical but real?"

"Please do."

"In Spain, as in other countries, the law is applied as it is interpreted by human minds subject to human weaknesses;

horror, pity, disgust, venality, the craving for vengeance, the urge to forgive. What is a particularly heinous crime to one man might be less heinous to the mind of another. Its punishment would be heavy or less heavy accordingly. If, in your set of facts, it is possible by the use of the money you mention, the exercise of influence or in any other way to determine the identities and personalities of the judges who will rule on the case, then I might give you a fairly accurate forecast of the decision they would render and the sentence they would pass. In the absence of that information I would be wasting your time and mine even to listen to a summary of the other circumstances."

"The circumstances would permit selection of the judges. I could not myself identify them, or describe them to you."

"Then only the person who will influence their selection can answer the question you have asked me, señor." The old man bowed courteously. "I am sorry not to have been able to help you. There will be no fee. My country is already indebted to you for four hundred million dollars."

In the afternoon Holland packed his bag, keeping out a toothbrush, toothpaste and comb to carry in his pockets with his passport. Afterward he gave the bag to the hotel concierge to send back to France, and checked out. He did not expect to sleep before the time came for the rendezvous, at the hotel or anywhere. In that latitude at that season dawn came around four o'clock. He would have to be in the Calle de las Hermanitas not later than three, better earlier. There was no point in going to bed when he could not stop his mind from worrying at the same meatless, profitless bone.

He found himself running over the blueprint, testing it for flaws. From the Barrio Chino to Barceloneta would take about fifteen minutes in a cab. Half an hour would be a safer allowance, with the cab hired ahead of time. Taxis could be hard to find in the Barrio at any hour, and had been known, when hurried, to lock bumpers with other taxis even in the middle of the night. Something like that, with a crowd gathering and the police asking for names and addresses, even identification papers—

He tried to take his mind off it in a flamenco tavern he passed while walking the night away. It was a small, crowded, noisy little dive near the waterfront. Gypsies sang and danced there, between performances wheedling the tavern customers for cigarettes, wine, money, an article of clothing, something, anything. It was as much a part of a gypsy's nature to beg as it was to dance the way their women danced, without restraint, to breathlessness and exhaustion in a whirlwind of swirling skirts, stamping heels and the machine-gun fire of hard quick handclapping helping out the rhythm of the guitars. One of the dancers looked a little like Micaela; just enough so that when her back was toward him and he saw only the loose black hair flying with the energy of her dancing he could picture her face as it would be beneath the hair when she turned. She had gold teeth in the front of her mouth that spoiled even the slight resemblance when she did face him. But she saw that he was watching her, and made the most of it between dances by coming to his table to flirt with him and drink his wine.

All the gypsy women were publicly bold. Most had husbands or lovers or brothers in the place, playing a guitar or serving drinks, so that the commercial flirtations were well observed and could be carried on only at the expense of a division of the cigarettes, small change and other loot they produced. Holland let himself be wheedled for drinks and cigarettes, not caring, submerged in the noise and smoke and wine-stink of the place until the warm, sweat-smelling girl pressed close against him on a bench under the watchful eye of her husband or lover or brother, whichever one it might be, whispered an unsubtle invitation to him to take her somewhere not under observation. He thought, before he knew what he was thinking, *I don't need you. I've got . . .* and stood up quickly to leave the place before the thought could finish itself.

He was in the Barrio Chino before three, with a cab standing by on the meter at the head of Las Hermanitas, a street too narrow for it to enter. When he whistled, the basket came down far enough to be visible in the dim glow of light from the street lamp, then went back up again into darkness. After that acknowledgment he had to wait five minutes before Magill and Candelas came out of the dark doorway into the street.

Magill was wearing his glasses. They gleamed like small headlights when they caught and magnified a reflection from the street lamp.

Holland said, "Take the glasses off."

"I can't see where I'm going without them."

"You don't have to see. You've got to keep from being seen. Hold on to your trained bear, if you have to."

Candelas said softly, "I'll owe you another clip on the ear for that, Dutchman. But do what he says, patrón. The glasses glow like moons."

Magill, grumbling, took them off, and held to Candelas' sleeve for guidance until they reached the taxi.

"Barceloneta," Holland told the driver. "We're not in a hurry. Go by way of the Ramblas."

The paseo, when they came to it, was deserted except for a pair of workmen sluicing it down with a hose. Before its flood the day's accumulation of peanut shells, matchsticks, toothpicks, cigarette ends and losing lottery tickets was swept away into the street gutters, leaving the Ramblas fresh, empty and glistening under its warm lights, waiting for another day to begin. Without its birds, its flowers, its gravel-voiced peddlers and shiners of shoes, it still kept an individuality. Magill said his hail and farewell to it aloud, musing.

"When we first came here, Marsha and Mike and I, before we had made any friends, we used to spend whole Sundays on the paseo; eating peanuts and granizadas and pickled squid; sitting for a while, walking for a while, maybe exploring the side streets, taking it all in through our pores. Mike was only twelve then, but she loved it. It was like a circus to her. One Sunday they were dancing sardanas in the plaza behind San José. A couple of kid soldiers wanted to take Marsha and Mike into the circle. They didn't know the steps but Marsha can dance anything, given a lead, and Mike never had any doubts about herself even at that age. The soldiers—"

"Take off those damn glasses!"

Holland, catching their glint on Magill's face in the light of a street lamp, knew that he had spoken too loud and too angrily even before the blink of light from the next street lamp and others that followed it with the regular, flickery march of frames from an old movie showed the cabdriver's alert, observing eyes in the rearview mirror. There was no help for it. He could not be prevented from seeing Magill's face with the glasses, huge-eyed; Magill's face hastily, guiltily, swept free of the glasses; in the next blink Candelas, scowling and tense; in the next, Holland himself trying not to show concern, not to notice the driver's curiosity or give away his own sinking insecurity because he had provoked it. It was Magill's own fault that he had. Magill shouldn't have got on the subject of Mike at the age of twelve, or Marsha's dancing.

He wiped his moist palms on his coat.

The damage wasn't fatal. It would be at least daylight before the cab driver could learn that the police were offering a reward for news of an elderly foreigner wearing strong glasses, if he learned it that soon. By daylight the blueprint would have carried them well to sea, barring further accidents. There could be no more accidents.

At Barceloneta he stopped the cab at the entrance to the little port, paid the meter fare, gave the driver the right tip and made sure that he had driven away before they went farther. It was still black night, moonless. The stars hung bright over the sea, less bright over the city where the metropolitan night-glow dulled their brilliance. Stars, a few bare electric bulbs hanging from standards on the mole, dim radiance from a port or hatch of one of the fishing boats at its moorings gave what light there was; enough to see by and be seen, without being identified as out of place for the hour and surroundings.

"I'm sorry about snapping at you in the cab," Holland said. "Those glasses are too conspicuous. The cab driver noticed them as it was."

"He wouldn't have if you hadn't forced him to," Magill answered testily.

"That's why I'm sorry, not because I hurt your feelings. You should have known better than to take an unnecessary chance."

"Look what I made you do," Magill jeered.

Candelas said imploringly, "Mother of God, this is no time to fight! Let's get under cover and gnaw each others' throats in comfort. Grab the tail of my coat, patrón. I need both hands to protect myself."

He led the way, Magill close behind, Holland following. The nets had been taken up, but the mole was cluttered with other gear—big wicker lobster pots, bait boxes and crab traps—so that they had to feel their way cautiously, distinguishing between shadows that were only shadows and others with sharp edges or damaging corners. Where the *Montserrat* lay moored, all was shadow.

Candelas, groping into the darkness, grumbled, "The pig, for what we're paying him he could burn an anchor lamp at least. All right, patrón; I've got my right foot on the bottom of the gangplank. There's no rail, so hold on to me and take it easy."

"Go first," Magill said curtly.

"I can give you a better hand from here, on solid footing."

"Go first," Magill said again.

Holland said, "Let me; I've done it in daylight," and pushed past the other men to feel his way to the gangplank. The *Montserrat's* deck was considerably higher than the level of the mole, so that the narrow footway rose steeply and had to be negotiated with caution. But he was able to reach back from the security of a grip on the deck railing to give his hand to Magill when Candelas passed him up, and felt oddly moved, he did not know why, at the tightness of the grip of Magill's thin fingers on his as he drew him up to the deck. The gangplank sagged under their combined weight, not dangerously, and sagged again as Candelas followed them. Standing together in the dark, they could feel the fishing boat adjusting the rhythm of its easy roll on the small waves of the harbor to the new balance it had taken with their boarding. But no one spoke to them out of the dark.

"Vicente's not here," Holland said. Candelas grunted, listening.

Magill said irritably, "You're psychic, too, no doubt."

"He'd be awake if he were. He isn't aboard."

"Someone is," Candelas said. "I hear snoring. Wait a minute."

His shadow moved away. They waited, intent, not moving, smelling fish and tar and salt, hearing at first only the lap and suck of waves against hull and mole, the faint creak of the *Montserrat's* timbers as she rocked, then a mumble of conversation in Catalan that followed on the appearance of a glow of light in the deckhouse and ended with a sharp, furious burst of blasphemy. Candelas came back raging and obscene.

"The son of a whore! The stupid dirty bastard son of a whore mother and a poxed father! For ten cases of cigarettes, ten lousy cases of cigarettes, he's bitched the whole business! I'll kill him! I'll—"

"Shut up," Magill said. The promises cut off in mid-oath. "Now tell us what happened."

"I'm telling you! A lousy ten cases of cigarettes!" Candelas turned the heat of his rage on Holland. "I spit in the milk of the mother of your blueprints! He took the money you gave him and put it into black market tobacco. I could have told you he'd try to squeeze an extra duro out of the deal if you gave him a chance, and somebody talked. The harbor cops pulled him in. They found the other money on him too, the cut bills. If they don't know all there is to know about us already, they'll bang it out of him before breakfast. We're futúts!"

His shadow was more distinct than it had been, a sharper outline against a graying of the eastern sky. Dawn was on its way, bringing a beginning stir of life aboard the other vessels of the fishing fleet. Their timing had been perfect. That much, at least, of the blueprint had been well drawn.

Holland said, "Is the boat fueled?"

"I don't know. It doesn't make any difference. We can't take off in it now, with or without the bastard."

"What's to stop us, if I buy the crew?"

"Gossip. Every big-mouth in Barceloneta will know that Vicente has been picked up, and why, and about the cut money, and everything else there is to know. They'll smell more than fish guts if his boat casts off without him. This tub is poison to us. The whole port is poison to us."

"We'd better get out of it, then," Magill said.

"I *told* you, patrón—"

"Never mind. It's a waste of time. We've got to move."

Holland said, "Before we move, let's make sure we know where we're going."

"Back to the Barrio Chino. What else?"

"That's poisoned for you, too, now. The cab driver will remember where he picked us up."

"We've got to find a hole somewhere until we can think of something."

"The hole needn't be in Barcelona. It will be a lot better away from Barcelona. Where's the nearest railroad station?"

"Five hundred meters from here," Candelas growled. "Buy

yourself a ticket and free us of your help, blue-printer. We can survive without you."

He was fairly visible now, a bulk rather than a shadow. Holland said, "We have enough time for this," and stabbed him solidly under the breastbone with extended rigid fingers. The blow was silent, easy to deliver and effectively paralyzing to the diaphragm. Seconds passed before Candelas could breathe again. After he was able to, he stood spraddle-legged and limp-armed, sucking for oxygen in hard-fought, hard-won noisy shallow inhalations that left him nothing over for protest, vocal or physical, when Holland said, "Only the people who pay me call me that."

Magill said, "I might as well be picked up for trying to find my own way as for being saddled with a pair of quarrelsome fools." He put on his glasses, peering first at Candelas, then accusingly at Holland in the growing light. "What did you do to him?"

"Nothing that won't pass. He can move. Let's go."

They went back down the gangplank and once more through the maze of lobster pots, bait boxes and crab traps on the mole, now distinguishable in gray depth from the shadows that were only shadows. Candelas was shaky still but mobile. Lights had begun to show on most of the boats, and brazier charcoal added another flavor to the port smell of fish, salt water and tar. One clattery diesel motor was already banging, warming up to be first out of the harbor.

Magill said, "If we do take the train, we can't go far on it. It's only a hundred miles to France. We'll have to drop off before we reach the frontier."

"The thing to do is get out of Barcelona as quickly and as far as possible," Holland said. "They know enough to look for you here, but that's all they do know." He added, "Or so it seems to me, although I don't suggest that my judgment is necessarily infallible. If you have a better idea, let's hear it?"

"You show promise," Magill said dryly. "But I don't have

a better idea."

At the railroad station they bought first-class tickets. Foreigners were always conspicuous in third class, the alternative. The first passenger train that went as far as the French frontier did not leave for several hours, but there was an early mixto for Gerona. It was far enough, if not possibly too far. A lot depended on the cab driver's curiosity, how long the police would take to trace them as far as the railroad station, other factors. With the widest possible safety margin they could still count on a safe couple of hours, and even a rattletrap Spanish mixto running on a poor roadbed covers half of a hundred miles in a couple of hours. It gave them time to breathe and to think ahead.

The first-class carriages were almost empty at that early hour. They had two full seats to themselves at the end of a car, with no one near enough to overhear their talk above the clatter of the car trucks on clicking rail ends.

Candelas said, "Now that I have my breath back and can break your skull if you try to give me another sore belly, Dutchman, I still say we should split up. You and the patrón are poison to each other. You and I are poison to each other. You have a passport, we have no passports. We are wanted by the cops, you are not wanted by the cops. Give us what further money you can spare and we will get off the train at Gerona. Stay on it, use your passport, go to France, buy us a bottle of wine if you like when we get there, and afterward I will show you a trick or two with the fingers you have yet to learn."

"No," Holland said.

"Why not?" Magill had put the glasses safely out of sight in his pocket and was squinting again, peering from one of them to the other. "It's at least a suggestion worth considering. All you do is veto it without argument."

"I took on a contract to deliver you in France. You don't have to like my help."

"I don't have to accept it, either, if I don't feel like it.

Have you any suggestions of your own—for consideration and discussion?"

"There are plenty of fishing boats on the Costa Brava. We can be in Palamós or Cadaqués this afternoon, and go on from there the way we started."

"No," Candelas said.

"Why not?" Magill snapped at him as he had snapped at Holland. "You're as bullheaded as he is. Think about it first and disagree afterward, if you have to."

"I don't have to think about it. We haven't any connections on the Costa Brava. You don't go up to the first fisherman you see on the beach and say, 'Hola, friend, we're running from the cops, slip us a ride to France.' For all you know the pig may be law-abiding. It's happened before now. You can't take a chance like that. You've got to have a connection."

"Where do you have connections, then, outside of Barcelona?" Holland asked.

"Andorra," Candelas said.

"No," Magill said.

"That makes it unanimous," Holland said. "Let's have your own reasons. Why veto Andorra?"

"You don't have to know the reasons. Andorra is out."

Candelas shook his head.

"And don't tell me to shut up, patrón, because this time it has to be said by somebody. Andorra is your best way, as we both know. But I'm wanted on both sides of the mountains there, Dutchman; Andorra is good for him but bad for me. So he says no, not to risk my neck for his."

"I still say no," Magill said. "It's as reckless for you to go back to Andorra as it would be for me to go back to the Barrio Chino."

"Let's do it the other way around, then," Holland said. "I'll take you out through Andorra, he can go back to the Barrio."

Candelas shook his head again, showing his strong yellow

horse teeth in a grin.

"You can't take him out through Andorra. There are two borders to cross instead of one, and he still has no papers. It takes connections, like mine. You don't have to like my help."

"All right," Holland said. "Let's compromise. Let's start in the direction of Andorra, see how close we can get to your connections without exposing you, then make up our minds what to do next when we've got that far. At least we'll be moving toward something instead of running away from it. If anyone thinks of something better while we're on the way, we can always change our minds."

"Good. But in my terrain we go my way, not yours. No blueprints. Is it understood?"

"We go your way as long as you know your way."

"Fair enough."

Magill was staring at the sea. The train rolled northward along the open Mediterranean shore, its track paralleling the flat beach. Even if he could have made out more than a blur without his glasses, it would have resolved itself into a ribbon of sand, another ribbon of white wave, the sea itself, a few clouds pink in the rising sun. Nothing more, not even a ship on the flat blue-gray monotony of water beyond which the coast of France was invisible. But the view, or the blur, seemed to hold his attention for a long time before he said, slowly, "I'd prefer taking my own risks to having them taken for me, if there were any other way to do it."

"There isn't any other way," Candelas said in good humor. "Besides, you have to take care of yourself on account of your señora and señorita, whereas who is to care if a couple of old stags like us land in a nice comfortable clink, eh, Dutchman? Or do you have a family of your own?"

"None that I've got to take care of myself for," Holland said. "Andorra it is, then."

VI

THE HAYCART HAD an odd switching motion when the donkey that drew it was trotting, like a flirt of its hips. It only happened when the donkey was going downhill and had to run to stay ahead of the force of gravity. The rest of the time the movement was more of a gentle sway back and forth between wheel and wheel, as conducive to sleep as the hay that mounded the cart and the sun shining on it. Holland and Magill had both slept for a long time while Candelas clucked to the donkey or got down from the cart to help the animal with his own shoulder at the cart's tail when the road climbed. The donkey was a little animal with slim deer-legs and tiny hooves. It had bells on its collar that jingled, a red plume mounted on its headstall that served no purpose but was traditional with Catalan donkeys, as Candelas explained it. Or maybe it was for good luck. He wasn't sure, not ever having been much of a jackass admirer himself. They were too liable to run the wrong way when frightened, or not to run at all. Like mules.

He slept now in his turn, while Magill held the reins and clucked to the donkey and Holland rode, walked or pushed from the rear as was necessary. It was a fair division of responsibility. Magill did not have the weight to give the donkey much assistance at the tail of the cart, but could help balance it against Candelas' larger bulk sprawled on the hay. The cart had a single axle slung between two high wheels that lifted its bed well off the ground, so that Candelas, weighing with the hay more behind the fulcrum of the axle than the little animal in front of it, would have lifted the donkey's hooves off the ground at every bump they came to without Magill sitting forward on the shafts as counterbalance. It was a clean practical application of a simple leverage factor, and it gave Holland a feeling of accomplishment that he had a hand in its success by helping the donkey in his own way. Otherwise he felt much like a third wheel on the cart; unnecessary to its function, unwanted by its passengers.

It was to be expected that Candelas would need little help in his own kind of terrain. To pass inconspicuously across a countryside of hay and haymakers he had bought the cart and donkey from a farmer, loaded from the first hayfield they came to, stuck a fork in the load, and so provided them with a bed and hiding place, if hiding became necessary, as well as transportation. To the cart he had added, in a village market, food and wine in a sack, a road map of the route they would have to follow, and the camouflage of rope-soled alpargatas to replace their shoes.

"The feet are the first thing they look at," he explained. "I had a pal once, picked up thirty kilometers inside the French border with a load of absinthe, half of it mine, too, because the dumbhead wore the wrong kind of shoes. You, Dutchman, your coat is too good for a countryman, but hide it in the hay with your socks and necktie and when your pants are wrinkled enough you can pass for a Catalan at a distance. You're the right color."

"I don't speak the right language."

"I said, at a distance. If you have to talk your castellano is no lousier than a Basque's or a Gallego's, and better than that of some of the other outlanders who come here for the haying. Patrón, I don't think it matters much now about the peepers, but it won't hurt to duck them into your pocket when you don't have need of them. Here's how we'll go." He pointed out their way on the map. "Bañolas, Ripoll, by train from Ripoll to Puigcerdá, easy. In Puigcerdá, well, we'll see what we'll see. It's no more than a hundred kilometers on the map, maybe twice as far the way we'll do it. We've got time, food, wine, transport, a bed to sleep in and good weather. What more does anyone want?"

"A cigar," Holland said, and was conscious of the pettiness of his thoughts.

Candelas dug down into the sack of provisions for half a dozen packages of cigarettes, all of them the most popular American brand and by far the most expensive on the Spanish market.

"They cost like the devil, but it's your money," he said cheerfully. "Eh, patrón? What's a little thing like American cigarettes to him, after forty-five thousand pesetas down the drainpipe?"

"Sixty thousand," Holland said. "And it's his money, not mine. He borrowed it from me."

"Mierda," Candelas said, yawning. "I forgot. One for your side, Dutchman. Have one of the patrón's cigarettes."

Now Magill and Holland sat smoking companionably on the seat of the cart, with Candelas snoring lightly behind them and the donkey's bells jingling musically along ahead. The country through which they were passing was fertile, well-watered, heavily farmed. They were already in the Pyrenean foothills, at the base of the watershed, and the richness of irrigated soil under a southern exposure was evidenced by the crops that grew all around them. Hay, corn, cane, wheat, vines, fruit trees, garden truck, patches of wood, meadow and pasture were watered by small streams that ran into larger streams in which there would be trout and crayfish. Holland, who had looked down on the length and breadth of Spain's aridity during more than a few plane flights above it, was unprepared for the productivity of its productive corner. He commented on it to Magill, when the long silence between them grew heavy.

Magill said, "Candelas would say, that's because it's Cataluña, not Spain. You heard him on the subject of Basques, Gallegos and other outlanders."

"How is it that you, even more foreign to him than a Gallego, control the kind of loyalty he gives you?"

"I buy it."

"For cash?"

"For cash and other rewards. A Catalan is a businessman, above all."

"What was the lie you told for him?"

"Lie?"

"To keep him off the rock pile."

"The police stopped two shipments of watch movements at the border, three or four years ago. I was carrying one, he was carrying the other; a coincidence. We had never seen each other before. I had an import license for mine, he had nothing. They were carting him off to jail when I saved him and his watch movements by claiming him as an employee under my license. It took a bit of bribery to bring off. Afterward he had no choice but to come in with me."

"Could I buy him away from you for more than you pay him?"

Magill was a while answering. He said finally, slowly, "I doubt it. When an old dog has lived for a time in a household, he becomes attached to the family."

"That sounds like a leading remark."

"We've got to discuss them, sooner or later. We can't just pretend that they don't exist."

"What's to be said?"

"I don't know. I don't know." Magill slapped irritably at the donkey's rump with the slack of its reins. "Have you—does Mike know?"

"Not yet."

"I suppose you're going to try to take her away from me?"

"I'm going to try to take both of them away from you."

"Marsha, too?"

"Marsha above all. I can't hope to win Mike from her and you together. You're too strong a combination."

"How do you propose to go about it?"

"If I knew, I wouldn't tell you."

"You might consider strangling me. Or have you?"

"I have. Marsha convinced me that it wouldn't do the trick. I haven't yet figured a way that will."

"You never will figure a way to come between Mike and me. I remember when she was only four or five years old—"

"Shut it off."

Magill made a sound of anger and frustration. Holland said obstinately, "I don't have to listen to when she was four or five years old. I don't have to listen to a damn word about her, or look at the pictures of her you've got in your wallet, or read your letter, either. I never asked to talk."

"It's going to be a long way to Andorra if we don't find something of common interest to talk about."

"Pick a neutral subject, then. What do you know about mining engineering?"

"Nothing."

"Good. We can't argue."

So Holland talked, endlessly; about mines and the engineering of mines; in Saudi Arabia, in the Saar, in Luxembourg, Thailand and Honduras, on the Cape and on Formosa; in Canada, Alaska and Colorado, everywhere he had worked except Peru, the first job of them all, the beginning of a career and the end of a marriage. He meant to bore both Magill and himself to stupor. But because he knew his job and was himself interested in it, he made it absorbing. Magill listened with interest, asked intelligent questions, stimulated Holland's memory to anecdote and further anecdote that took them a good three hours on their way over the slow back roads of the Catalan farm country before Candelas woke up to yawn, stretch and paw through the hay for the wine bottle he had burrowed into it.

Magill said, "You sound like a man who knows his job."

"I do," Holland said, in honesty. "I've piled up almost a million dollars working at it; in fees, bonuses, stock option deals that turned a profit when I brought in something good. No income tax on most of it, and expenses paid. I've got a reputation in the trade that's worth another million, too; Hard-nose Holland, the man who never takes his face off the grind-stone." He laughed, genuinely amused. "I've never thought of it before, but I'm a success. I've made good. I'm the one you read about in advertisements for correspondence school courses."

"An earned million dollars isn't anything to mock," Magill said.

"No? What will you give me for it?"

Magill was silent.

"So now you know what it's like to be on top of the heap," Holland finished. "Hand me up the bottle, you in the hay, before you drink it all. How far will we have come in three hours?"

"Twenty kilometers, maybe. Have I slept that long?"

By nightfall they had covered another thirty kilometers without particular incident, and were near enough to Ripoll and the railroad line to see a plume of sparks and the glare of the engine's fires as a train pulled out of town for the winding climb into the mountains. Candelas had a connection in Ripoll. He left them at a fonda outside of town where they were not asked to fill out the usual police registration forms before being taken in and fed, then drove the donkey and cart away to turn them back into cash.

"At a profit, too, unless these Ripollos are a lot harder to pluck than they used to be," he promised. They knew that something had gone wrong when they heard the quick jingle of the donkey's harness bells coming back to the fonda half an hour later.

"The guardias are looking for us." Candelas wagged his head in puzzlement. "I don't get it. Mother of God, how did they track us so fast, before we even got here? They must be reading tea leaves."

"What did you learn?" Magill said.

"What I'm telling you, patrón. I went to see my pal, first, lucky for us that we didn't show up together or the crook would have sold us like a shot, and he says the guardias are asking for identification papers on the train, in the station, wherever they feel like it, since this afternoon. Three men they want—a Catalan who looks like me, that means nothing because half of Cataluña looks like me, but also an American who looks like a Catalan and an American who looks like an American, with glasses like bulls'-eyes. Five hundred thousand pesetas for the package. Jesus and Mary, money like that isn't to be believed."

Magill, who had been wearing the glasses, sighed and took them off.

"Vilasar," Holland said. "It has to be, for that kind of reward."

"I'm afraid you're right." Magill rubbed his eyes. "The police wouldn't offer so much money on their own, nor be able to link us together quite so surely with nothing to go on but the word of a cab driver."

"At least your doubts about Carlos have been resolved. Since you don't want the clan on your side, he's organized it against you."

"But to what end?"

"The same end as always, with the added incentive of revenge." Holland described his humiliation of the marqués at the casino in Cannes. "A chance to scoop us both in together, you to be levered out of prison as a wedding present for Micaela and me to be kept there for obstructing justice as well as the Vilasars, would appeal to his sense of the fitness of things. Or am I exaggerating my own importance to him?"

"No. He'd never take a public slap in the face like that without hitting back."

"So we can be reasonably certain that the net is out for us at least as far as the frontier, and may extend into France if the family has that much influence. Does it?"

"I don't know. I doubt it. French justice isn't easy to buy. But Carlos doesn't need to exercise influence in France. I can't legally be in the country without papers. All he has to do is let the authorities know that I am, as soon as we get there."

Candelas, puzzled, said, "I'm thicker in the head than usual tonight, patrón. We're talking about the marqués, true?"

"Yes."

"But he is a friend, true? It was he who was digging to get you clear with the cops before this one talked you into making a break, true?"

"There was to be a payment for his help. The payment isn't going to be made. He has become an enemy instead of a friend."

"And this one becomes a friend instead of an enemy?"

"For the time, yes."

"Then you were right not to tell me what is none of my business." Candelas thumped the side of his head with the heel of his hand. "Friend, enemy; enemy, friend. We'd better get out of here before news of the reward leaks down from town."

"We'd better think of a new way to move first," Holland said. "A haycart and a donkey won't carry us far ahead of news of half a million pesetas."

"That does not have to be explained to me, either, Dutchman. They will carry us as far as the railroad, which is all that was ever expected of them. Come on, patrón. Grab the coattail again. Here we go."

They were in Puigcerdá, high on the Pyrenean slope, before midnight. More accurately, they were a kilometer and a half short of Puigcerdá, building a fire of cornstalks in a culvert under the railroad track to warm themselves after an unforgettable train ride. It had lasted only a couple of hours, but the hours had been wearing. Most of the time they had spent spread-eagled on top of a rocking boxcar behind an ancient coal-burning engine that belched smoke, sparks and glowing cinders like a fountain of fireworks, so that they had to slap fire out of their clothes with one hand and hold precariously to safety with the other. The train was not fast, but the windings it followed behind an earsplitting whistle up into mountains came often and sharply on a badly ballasted roadbed. And there had been more activity to the ride than slapping sparks, catching cold bullets of condensed steam in the face and hanging on. The train stopped twice before Puigcerdá; once at a junction where a yard crew split it in two, once at a station where the top of the boxcar could be too easily overlooked from a signal tower. Both times they had to drop off when the engine whistled for the stop, make their way around the station in darkness on strange ground where dogs barked at their going, then board the train again as it pulled out. Holland and Candelas worked in tacit teamwork to aid Magill in the boardings, Candelas swinging first to the irons and from them reaching to pull Magill's weight to security and hold it there while Holland scrambled up the following set of irons to lend a hand from the top of the boxcar before the train began to rock too dangerously for climbing. Magill had to make his own jumps, the glasses tied to his head for safety with a string from one of the alpargatas, and take his own bruises when he stumbled and went down with his hands over the lenses to protect them instead of his flesh.

"I'll heal," he said briefly of a torn ear while they hunched over the burning cornstalks in the culvert, sheltered from the cold Pyrenean wind. "The glasses won't. They've got to last for a while. A spare stops being a spare when you have to use it."

Holland said, "What's to stop us from walking around

Puigcerdá, the way we've already walked around two other towns tonight, and following the railroad track straight into France? It can't be more than half an hour from here, and even Vilasar hasn't enough money to buy patrols for a whole frontier."

Candelas was scuffing his hands over the flame. His face was so begrimed by soft-coal smoke that his yellow teeth looked white in contrast.

"You don't know the racket," he said.

"Tell me."

"It isn't just crossing a border that counts when you haven't got papers. It's the hundred kilometers on the other side. You have to get over those without making some nosy Nellie curious about your clothes or your haircut or your accent or the way you spit. The marqués doesn't have to have tipped the French cops for them to be watching their side of the mountain for immigrants. If they pick us up without papers—cataplungún! Back we go. Officially, in the salad basket."

"We covered the last hundred kilometers without too much trouble."

"This isn't France, Dutchman. This is Spain. Spanish cops don't have to watch for people sneaking into the country, except importers with packs on their backs. Everybody who can is sneaking the other way; a lot of them, as we are, through Andorra."

Magill said stubbornly, "We haven't made up our minds to Andorra yet."

"Patrón, we don't have to make up our minds now. The marqués did it for us when he put up the five hundred thousand pesetas." Candelas tossed a bundle of cornstalks on the fire, and by its light sorted three cigarettes from a package to hand around. "We've got to get out of Spain fast, we've got to go into France carefully. Tell me any way to do it without stopping to take a breath in between, and I'll listen."

Reaching for a coal at the fire's edge, Magill said nothing. His face was drawn and tired. Dark blood from the torn ear had coagulated on his cheek. He held the coal for all three cigarettes, then tossed it back in the fire.

Holland said, "Are you certain you'll be better off in Andorra than out of Andorra? What about papers there?"

"Papers?" Candelas laughed his musical laugh. "The only papers they care about in Andorra are the kind that have numbers printed in the four corners, and you can get along without those if you know how."

"How do we get there?"

"Walk."

"How far?"

"A jaunt. Thirty kilometers."

Magill said, "I could use some sleep first."

"Patrón, listen to me, just this once—"

"I know, I know," Magill said crossly. "Just this once, and once more, and once again after that. I only said I could use some sleep, not that I expected to get any. Kick out the fire and let's get started."

They walked for the rest of the night; most of the way by road, at the end stumbling and heavy-footed with fatigue over footpaths, when footpaths became visible in the early light. The way took them into the shelter of pine forest that more and more began to cover the mountain slope in place of farm and vineyard. The walk was up and down all the way, but up much more than down, so that at the end of the night they had gained enough altitude for Holland to become conscious of increasing cold and a slight shortness of breath. Two years at sea level or below it in the Arabian desert had not conditioned him for a night-long climb in the mountains, a climb that was made the more tiring because he was not wearing the right kind of shoes for it. The soft rope-and-canvas alpargatas were comfortable enough on the foot but gave no support to it, and were inadequate protection against sharp stones. Still, he was twenty years younger than Magill, in far better physical condition, without need to peer through strong lenses even to see his way. He refused to be the first to confess that he was done in and barely able to keep moving when the sun came up to give them light and warmth at last and Candelas, picking out a rock face that would store and reflect the warmth, dropped down against it like a tired dog.

"That's all for this leg," he said. "We've got to eat again before we tackle the rest, and pick up a bit of camouflage. Patrón, stick your back against the rock here and you'll think you're a fried egg when the sun gets a little higher. You, too, Dutchman. There's room for all of us."

Magill collapsed against the rock without a word. His face, still with its stain of blood, grimed by smoke and coal dust and grayed by a day's growth of beard, was shocking in its colorlessness under all. He looked like a dead man. Without lifting his hands even to remove the glasses, completely inert, he closed his eyes and was asleep.

Holland lowered himself achingly to the ground, grateful for the hard support of the rock at his back. It would be better when the rock was warm, but even to sit down and lean against something was an animal pleasure. He had never been so tired.

Candelas said, "I didn't think he was going to make it this far," and reached for the knife sheath at the back of his neck to pull it around to his chest before settling into a position of maximum comfort. "Jesus and Mary, what a day."

"I didn't think I was going to make it," Holland said. "I don't know how he did."

"He can't afford to quit. You can. You've got a passport."

"We've been over that before."

"This time I'm asking for an answer, not a punch in the gut. Why don't you use it?"

"Too dangerous." Holland couldn't keep his eyes open. "The marqués is after me now, too."

"So you told us. But why? Why make yourself an enemy like the Vilasar?"

"You said you didn't want to know any more about it"—Holland yawned uncontrollably—"than you do."

"Is it for the daughter? Or the mother?"

Holland opened his eyes, rolling his head against the rock to look into Candelas' dirty face, stubbled now like a grizzly's snout. Candelas said, "He killed one man for her already. You wouldn't think he had that in him, either, would you?"

Holland's eyes closed again, for all he could do to keep them open. He was too tired even to think. Candelas said, "Profit, revenge or a woman, it's got to be one of them. Whichever it is, God be thanked I don't want it as much as you do, Dutchman. Pass a good night."

He closed his eyes and began to snore. Holland was asleep before the snore was repeated.

He awoke when the sun had passed behind the rock face and the rock began to cool instead of gaining heat. Magill slept on. His color was better, although his body still lay in the same position of inert helplessness, a dropped bundle. Candelas was nowhere in sight. Somewhere nearby a stream of water made a whispering noise on pebbles, and a jay screamed at intervals from a pine. There was no other sound, not even wind in the trees. Around them the mountains were high, still and peaceful.

He sat for another five minutes, easing himself bit by bit from the cramp that stiffened his arms and legs. His head ached, his back ached, his feet were sore, he was hungry. Otherwise he felt in fair shape, or would when the cramps had worked themselves out and he had brushed his teeth. He was searching his coat for the toothbrush he carried there, finding more cinder burns than the coat could survive for long, when Candelas came around a corner of the rock. His face was clean, and his hair and grizzly's beard dripped water.

"There's a spring back there," he offered hospitably.

"Don't look at yourself in it, unless you've got a strong stomach."

"Thanks for the warning," Holland said. He rubbed his stiff bristle of black whisker, looked at the smut that came off on his hand, and got up painfully, still cramped, to go and give himself a rough scrubbing with sand and water from a pool below the spring before he brushed his teeth and combed his hair.

When he came back Magill was painfully working out his own cramps. He had taken off the glasses, and the pale circles their removal left in his smoke-grimed face gave him a clownish look, like a panda.

He said, grumbling, "I can't feel my legs."

"You'll feel them fast enough when the blood gets moving," Candelas promised. He picked Magill up, propped him against the rock and took the glasses from him to polish on his shirttail. "There. Put on the peepers now, and I'll show you where we're going. Just over there, behind those two peaks."

They were on a shoulder of mountain overlooking a long river valley that descended, widened and became flat farmland. Candelas pointed out a town in the valley, fifteen or twenty kilometers from where they stood but plainly visible in the thin mountain air. They could see the small moving dot of a bus coming from the town up a road that paralleled the river, a couple of smaller dots going down that were automobiles, another slower-moving dot that was a farm wagon.

"That's Seo de Urgel." Candelas held out his broad hands cupped together, fingertips tipped higher than the base of the palms, as a man would hold a book he was reading. "Put Seo on the left pulse. Andorra is in the hands; a little bigger than mine, not much, all of it on this side of the cordillera except the right thumb. You have to bust that at the knuckle to make it hang down right on the other side. The fingertips are the peaks of the cordillera, where France begins. The road goes up the wrist here, from Seo, into the palm of the left hand, and forks. One fork goes another five kilometers into the palm and dead-ends. The other branches off across the right hand at the base of the fingers, crosses the watershed at the hump of the busted thumb and follows the thumb down into France. That's the highway system, except for mule tracks and foot-paths."

Holland said, "Railroad?"

"No railroad, no airfield, no navigable water and no French road connection most winters. The pass over the watershed is at twenty-four hundred meters, and it generally snows in from October to May. You can get in and out from this side all year, because this end is lower, but every once in a while the big brains in Madrid close the border to control contraband—they're real clever that way, in Madrid—and then contraband becomes good business because it takes a professional to get it out the hard way, through the hills, instead of tucked inside some dame's dairy or under the back seat of a car."

"What does a country of that size produce that's worth smuggling?" Holland asked.

Candelas laughed. Magill said, "What do you know about the import-export trade?"

"Nothing."

"Good. We can't argue."

The lecture was even more interesting to Holland than his own, he was sure, had been to Magill. He had known in a vague way that Andorra was microscopic, mountainous, land-locked by France and Spain and uninfluenced by the laws of either country insofar as they had to do with the payment of customs duties. What he learned further was that Andorra had no customs duties of its own, and with a permanent population held to around seven thousand people by the limited productivity of its soil, mostly in tobacco cultivation, was allowed by France and Spain to import, or could not be prevented by France and Spain from importing, enough untaxed, duty-free manufactures of other countries, including those of France and Spain, to supply a population fifty times greater than its own. The bargain-priced excess annually brought several hundred thousand French and Spanish buyers up through the Pyrenean passes when passes and frontiers alike were open. When they were not, the same untaxed goods went hunting for French and Spanish buyers, along with untaxed Andorran tobacco, by way of mule tracks through the mountains, in evasion of the armed guards with which France and Spain ringed the country to hold a check on the traffic they could not eliminate.

"That's why we won't have any trouble getting in," Candelas explained. "Nobody ever heard of contraband moving in the wrong direction. All we need is a pack-load each of whatever is hottest on the market right now, and we're practically there. If they catch us going in, they think we're coming out, and chase us back the way we want to go. Not bad for a dumbhead, eh?" He beamed.

"What are the odds on getting shot instead of chased?" Holland asked.

"None, if you know what you're doing. On this side, when they see you they shoot in the air first, and when they shoot in the air you dump your load and run. They only shoot at you if you try to get away with the stuff. On the French side, they carry guns for ornament."

"What does that mean?"

"Well, who but a Spaniard would want to put a bullet in some poor bugger because he hasn't paid tax on a little alcohol or tobacco? Not the froggies. They're too civilized. All you have to do is outrun them."

"It sounds easy enough. Where do we get the packs?"

"You don't. I do, down there." Candelas pointed out a plume of smoke below them, another nearer the valley where the road came up. "That's La Llosa, that's Bescarán. Both of them are drops."

"That's where you'll be most easily recognized then," Magill said worriedly. "It isn't as simple as it sounds. You're known in this part of the country, and five hundred thousand pesetas will sharpen a lot of eyes. I don't like it."

"Eyes can be dulled, too," Holland said. He felt inside his shirt for the buckle of the soft leather belt he wore next to his skin, and brought the belt out. "Do they know what a fifty-dollar bill is in these mountains?"

Candelas said, "The whole world knows what a fifty-dollar bill is, if only by reputation. Mother of God!"

Holland had unzipped the compartments in the money belt and was taking out packages of currency. He gave Candelas four of the packages.

"That's six hundred thousand pesetas at any bank, anywhere. Overbid the reward, if you have to, and promise more. You'll have to decide for yourself how to protect against a sellout. The knife trick is as good as any, if you can work it."

"Mother of God," Candelas said again, staring wide-eyed at the money in his hand.

There was a constraint on him afterward, when he had put the packages of bills inside his shirt and Magill, still reluctant, had been persuaded that it was no more than sensible for him to go down the mountainside alone and come back for them if the way was clear. If it was not clear, they would know about it when he did not return. A certain amount of risk was inescapable. He gave them explicit directions as to the way they were to go and the paths they were to follow without his guidance, if it became necessary.

"The packs would be the safest, but you can get through without them if you take your time." He drew a rough map of the route on the ground. "Lie up on the hill, here, until you've got the guards spotted. They'll be along here, and here, and here. If the weather is good, wait until daylight and follow the hill crests. That way they'll see you, but you can watch both sides of the crest and see them coming, then go the other way.

If it clouds up, go in at night and keep to the stream beds. They've got dogs, you'll hear them yowling, but they keep them on a chain so nobody can steal them and sell them back. Dogs can't smell through running water. Just don't let the yowling come too close. If they shoot, remember to run uphill when they're below you, downhill when they're higher; a rifle always overshoots from above and the other way around. And when you get there, both of you, remember that half a million pesetas is just as big a potful in Andorra as it is here. You could both be sacked up and brought back for sale like any other contraband. Keep your backs together and your guard up."

"We'll remember," Holland said. "Anything more?"

"That's all. Except—" Candelas hesitated, shrugged and finished, rudely, "Mierda. That's all. Cigarettes and matches are on the rock where we slept, with the spare peepers. Take care of yourself, patrón. If I come back, it will be before nightfall."

Magill said nothing.

They stood and watched him go down the hill, taking long plunging steps. Once he stopped to re-tie the strings of his alpargatas, but he did not look back.

When he was out of sight, Magill went over to the rock for a cigarette. He offered Holland one, and accepted a light.

"Will he be back?" Holland said.

"Your guess is as good as mine."

"I don't mean only if he isn't picked up."

"Neither do I."

They smoked in silence for a while.

Magill said slowly, "I don't think even he knows, at this point. The answer is the answer to the question you asked yesterday, about buying him. We'll both know."

"If it makes a difference, I wasn't trying to buy him."

"It doesn't make a difference. The answer will still be the same."

Some time later Magill said, as an afterthought, "Add the money to what I owe you."

"No," Holland said. "If I've bought him, I'll pay for him."

Magill did not argue.

They sat in the sun and waited. Jays screamed from time to time; shadows moved and lengthened from right to left. Clouds began to form on the mountain peaks. A thin steady traffic of cars and trucks moved up and down the far-off road in the valley below them. Several times during the afternoon Holland went to the spring to drink heavily of the cold water, numbing the ache of hunger that was growing in his belly. When he suggested that Magill do the same, Magill seemed to be less gnawed by hunger than by his thoughts.

He said abruptly, "We've got to talk about Marsha, whether you like it or not."

"What is there to say?"

"She told you what happened?"

"Yes."

"Any of the details?"

"Enough."

"In this country, more even than in other countries, public opinion is on the side of a husband who commits murder for his wife's virtue. It isn't a defense, but it's extenuating; an interloper in a man's home presumably deserves whatever he gets. It could save me from the garrote if I ever got taken to trial."

"Go on."

"The trouble is, I'm an interloper myself. That won't look so good. She's still married to you."

A hawk soared lazily over their heads, hunting. All the jays screamed at once in warning and were quiet, safe in the foliage of the pines. The hawk made a swooping circle of reconnaissance, then soared away to a more rewarding part of the mountainside.

After it had come and gone, Holland said, "I knew. When

did you find out?"

"Before we came to Spain. Divorce is questionable here when it's recognized at all, so I had to check to make sure that she and Mike wouldn't be humiliated or left in an embarrassing legal position if something happened to me." Magill tossed a stone and watched it roll down the hill slope. "I found out that she was without the stigma. Merely a bigamist."

"She could have gone back to Peru and divorced me any time you wanted her to. She's still legally resident there."

"I didn't want her to know. I didn't want Mike to know I wasn't her father. I rewrote my will to protect them, and let it go at that."

"She knows now. I told her."

"What did she say?"

"She thought it was unkind of me not to do what you had done, and keep it from her."

"You and she and I are still the only ones who do know, then."

"What does that mean?"

"Whatever you want it to mean, I guess." Magill tossed another stone. "Mike's at rather a bad age to learn that her father isn't her father at all, just a man who's been living with her mother since before she was born, and a murderer for another man's wife."

"Not to mention the effect the disclosure would have on a Spanish trial court."

"I said that in the beginning. If they take me, you can be the most damaging witness against me. You'll never win them from me that way, though. You'd only alienate them forever."

"I hadn't thought of doing it that way."

"Something more subtle? A shove off a cliff?"

"I still haven't made up my mind, but the cliff is out for the moment. Your watchdog is coming back."

Magill lifted his head to look. Seeing the unmistakable squat figure far below, toiling up the mountainside with a pack on its back, he said, "So now we know that much, at least."

"Now we know that much," Holland agreed. The sun had gone behind a mountain peak when the climber reached the shelf where they waited. He was sweating from the climb. Holland took the weight of the knapsack he carried as he eased out of the shoulder straps.

"Thanks, Dutchman." Candelas wiped sweat from his curly stubble of beard. "I'm carrying more blubber than I used to. There's food, wine and blankets in there, also your money, and a heavier load to bring back up a mountain I never carried. Take it away from me before I think more about it."

"You could have kept it," Holland said. "Even coming back, we needn't have known that you didn't have to use it."

"Eh, but I'd have had to make up a better story than the real one, and that's not in me. Wait until I have a pull at the spring and I'll tell you."

He came back from the spring with his face and shirtfront wet. He was grinning.

"When you've got luck you can live with you-know-what for brains," he said. "They were looking for Candelas down below, as we all expected. They took him, too, poor clown. A couple of hours before I got there."

"What?"

"God's truth. Another dumbhead like me, as I was fifteen years ago, with the same weak mind for business and the same strong back for burdens. The guardias put up a price, not the whole reward by a long shot but enough, and in their own brainy way took the first one offered who fit the description. Being in his business, naturally he was too dumb to convince them that he was no more than an honest importer. They've been slapping him around ever since to get him to tell where you two are hiding. I went in under their fat asses and out again like a rabbit. We're all fixed."

"Where are the packs?"

"Down below, safe. I had to invest the last of your whole

pesetas, Dutchman, but we'll get some of them back on the other side." Candelas looked calculatingly at the clouds that were piling up around the mountain peaks. "It's going to be a wet night, good for business. Let's eat while a fire will burn."

They made the fire behind the rock face, convenient to the spring and invisible from the valley below. The fallen pine needles Candelas gathered to start a flame were not dry, and caught fire so slowly that Magill, impatient, said, "Did you invest the half-pesetas, too?"

"Those are beyond investment. I was too clever with the knife."

"Then push them under the pine needles and let's get what value out of them we can. You'll be all night with it otherwise."

Candelas, blowing carefully on the smoldering tinder, said, "Because I brought back the Dutchman's six hundred thousand when I didn't have to, patrón, will you give me instead of the fire your waste paper?"

"What good is it to you?"

"Nothing, now. But the other half is still in Barcelona somewhere. It could be that the two halves will have an attraction for each other when I go back."

"Your half could win you a beating from the guardias and a jail sentence. You'd do better to throw it on the fire."

Candelas hunched his thick shoulders in a shrug, still coddling the flame.

"A beating, what is that? As for jails, they do not frighten me too much." He blew strongly on the glowing pine needles. They caught and flared at last, lighting the gravity of his bearded face. "I was a rich man for a few hours today, patrón. Let me dream of being a rich man again, in a small way. It costs nothing you would not throw on a fire."

None of them ever referred again to his descent of the mountainside, or the fact of his return.

He had brought meat, bread, salt, wine and onions in the

knapsack, and three strongly woven wool blankets. The meat they roasted on pine twigs; the blankets Candelas made into ponchos, while they ate, by cutting a head-slit in the middle of each, so that the blanket would cover both the man who wore it and the pack he carried on his back. By the time they had finished their meal the ponchos were necessary. With nightfall, a light drizzle of rain began that grew heavier as they went down the mountainside to where the packs were hidden.

"It's all pretty heavy stuff," Candelas apologized. "I had to make the monkey I bought it from think I was running it into Lérida by truck, and I couldn't hold out for light goods without giving him something to think about. Heft this one, patrón. It's full of stylos, the best I could do for you. Can you manage it?"

"I'll carry it until I can't," Magill said.

"If you have to dump it, just slip the straps and run. But don't dump until I tell you to. This one is yours, Dutchman. Guess what you're carrying."

Holland lifted the pack. It weighed in the neighborhood of twenty-five or thirty kilos and was full of what felt through the canvas like cartridge boxes. He said, "Ammunition?"

"They put you in prison for that." Candelas showed his strong yellow teeth. "No. No. Guess again. Closer to home."

"I give up."

"Candelas," Candelas said, and laughed. "Now you will know what it is to be a dumbhead."

It was with those loads, in an intermittent drizzle pierced by enough watery moonlight to show them their path from time to time, that they made their way out of Spain. They were not challenged, nor seemingly in danger of challenge even when, as happened several times, Candelas cautioned them to silence and immobility while they listened to dogs bark at a distance, judging the distance and the animals' direction of movement before choosing their own. Once, when they had been an hour on their way, they heard shouts and several shots, not too far off.

"It could be business, it could be a bluff," Candelas said. "A night like this, sometimes they hear something or think they hear something, they'll snap a cap into the dark and hope to scare somebody into dropping his pack." He added seriously, "You can't trust a customs guard."

They went on, pacing themselves to Magill's ever-slowing progress. He breathed hard and heavily, and was either already too tired to lift his feet or having trouble seeing his way through the rain that misted his glasses. He kept stumbling, two or three times going to his knees in the mud and water of the stream bed they were following. Holland was better off, but not much. On level ground the heavy pack he carried would have been more than a comfortable load. To climb with it, over footing that was rocky and unreliable when it was not wet and slippery beneath the inadequacies of the cloth-and-rope alpargatas, was real hardship.

"We'll drop part of your load when we get a little farther along, patrón," Candelas promised. "It isn't safe yet. Back up against the bank there and take a blow."

"How much farther?"

"Another hour, maybe."

"I won't last another hour." Magill was a stooped shadow in the rainy dark, grotesquely humpbacked under his soggy poncho. "The pack is too much for me."

"You've got to keep the pack. It's your insurance. If they catch you without it, they'll know you have no business in the mountains. They'll shoot you in the leg just to find out what you're doing here."

Magill splashed toward the bank of the barranco in which they had stopped, to lean the weight of his load against its slope. Either he or the pack failed to find solid support, because they heard him slip and fall in a collapse of earth. When they went to him he said dully, "I've lost my glasses."

Candelas found them, pawing through mud and rubble.

A break in the drizzle and the temporary emergence of the watery moon helped, but they had to leave Magill where he had fallen until it was safe to plant their feet to help him, after the glasses had been found. He made no move to help himself, but lay inert until they pulled him up between them.

Candelas, scrubbing the glasses on his poncho, said anxiously, "They feel all right. Here, try them, and see if our luck is still running. Thanks to God we still have the" spare."

"We don't have the spare," Magill said, in the same dull voice. "I left it on the rock where we slept. And it doesn't do any good to be able to see where you're going when you can't lift your feet."

"Take the stylos out of the pack and stuff it with the ponchos," Holland said. "They're too wet to be any protection now. They'll give the knapsack shape."

"It's the stylos that count, not just the knapsack," Candelas insisted. "The rules are, if they see you and shoot—"

"Never mind." Holland was himself too weary to argue. To Magill he said, "Give me your pack. He can take it for a while after me, until you get your wind back."

"You can't carry two packs," Magill answered irritably. "Don't talk nonsense."

"I can carry anything I have to carry." Holland ached with fatigue and frustration. He knew as well as Magill that he would scarcely be able to stagger under the double burden, but between Candelas' stubbornness and Magill's physical limitations there was no choice but to make the effort. "Give me the pack, damn it! We've got to move!"

"I've changed my mind." A frosty new vigor was in Magill's voice. "I think I'll be able to carry it after all."

After that they saved their breath for climbing, following along behind Candelas' blanketed shadow in their own dripping blankets. The crude ponchos, having absorbed all the water they could hold, were an encumbrance and an additional burden, but it would have taken a deliberate expenditure of energy to throw them off and they did not have the energy to spare. They climbed like animals, on all fours where the going was steep; stopping every few minutes because they had to stop, because it was impossible for flesh and blood not to stop, but only long enough to get their wind before going on; not resting, only catching up on the arrears of breathing. Candelas, bull-strong, grumbled at even those halts, chivvying them to keep moving, but the intervals between breathers grew shorter and shorter as Magill's reserves ran out. The sound of his hard-breathed stumbling progress in the dark was painful. It made Holland think of pack horses he had known to kill themselves of overwork in the heights of the Andean peaks because they would not, like tougher-hided mules, stop to rest even under the whippings of their drivers. Was Magill horse or mule?

He put the thought away, but it came back. Magill was horse. He himself was horse. Pride goaded them both. But Magill did not have his strength, his heart, his younger arteries, his vitality. If he drove himself to the breaking point, would not Magill, rather than again confess inadequacy, inevitably break first? His own breaking point was not far off, and it was Candelas who urged them toward it, not any volition of his own. Nobody, not even Marsha, could possibly blame him if it happened that way. He could even safely hurry it; a small increase in the pace; another rowel, subtly applied —the perfect, undetectable, unpunishable murder—

Panicked, he gasped, "I can't go on!" at Candelas' back, and stopped in his tracks to block the way for Magill behind, so that when he leaned his pack into the bank of the barranco they were climbing and accepted the enormous relief of its support for his load, Magill was obliged to take advantage of the same surcease. They rested elbow to elbow, speechless, slack-muscled, sucking air in great gulps, while Candelas cursed and complained at the delay.

"Jesus and Mary, we don't dare stop now," he pleaded.

"They patrol these rabbit runs from the bottom up. If we don't keep moving ahead of them, they'll run us down from the rear and see the whole trick. Come on, come on, come on! It's only another couple of minutes to the top!"

He stopped to listen anxiously for dogs.

Holland could hear only the flow of water down the barranco, the raggedness of Magill's breathing over his own, the thump of his own pulse in his ears. They had come much too close to it that time. He did not move, nor allow Magill to move by him, for all Candelas' urgings, until they were both breathing normally. Afterward they climbed for another quarter of an hour to where the barranco flattened to a swale and they stood in a saddle of wet meadow looking down into a valley where house lights unexpectedly twinkled through the rain and motor traffic moved on a single road.

"That's it," Candelas said in satisfaction. "I told you it was only another couple of minutes. Now for a bit of easy going downhill, and we'll be getting some of our money back on the merchandise. Was I so dumb to make you hang on to the stylos, patrón?"

VII

THE BARON WAS a slight dark man, smaller than Magill but without Magill's stoop, and patrician. His family crest was a shield of elaborate quarterings; his family name, Montaner-Engordany, had the ring of medieval trumpets in it. The Engordany half of the title, according to a genealogy Holland found while browsing in the baron's library, had been granted by Charlemagne in the ninth century, for services rendered. Candelas addressed him as "Excellency" and used the "thou" of a social equal to him, as he never did with Magill or Holland. The baron had given Candelas his nickname fifteen years earlier, before buying him out from under the burden of the Andorran spark-plug monopoly. According to Candelas, the baron was a master among contrabandists; he paid duty on nothing and smuggled everything.

He was a widower, still in the black of first-year mourning, who lived with three hunting dogs and five servants in a big stone house like a castle on the mountain slope above Ordino, a hillside village placed almost exactly halfway between France and Spain on the single dead-end fork of Andorra's single highway, convenient to both frontiers. The castle, in part, predated the discovery of the Americas; the date 1450 was cut into the stone lintel of the Gothic door that led from its stone-flagged courtyard into its stone-pillared wine cellar. Half of the wine cellar was full of ancient musty barrels, the other half stocked with modern packagings of imported merchandise waiting its turn for re-export. The cellar warehouse absorbed the packs that Candelas and his two tired bearers brought to it, at cost to them and a loss to the baron, who would have to pay for the return of the goods to Spain. In his view it was a small price for the pleasure of their company.

"You're a break in the monotony," he told Holland, the afternoon after their arrival. They had been allowed to sleep as long as they chose to sleep, which was until late in the day. "There's nothing duller than a business that runs by itself, even from customs guards. How long are you going to be around?"

"It's up to Candelas. Probably not more than a day or two."

"Stay until the weather changes and I'll show you some shooting. We've got chamois and a few bear. Wild hen, too."

"I'm afraid I'm not much of a hunter. I haven't shot a gun in almost twenty years."

"Time you tried your hand at it again."

"The last animal I shot took too long to die," Holland said. "Chess is my sport. Do you play?"

The baron gave him a single sharp look and spoke no more about shooting. "Chess, certainly. Although I warn you, you will have to be good to beat me. It's another trouble with having time on your hands. You get to be too clever at games. What would you like to drink?"

"What is there to drink?"

"Oh, Scotch, bourbon, rye, Irish, cognac, calvados, absinthe, aquavit, slivovitz, ouzo, raki, vodka, wine, beer, what you like. It will be in the cellar some place."

Holland stretched cautiously, feeling the sore muscles of his back twinge. From rags to riches was not an unpleasant change, and he liked the baron. He said, "Coffee to begin with, I think. And a hot bath would be welcome, if it's not too much to ask."

"It's your house," the baron said, in the formal Spanish way. He pulled a bell cord.

Holland's room was one of three that had been opened, warmed and aired when they came stumbling down the hill out of the rain to drop their packs in the baron's courtyard. The baron had asked no questions, then or later. They had been taken in, fed and given beds, although not soon enough to prevent Magill from falling asleep while he was still eating. He looked small, shrunken and ugly asleep in the baronial dining room; his mouth slackly open, his glasses magnifying the hollows into which his eyes had sunk. Candelas had picked him up like a child, without waking him, and taken him away.

Holland, eating hungrily, had apologized to the baron for his own table manners while continuing to wolf his food. He knew that he would himself fall asleep within minutes, and for some reason it seemed highly important that he should make it as far as a bed on his own legs, even though he was barely able to pull his clothes off when he got there and gave no thought to washing. Now, rested, with a pirate's growth of black beard on his face and the sweat, grime and mud of three days' flight on his body, he had time at last to be clean.

The bath that arrived in answer to the baron's ring was as medieval a survival as the baron himself. It was brought in by two maids, a deep wooden tub which they set before a fireplace before filling it with steaming water carried in from a kitchen boiler in copper pots. One of the maids was a middle-aged mousy woman, the other young and very pretty, an authentic Catalan beauty with lustrous eyes, lustrous hair, clear white skin, a white flashing smile, a trim full-figured body as attractive as a ripe peach. She startled Holland by bringing him his coffee after he had climbed into the tub and was soaking the ache out of his muscles, and twice came back afterward with more hot water to warm the bath. But she did not seem to be even slightly embarrassed by his nakedness, or to consider her own function an unusual one. He decided that the baron's feudal way of life had much to be said for it. He wondered if a lackey would be sent to shave him, and was disappointed when the mousy maid, as indifferent to him as the pretty one, brought a good Japanese imitation of an American electric razor, still in its original package.

Candelas was freshly shaved and clean when he came into the room between the filling of the tub and its first rewarming. He looked appropriately medieval in a cowled robe like a monk's habit.

"Sainted Mother of God, why did I not think to ask for a tub?" he said of the pretty maid, when she had come and gone once. The second time he paid her the favor of an elaborately heavy-handed piropo, the flowery compliment with which a Spanish gallant pays tribute to a pretty girl: "With plumbing like you in my house, little fountain, I would bathe twice every day and three times for fiestas." The girl blushed and smiled, but did not come back to give him another opportunity. To accept piropos gracefully was one thing. To invite them sometimes led to misunderstanding.

"How is he?" Holland asked of Magill.

"Still sawing away."

"How long before he'll be ready to move on?"

"You're in a hurry, after that load of pig iron you packed up the mountain?"

"I was supposed to deliver him in Marseille two days ago. His family may be wondering what happened."

"You could telephone his señora. I expect that's what he'll want to do himself, when he wakes up."

It had not occurred to Holland that a fifteenth-century baronial keep would contain a telephone. The possibility that it did made him sharply impatient to call Marsha before Magill could. He climbed out of the tub, dried himself, and could find no clothes, only the things that had been in his pockets. A carved medieval armario gave up slippers and another of the cowled robes such as Candelas wore. Robe, slippers and the three-day stubble of black beard he had not yet taken time to shave made him look rather like a debased monk in the mirror of the armario; Rasputin, perhaps. The money belt he had strapped around his waist after the bath gave him, in the straight lines of the robe, a small monkish paunch.

On impulse, he took the belt off and tossed it.

“Keep that for me, will you?” he said. “Twenty-five thousand dollars is too much to wear around the middle without a pair of pants to cover it.”

He left the room before Candelas could answer or object, not sure why he had done what he had done but curious to know what the outcome would be. It was said that every man had his price, and Magill’s man had wavered at six hundred thousand pesetas; ten thousand dollars. Two and a half times as much ought to buy—what? He wasn’t sure what it was he wanted to buy.

The calves of his legs and the muscles in the small of his back still hurt, but he could walk without limping after the bath. In time he found the baron, giving orders to a mayordomo about dinner and the proper wines. The baron said, again, that his home was his guests’ along with everything in it, including the telephone to be found in the library, but that the line was useless for the call that Holland wanted to make.

“We’re part of the Spanish system here,” he explained.

“The only direct line to France is in the French post office in Andorra la Vella, down the road. You could, in theory, reach Cannes from here by way of Barcelona, but nobody has ever had the patience to wait for a call to go through that way. It would take days. You’ll do much better to let my man run you down to La Vella.”

“I haven’t any clothes. Mine have disappeared.”

“The maids took them to clean. I’ll see if they’re passable.

I'm afraid there's nothing else in the house to fit you."

His suit was being made ready by the pretty maid. She had got most of the mud off it, and was trying to do something about the cinder burns and brush rips with a needle and thread. He had to wait for a few minutes for her to finish.

While he was waiting, Candelas found him. He carried the money belt in both hands, as if it were venomous.

"Were you thinking when you said twenty-five thousand dollars, Dutchman?" he asked seriously.

"I'm not sure."

"For a smaller fortune than that many men would cut your throat without a second thought."

"Perhaps I was protecting my throat by giving it away."

"A man who worried overmuch about his throat would not carry so much around his middle."

"I thought I might need it to buy your patrón free."

"And since you did not, why do you tempt me with it?"

"I don't know. It was an impulse."

"That kind of an impulse could be dangerous for both of us." Candelas held out the belt. "This I can do once, at least, but do not count on me to do it again. I owe you nothing, neither loyalty nor friendship."

There was a massive dignity about the gesture that made Holland feel vaguely shamed. He took the belt back without further words, and when he unzipped it in the privacy of his room to take a few bills from one of the sheaves of fifties, refused to permit himself to check the contents further.

After he had shaved and dressed, the baron's chauffeur drove him down to Andorra la Vella. The road was winding but good, the chauffeur a careful driver who took no chances on the curves. During the drive Holland asked, "What kind of money do you spend here?"

"Pesetas and French francs, señor. Either is acceptable everywhere except at the post offices."

"Why not at the post offices?"

"One is French, one Spanish. They take only their own money."

"Doesn't Andorra have a post of its own?"

"No, señor. Spain and France generously assume the burden of our mails, such as they are, for the privilege of printing and selling our stamps. It helps them to recover some of the money they lose to us in other business transactions."

"What else does Andorra lack, besides money and a post office?"

"A number of refinements, señor. We have no army, no military service, no taxes, no customs-house, no diplomatic service, no passport controls, no currency restrictions and no crime."

"No crime?"

"No, señor. Where there are no laws to break, none are broken. It is only when you pass beyond the borders of our country that you find mercenary men engaged in smuggling, black-market exchange and the evasion of taxes."

Holland laughed. The moral atmosphere of Andorra was as refreshing as its mountain air.

In Andorra la Vella the chauffeur recommended a money-exchange house, then pointed out the twin post offices facing each other across a little plaza beyond. But when Holland, not wanting to impose further on the baron's hospitality, attempted to dismiss the car with thanks, the chauffeur refused to be dismissed.

"My orders are to bring you here and to bring you back, señor," he said. "They were given to me by his Excellency. I may not disregard them."

"What further orders did his Excellency give you about me?"

"To see that you were not watched, followed or approached from the rear without warning."

"Did he tell you why?"

"No, señor. His Excellency does not find it necessary to

explain his orders."

"What steps are you prepared to take to see that his orders are carried out?"

"Whatever steps may be necessary, señor." The man made a small motion toward his waist. "I am armed. You need have no fear."

"I have none," Holland said, truthfully. He could not think of Carlos as a physical threat to himself. At the thinking level his mind recognized the danger of the enmity of the marqués, but emotionally Carlos failed to disturb him. It might have been because his emotions were otherwise engaged.

He felt strangely excited by the time he had changed a bill into francs, and had to remind himself, It's only a telephone call; maybe not even that much, for a while yet. The French post office was very French, down to the inadequacies of its telephone connection. He was told that the call would take at least half an hour to go through. He passed the time looking into the inviting shop windows of La Vella's one important street, unobtrusively trailed by the baron's chauffeur.

Andorra la Vella would have turned Ali Baba's attention away from the cave of the forty thieves, although there was nothing of the Thousand and One Nights about the brisk, businesslike little capital city except the variety of treasures it displayed. Holland burdened himself only with a handful of Havana puros and new linen to replace what he had been wearing since Barcelona, but in other circumstances he would have been tempted by the reminder of Micaela's birthday to come. Swiss chocolates, French perfumes, Italian silks, Swedish crystal, Danish silver were all to be had for her. So also were German cameras, Japanese radios, English tweeds, Spanish wines, Italian typewriters, American phonograph records, Kashmiri prints, a hundred other luxury products of the world market, in quantity and variety at prices which accounted for the steady stream of cars with foreign license plates coming up the single highway from Spain or down it from the mountain pass that led to France. Other goods were offered for a less conspicuous traffic; small ball-bearing assemblies, watch movements, packaged antibiotics, stylo pens, radio tubes and, inevitably, spark plugs.

His back began to ache again at the spark plug display. Although the half-hour was not yet up he strolled back toward the post office, then hurried when he saw the clerk in the doorway beckoning to him. As unpredictable as always, the French telephone system had functioned efficiently.

The concierge he had fought was on the line, neither polite nor impolite when he asked to know who was calling and went to bring Marsha. Her voice came faint but clear over the wire when it wasn't drowned by a spatter of static from an electric storm somewhere in the Pyrenees, and her first question was immediate and unequivocal: "Is he all right?"

"He's all right. Done in, at the moment, but all right."

"Where are you?"

"Andorra."

"How did you get there? What happened?"

"It seemed like the best way out. The boat trick blew up in our faces."

"I've been worried." Even through the noisy filter of an electric storm he could hear the relief in her voice.

"Carlos called, from Barcelona, the day before yesterday, to say that Harry had disappeared from the Barrio Chino in what he called, oh, disturbing circumstances, and when I didn't hear a word for two days I—I thought—I didn't know what to think. You don't know how glad I am to hear your voice, Andy."

"What did you tell Carlos?"

"Nothing that meant anything."

"You're sure?"

"I'm sure. He was insistent about knowing why you had gone to Spain, what connections there were between you and Harry, anything else he could learn. I said you were an old friend going to see an old friend in trouble, and that's all I knew. Is it important?"

"He's been chasing us."

"Carlos *chasing* you?"

He explained, conceding that the conclusion was a deduction from the size of the offered reward, but the only reasonable conclusion. "Both your husbands together aren't worth that much money to anyone else, in or out of jail. It has to be Vilasar money."

"But then—" She was drowned out by a burr of static, until her voice came through again, eager "—never forgive him, Andy. All we have to do is tell her—"

"Tell her nothing. Not yet."

The static stopped abruptly. Her faraway voice, incredulous, said, "Why?"

The chauffeur-bodyguard waited just inside the door of the post office, inconspicuously watchful. He was a solid, sensible-looking man, not at all the type to stand on the alert for dangers which did not exist. Choosing his words, Holland said, "I'm not absolutely certain that we're right; not near enough to certainty to condemn him, anyway. If we're wrong, an injustice would strengthen him with her, not weaken him. If we're right, he's out to win this race without respect for the rules. He sees Micaela as the silver trophy at the end of it. If he were to learn from you or from her or from anybody, at this stage of the race, that he isn't going to get her, that he hasn't a chance—I don't know. His ego is pretty close to the skin. I think it's at least possible that he might go off the road and start smashing things."

"But what could he do? You've lost him, haven't you? And you're not in Spain."

"I don't know that we've lost him. I don't know that he wouldn't begin smashing in Micaela's direction, or yours. I don't know that he won't be able to drag your husband back to Spain, by extradition or otherwise. If he ever does, there'll be only one form of insurance you can count on against the dawn ceremony you described so graphically. That will be Carlos, as before. Do you still think she should be told?"

If she answered, the answer was drowned by another spatter of static. When the line cleared, he said, "Where is she now?"

"Out with Larry somewhere."

"Tell her that her father—" he grudged the word, but it had to be used— "had to get out of Barcelona for reasons that haven't been explained to you; that he couldn't wait for Carlos' help but had to take mine instead, and that we're in Andorra; safe, well, on our way to France. That's all she need know for the time being. I'll have him call you back after I've primed him. Tomorrow morning."

"Couldn't we call you this evening? She'll be anxious to talk to her—to him." Marsha added in the same breath, "And to you, of course."

"Of course."

Why "of course," he thought; not resentful, but let down. There wasn't anything for him to talk about with his daughter except the truth, and the time had still to come for it. He explained why a call from the French end of the line was impractical, promised faithfully that Magill would call back in the morning and broke the connection quickly, before she could thank him or say good-by.

One deception, at least, was inadvertent. Magill was not all right. A man carrying the black bag of a doctor had just gotten out of a car in the baron's courtyard when the chauffeur-bodyguard brought Holland back to it late in the day. After he had disposed of his purchases he found Candelas, still in the monk's robe, waiting with the baron outside the closed door of Magill's room. The baron was solemn, Candelas jittery.

"He's red-hot with fever," Candelas said. "I took him a bowl of soup a couple of hours ago and even his eyes were flaming. He couldn't see me, or didn't recognize me if he did. How good is this pill-pusher of yours, Excellency?"

"The best in the Pyrenees," the baron said. "I imported him."

"From France or from Spain?"

"From Poland. A political."

"I would have more confidence in a Frenchman, but so long as he is not Spanish–" Candelas beat his two fists together, hard. "Sainted Mother, I could stab myself. The little doll in the kitchen had me doing tricks for her when I should have been wondering why he slept so long. You remember what I promised you if something happened to him, Dutchman?"

"I remember."

"I promise you the same thing for myself if it happens because of this."

The baron said, "A fever means nothing. The whole world runs a fever from time to time. It survives."

"You didn't feel him as I did, Excellency. He was burning up. He didn't know who I was, or where he was, or how he had got here."

"I told you, this is the best doctor in the mountains. Now run off and do more tricks for Paquita if you can't wait to have something to worry about. I'll tell you what the doctor has to say."

"I'll wait for him myself, Excellency. With your permission."

"It's your house," the baron said. "As long as you don't crack your knuckles." He gave Candelas a ferocious scowl of impatience. "In the name of God, man! Your friend has a fever, we have a doctor for him, the doctor will tell us what more may be wise, and that, too, he will have. What is to be gained by uselessly beating your paws together?"

"Nothing, Excellency. Excuse me. I will not do it again."

They did not talk further until the doctor came out of the

room. He was a capable-looking man who spoke excellent French and inadequate Spanish. Holland translated for Candelas when the doctor said, "His temperature is forty degrees; not good, but it will come down. I have given him an injection."

For himself, Holland translated the fever into Fahrenheit. He had never learned to think efficiently in terms of centigrade. He got 104; not good, as the doctor had said.

"What's the cause of the fever, Doctor?"

"A congestion of the lungs. I have taken a sample of his sputum for analysis. I will be able to tell you more later. Meanwhile, he needs rest and liquids."

"When do you think he will be back on his feet?"

"I would hesitate to say, at this point."

"What's the earliest possible date?"

"Several days away, at the least. At the other extreme, a matter of weeks."

"Is he in danger?"

"A sick man is always in danger, monsieur. Sickness is danger, by definition. If you mean do I think he is going to die, I am here to see that he does not."

"Is there anything special we could get for him in the way of medicine?"

"Special?" The doctor raised his eyebrows. "What is special?"

"Penicillin," the baron said. "Streptomycin, aureomycin, terramycin, cortisone, hydrocortisone—"

"I'm sorry," Holland said. "I forgot where we were. Only one thing more, Doctor. Can I talk to him?"

"He's lightheaded. He may not be wholly rational. But there is no harm in it, if you do not tire him by making him talk to you, or worry him. He has been through a painful and exhausting experience, beyond his capacities. His reserves of strength are used up."

When that was translated for Candelas, he beat his fists together in futile despair even with the baron scowling at him.

"Jesus and Mary, I would have carried him here on my own back if I had known this was going to happen," he said. "What do we do now, Dutchman? Pray?"

"It can't do any harm. I've got a message for him from his señora that will help. Let me see him alone."

"I'll be in the chapel," Candelas said moodily. "If I haven't forgotten the words."

Magill was flushed, hot and very sick. His glasses were on a table by his bedside and his eyes were closed. He opened them without turning his head when Holland came into the room. They were drugged; the pupils expanded, the whites unclear. He said thinly, "Who—?" and let it go.

"Holland. You're not supposed to talk. The doctor says you'll be all right in a few days. There's nothing to worry about. I talked to Marsha on the phone. She and Mike are both doing fine and send their love. Candelas is in good shape. So am I. There's nothing to worry about."

"—are we?"

"Andorra, the baron's house, above Ordino."

"—remember." The dry lips moved painfully, shaping the words. "Thought we went France. Fell."

"France comes later. All you have to do now is rest. I'll look in on you later. Go to sleep."

"—a minute." Magill's drugged eyes still stared unseeingly at the ceiling, but his hand stirred on the bed covers. "Didn't fall cliff?"

"You didn't fall off anything. You caught a cold, you've got a fever and you have to rest."

"—nightmare. Always fall cliff nightmare. Andy Holland this one."

"It was only a dream. You're safe in Andorra. Go to sleep."

"—sorry Holland." Magill sighed, abruptly and heavily. In a voice of infinite sorrow and pity, he said, "Poor dog."

His eyes closed again. Holland left the room and closed the door quietly.

Poor dog, he thought; poor dog to a poor dog of a sick man, in delirium and nightmare. How poor a dog can you be, poor dog? He felt a sudden strong conviction that Magill was going to die, through no fault of his and in circumstances for which he could be neither reproached nor punished. It was the perfect solution to his problem, and it left him feeling depressed. There was no sense of accomplishment in it, no triumph. He did not call Marsha the next morning. Magill's fever was higher, wavering up toward 41 degrees. He was delirious most of the time. The Polish doctor was worried, and did not try to hide his worry, that the virus in Magill's lungs was not responding to treatment. He stopped by at intervals of an hour or two during the day to look in on the patient. One or the other of the maids sat by Magill's bedside all the time, with Candelas doing regular penance in the chapel and the baron, occupied by the demands of a business that ran itself only after it had moved out of his wine cellar and courtyard, in the courtyard cautioning his men to make as little noise as possible with the mules, jeeps and trucks that brought merchandise and took away contraband. Holland browsed restlessly through the baron's library, explored the baron's liquor cabinet, wrote a number of letters that did not need writing, and smoked more cigars than was his habit.

He found, to his astonishment, that he did not want Magill to die; not then, in any event, nor by the operation of Kismet. Magill's ceasing to exist was still the most practical answer to their problem of a mutual wife and daughter, but not before the contract had been worked out according to its terms. Anything else was a cheat. He felt an enormous lift of spirit when, in the evening of the day, Candelas' calliope roar of gratitude for favors granted came ahead of Candelas into the library, where Holland was dulling the unwelcome activity of his mind against eleven hundred years of Engordany genealogy, and he was wrapped in a Catalan abrazo that made his ribs squeak.

"It's over with, Dutchman! He's run it out! The sawbones says there's nothing more to it now than getting well!"

"You've seen him?"

"I just talked to him! He's sweating bullets, as shaky as a picador's horse, but he knows who he is and he's hungry! I tell you, this prayer business is better than having money in the bank! He's going to be all right!"

The doctor confirmed it. The fever was broken, the crisis over, convalescence assured. How soon Magill would be up and able to move about depended on Magill; perhaps within a week, certainly within two weeks. It would not be wise to hurry his recovery.

Conscious of his responsibility for telephoning Cannes, Holland forgot the possibility of danger beyond the protection of the baron's castle walls until he was halfway down the road to Andorra la Vella with the doctor. Caution because of Carlos was still something that came to him at the thinking level, not from fear, and when he did remember the need for caution it was easy to rationalize his failure to remember. Magill, not he, was Carlos' primary quarry. As long as he gave Carlos no chance to follow him, left no trail back to the baron's courtyard, Carlos could not move effectively against either of them, even if he had traced them as far as Andorra. Waiting for his call to go through, he paid less attention to the contents of La Vella's inviting shop windows than to the reflections in their panes that might show some sign of attentiveness at his back. There was none that he could discover.

The bright window of a jeweler's shop reminded him again of Micaela's birthday. The fourth of the month, Marsha had said. He had lost track of the calendar, but it could not be more than another week or so. Eighteen was an important age to a girl; maturity. At least, as Marsha had said, a kind of maturity. He considered buying out the jeweler's shop, to make his first birthday gift to her one that would outshine all the birthdays that had gone before, but thought better of it. Magill would not have been extravagant. Birthdays would have meant a wrist watch, probably, or a bicycle, a savings bond, something like that. She would not think of spectacular extravagance as a fatherly attribute.

He bought her a necklace of good Italian craftsmanship in pure gold, a gift that had beauty and at the same time a sound investment value. Fathers had to think of those things for their daughters. In the clarity of his mind's eye he could see himself clasping it around her brown throat. But then, confusingly, the picture blurred and it was Marsha and Marsha's throat, twenty years before, that he saw. The gift of visual recall that had always been his asset was beginning to play tricks. He could no longer hold clear separate pictures of his wife and daughter in his mind. They had a tendency to flow into each other and merge, like images coming together in the range finder of a camera.

He thought his eyes as well as his memory were beginning to trick him when, in another shop window, he saw Odile; honey-gold, pink-pretty, provocative Odile, true to life right down to rose-petal fingernails and champagne-bubble hair, but a foot tall, and stuffed. He had seen the clever French dolls before; slightly wicked, most of them, and not meant for the juvenile market. He had never before seen one that so much resembled a living person, and could not resist buying it for her. Then, because he had gifts for two women, he bought a third, the largest available flacon of the perfume Marsha favored. It held nearly a liter, and was faintly fragrant even through its green and white packaging. The fragrance was under his nose when he took the call at the post office, so that when Micaela came on the line he spoke to her with her mother's scent in his nostrils and could picture neither one of them, only the merged image that was both, Marsha-Micaela.

"What happened?" She was far off but clear, and as clearly upset. "We've been waiting by the phone all day in relays, worrying. You promised Mother that Dad would call this morning. Where is he? Is something the matter?"

"Nothing is the matter now. He's been under the weather. I didn't want to let you know before. Where's your mother?"

"It's her turn to have dinner. I'll call her in a minute. You're sure Dad's all right?"

"I'm sure. He got his feet wet and forgot his vitamins. He's back on schedule now."

Marsha-Micaela had his hair, her eyes and, damnably, Magill's direct way of asking for the answers. She said, "I do wish I knew what this is all about, Mr. Holland. Mother told me how much help you've been to Dad in getting him out of Barcelona, and I'm sure he wouldn't have gone chasing off to Andorra of all peculiar places if it hadn't been necessary, but why was it necessary? Carlos would have had everything arranged in a week or two, if Dad had just been patient. He promised me."

"Your father decided not to wait for Carlos' arrangements. That's all I can tell you. You'll have to ask him his reasons when we get to France."

"When will that be?"

"Probably not for a week or so."

"Why so long?"

"He's had a fever. He's still pretty shaky for travel."

"Will he be here for my birthday?"

"I'll try to get him there. What else would you like for your birthday?"

"Just Dad, thank you."

There was no storm in the mountains this time. He could hear another voice behind her, Marsha's, questioning, anxious, and her reply of assurance. He said quickly, "You're pretty fond of your dad, aren't you?" but got no answer. She had already given the receiver to Marsha.

He explained the situation once more, assured her that Magill was out of danger and made an arrangement by which he would call, or try to call, or have Magill try to call as soon as he was able to, during either of two periods of the day; one early in the morning, one late in the afternoon. Both were at hours when a connection could be expected to go through with minimum delay. But he warned her not to worry if they were not heard from for a day or two, or three. It would be that long at least before Magill was out of bed, and they had not yet made any plans for crossing the French border. These would still have to take shape. Because he knew Micaela would be following the conversation at her end, he was purposely vague about dates and places.

On the morning of the third day of Magill's convalescence he was still, by the Polish doctor's orders, in bed; fretful, in waspish temper at his confinement and to all appearances as good as new. He had a long list of questions for Marsha about Micaela's schooling, her teeth, their finances, other personal matters that were not overly urgent but which had taken on an exaggerated importance in his mind during days of inaction. When his insistence on speaking to Marsha about them grew so strong that he was demanding his clothes and cursing Candelas for not bringing them, Holland commandeered a jeep from the courtyard—the chauffeur had driven the baron off earlier in the morning—and himself took the list down to La Vella to relay it, question by question. He felt no twinge of jealousy while writing down Marsha's answers. It seemed quite natural to be discussing with Micaela's mother the advisability of enrolling their daughter temporarily at a private school in Cannes until a more permanent arrangement could be decided on, along with subjects like orthodonture and summer wardrobes. His mind, preoccupied with parental responsibility during the ride back to Ordino, did not absorb the significance of another car, a Mercedes, that followed the jeep at a distance until the Mercedes was turning into the baron's courtyard behind him. He saw it then, its Barcelona license plates, and was prepared for Carlos before Carlos got out of the car. He was not prepared for the other two men.

They were, he guessed, Spanish guardias civiles out of uniform. Both were bigger than the average Spaniard, better fed, and wore the guardia air of arrogant authority even without the guardia badge. One had a bleached narrow ugly face like a skull. The other looked like an alley fighter, with a brawler's flat nose. They stood behind and on either side of the man who had brought them, a pair of well-trained hunting dogs.

Carlos said, "I didn't think you'd get this far. Congratulations."

"I was stupid to let you follow me. You picked me up at the post office, of course."

"Of course. One of you was certain to make a call to France."

"What are your plans?"

"They will depend on your own."

"We're still thinking about them," Holland said.

He felt certain that a sharp demand for something more than thought was imminent. Except for his jeep and the Mercedes, the courtyard was empty; of trucks, of cars, of mules, of merchandise. The baron was in the process of acquiring a new stock of trade goods, his chauffeur was with him, his mayordomo was an old man. Otherwise there were only three women in the castle, with Magill in bed and, Holland hoped, somewhere nearby, Candelas. Candelas was going to be badly needed if the hunting dogs went after Magill. They had no authority outside their own country, but Spanish guardias had been known to make their own authority before then, and these would be armed. For the reward the marqués was offering, they would not hesitate to move if he gave them the word.

Carlos smiled, showing his good white teeth.

"You need not think too long," he said. "I have no intention of trying to take him away from you. Now that you have succeeded in smuggling him out of Spain, I am as eager to have him reach France as you are."

"So you can have him extradited?"

"Extradition is an arrangement between governments. I am not the government of my country."

"But as a private citizen, not wholly without influence."

Carlos shrugged. "I gave Micaela my word that he would be safely returned to his family."

"He can be safely returned to his family without your help."

"I have given my word."

"Micaela is not going to think much of your word when she is told how you have tried to trap him ever since Barcelona."

"Then I have nothing to lose by keeping my promise to her, as a gentleman should." Carlos was still courteous, still smiling, still the hidalgo. "Tell me one thing. It is what I came here to learn. Why have you set yourself against me, whom you do not even know, and how have you turned him against me, who knows me and has been my friend?"

"I can't answer that."

"You don't think you owe me an explanation?"

"I think you're entitled to an explanation, yes. I don't think I could make you understand it if I gave it to you."

"Try."

"All right. Micaela's father is not going to allow his daughter to marry you."

Carlos frowned, puzzled. "Micaela's father will have nothing to say about whom she marries after she is eighteen. Even if he could control her choice, how would it concern you?"

"I told you you wouldn't understand."

"Perhaps I understand more than you choose to say. Micaela is not for you. Never."

"She is not for you."

"There you are wrong. She is going to marry me. She has already done me the honor of accepting me."

His manner, his confidence, the hidalgo assurance had become too much for Holland. He said cruelly, "As pretty little Odile, waiting for you in her charming suite at La Belle Poitrine, will no doubt have done you the honor of giving you back?"

Carlos' face turned gray. His mouth took on an ugly look that would have been a pout if it had been less ugly. His lips trembled, but his voice was steady enough when he stepped back between his hunting dogs and said, "Beat him."

Holland knew it was going to be bad when the guardias drew apart rather than together to close in on him. They knew how to work in pairs, the guardias. An active man could take one of them out of action without too much trouble, if neither shot first. They did not know how to defend themselves against experienced attack with the hands and feet. But whichever one was faced, the other could not be faced, and they did know how to hit with a billy or pistol-butt. After that, one or both paid you back on the ground for what you had done to either, and sometimes you did not walk well afterward, or see well, or think clearly. He felt naked and inadequate, backing away from the flanking hunters. The wall of the castle was behind him. Before it checked his freedom of movement he had to arrive at a decision.

He chose the skull-faced man. The alley brawler looked slower-moving; dangerous enough but less dangerous to have at his back. The skull-face had his hand under his coat, gripping whatever it was he meant to hit with; a pistol. Holland half turned away from him, feinting a movement of panic in the direction of his partner, then turned back again as the skull-face jumped in, his arm wide rather than high for the blow at the base of the skull. Holland took the risk of a savate that would finish the man in one strike. The kick failed only because the guardia had moved fast enough to run into it, catching it on the thigh instead of in the pit of the stomach. It caved his leg in under him and threw him into a twisting fall, the pistol jerked from his hand to ring dully on the flagstones of the courtyard.

Holland needed no thought to charge the man rather than the gun, but reason, if he had had time for it, would have sent him the same way as his antipathy for guns. To have touched the pistol, even moved toward it, would have invited a bullet in the back instead of a blow. Expecting the blow at any moment, mentally cringing from it, he had still to finish the first enemy before he could turn to the second. He did it with his knee while the skull-face was scrambling up off the flagstones; still half crouched, rising, neither up nor down but wholly defenseless when Holland brought the knee up hard under his chin and struck simultaneously downward with both hands at the back of the man's head. He knew from the solid impact between bone and bone that it was enough. Still cringing from the blow that had not been struck, still expecting it, already wondering why it had not yet fallen, he ducked away from its imminence and whirled about to see Candelas, in cowled house robe and sandals, standing like a medieval monk-at-arms between him and the second guardia. Candelas held the vegetable slicer low, point down, haft loose in his palm for a quick upward flip into the man's belly, and was inviting him to take his hand out from under the skirt of his coat.

"With or without the pistol, mierda," he said. "It's all one to me, but if your hand is not empty you will want a basket to carry your guts with you when you leave. Make up your mind."

The guardia seemed immobilized more by surprise than by indecision. From his expression, and Carlos', Candelas had dropped almost literally out of the sky. An open window above him showed where he had been an observer of what went on in the courtyard, in all probability grinning his yellow-toothed grin at Holland's tight squeeze until the time came for intervention.

Nobody moved, the guardia not so much as by a blink of his eyes, before Holland said to Carlos, "Call off your dogs before somebody is hurt more badly than you planned. Mine doesn't have the brains to be afraid of them."

"You will not always be so lucky," Carlos said. His mouth still held the ugly pout. "I give you my word now, Mister Holland. In the end, I will defeat you."

He spoke to the guardia, who brought his empty hand carefully, not too suddenly, into the open. Between them they lifted the other man, still limp, into the Mercedes and drove away. Candelas did not return the knife to its sheath under the cowl of his robe until the car had left the courtyard.

"Lucky for you I wear a potato peeler instead of a money belt, Dutchman," he said. "Those two mierdas could have given you a bad time, quick as you are with your feet."

"I know they could," Holland said. "I owe you something. More than just thanks."

"Nothing, unless we have another go with them. Next time, let me have the skull-face." Candelas grinned. "I like the shape of his head. It would make a nice ashtray."

Holland was unable to smile in response to the joke. Carlos' gray face, with its ugly pout and trembling lips, was still too vivid in his memory. He had learned what it was to be afraid of the Marqués de Vilasar in his glands, instead of only with his mind, and he did not like the feeling.

That same afternoon the weather, until then variable, cleared enough for the shooting trip the baron had promised. Holland, declining the offered loan of a rifle, was not pressed by the baron to accept it, but was urged to go along if only to see the countryside. The baron promised that his chauffeur and mayordomo together could hold the castle against assault, if Carlos attempted assault, even without the help of Candelas, who stayed behind ostensibly to meet Magill's demands for attention and service, actually to claim as much as possible of Paquita's attention in his own right. She was weakening, he told Holland, under the pressure of a sustained Catalan courtship, "—and to abandon one pursuit for another in the middle of the chase is not only bad hunting but bad luck, Dutchman, as even his Excellency will tell you, although you need not tell him that I find his serving maid's company more to my mind than his and yours. You hunt your kind of rabbit and leave me to mine."

They went in a jeep as high up into the cordillera as the jeep could take them over an ancient mule trail that crossed centuries-old arched stone bridges barely wide enough for two laden pack animals to pass and ran along cliff-edge cornices no wider. From the mule trail they went higher on foot, beyond the tree line, to high windy mountain meadows where wild hen fed. The baron missed a snap shot at a running chamois, and they saw no bear. He did not seem to be particularly disappointed. Climbing higher still, they came at last to a bare rock slope patched with snow where a runnel of icy water dashed down the steep flank of the cordillera's backbone. The stream, according to the baron, came from a tarn at the crest of the cordillera which was also the source of another stream flowing down the far side of the mountain, so that the same water ran at once northward into France to the Atlantic and southward through Spain into the Mediterranean.

"It has been remarked with some truth that Africa begins at the Pyrenees," the baron said. "We can climb up and look over into Europe, if you like, but it is a hard climb to make, and here in my country we do not go any higher than is necessary for the business at hand. In our case, that is a view of the child of two continents." He made a frame of his hands to outline the valley of Andorra, all twelve by fifteen miles of it, laid out neatly and compactly below them like a toy landscape, and quoted: "The great Charlemagne, my father, from the Arabs delivered me."

"What's that?" Holland asked.

"The first line of our national anthem. Is it strange to think of seven thousand people with a national anthem?"

"No stranger than to think of a nation of seven thousand people all breaking the same laws."

The baron laughed.

"Not quite true, but true enough. Between one world and the other, we are a window of free trade."

"How do you get away with it? Or is that a trade secret?"

"We are tolerated. If France and Spain really wanted to put us out of business, it could be done easily enough. Only a certain number of passes exist through which a man can carry a pack or lead a mule, and they are all known. A certain expenditure of money and manpower would bottle them tight. Or a road tax could be placed on legal imports to make illegal exports unprofitable; we are inaccessible except over French and Spanish soil. The trouble with either effort, from the viewpoints of France and Spain, would be the cost of enforcement weighed against a doubtful benefit."

"How doubtful?"

"In terms of accomplishment; profit on the investment, so to speak. What do we smuggle into France? Cigarettes, a little sherry, coffee, a few bottles of absinthe. None of it does anyone any harm, and all of it, if taxed, would not contribute greatly to the French national budget. We do not attack the French national morale with opium or cocaine or hashish, as do even some of France's own colonies. On the other hand we do buy quantities of French products which are taxed out of the market in Spain—perfumes, cognac, medicines, radio parts, small machinery, cosmetics, a hundred small luxuries that most Spaniards would be denied except for us. Do you wonder that we have friends on both sides of the mountains, and few enemies?"

"But some enemies."

"The man in uniform is always an enemy. Periodically they trap a pass for us, to show us that they can stop us whenever they choose to. It is one of the occupational risks of the business."

"What happens?"

"In a trap? Oh, I lose the merchandise, the men are arrested and fined, I make up the fines to them along with a small bonus, they change their names and try the other side of the mountain for a while."

"Why change the names?"

The baron turned his look from the valley to Holland, smiling. "You are thinking of going into the business for yourself?"

"In a way, yes. My friend still has to cross the French border, and he has no papers."

"Of course." The baron nodded. "Excuse me. I was preoccupied with the view. My men do not carry papers, either. I do not permit them to carry papers, because with papers you can be too easily identified as Spaniard or Frenchman, by name as well as in the police records, and the fines grow progressively higher as the record grows longer. In time, you earn a jail sentence over and above the fines. Without papers you are only Juan Pous or Jean Plandolit of Andorra, where papers are not required, and until you have been taken so many times that they recognize you by sight you are safe from jail, although, unfortunately, not at all safe afterward. That is what happened to Candelas. Of course he is more easily recognizable than some, as you and your friend will be. Unless the Marqués de Vilasar has forgotten to give your descriptions to the French authorities, as I am sure he has not."

Holland looked sharply at the baron, who was enjoying the view again and did not turn his head.

"How much do you know about us?"

"All that Candelas does, I think. You need not tell me more. I did not urge him to tell me what he did."

"Tell me something. How should we go from here, when we go?"

The baron pointed at the valley below them, tracing the line of the road that came up from Spain as Candelas had traced it once before, climbing from his wrist over the heel of his hand to fork in the hollow of his palm.

"You take the right fork if you have papers, the left if you do not. Or you gamble."

"What kind of a gamble?"

"Without papers, sometimes—it has been done—a man will take the right fork and arrive properly by road at the French frontier. There he will say, 'Messieurs, I have no passport, no carte d'identité. They were taken from me by the Spanish police, who persecute me unjustly. I am in flight from them. Permit me to pass,' and be permitted to pass. On other occasions he will be seized and handed over to Spain, with regrets. The French are unpredictable except in their manners. They are always polite."

"My friend can't afford to gamble. What about inventing papers for him?"

"It could be done, certainly. But invented papers are only good when they are not known to be invented, and that is another gamble you would have to take, with the odds very much against you if, as we must assume, the French have been put on the alert for unauthorized visitors answering certain descriptions. Your friend can rely only on genuine papers, and not too long even on those. The French and Spanish governments are currently on excellent diplomatic terms, unfortunately for your friend."

"He'll be a lot less in danger of extradition after he has papers than he is of being picked up and sent back before he can get them. A passport isn't available to him this side of Marseille."

"You could go to Marseille for him. You have a passport."

"I can't get one for him. He has to make statements for

himself, under oath."

"Then the answer clearly is to get him to Marseille without one. You have friends in France with a car, who could meet you at an agreed rendezvous?"

"A rendezvous could be arranged."

"Arrange it, then. Discuss it well with your friends and among yourselves, draw up a careful blueprint, as a good engineer does—" the baron smiled, putting his hand on Holland's forearm to show that he meant no offense— "and do not follow it."

"I will have it out with Candelas later. Go on."

"I have told you that for a given expenditure of money and manpower the passes can be stopped. All of them. The French have the manpower; the marqués, it appears, has the money and the determination to beat you. I do not know that these factors can be brought to work together, the French being as stiff-necked as they are about national integrities and such things." The baron kept his hand briefly on Holland's forearm. "Neither do I know Vilasar personally, or how or why he has become your enemy, and I have already said I do not wish to be told more than I have been told. But Vilasar's kind is familiar to me, as a type, and I tell you in seriousness and honesty, I am afraid for you and your friend. We have a saying in these mountains that a Spaniard is the best friend and the worst enemy a man can have."

"We're afraid of Vilasar for ourselves."

"Good. Fear is always a good beginning." The baron smiled again. "In any event, you know that you are opposed by a man of will, intelligence and power. He will have you watched and listened to while you are here. Therefore the blueprint. Paquita will hear of it from Candelas and let news of it go further. In that way you will let them discover a track to follow in the wrong direction, and may with luck and foresight escape them in another."

"Which way should the blueprint lead?"

The baron studied the valley below, stamping his feet gently against the cold of the snowy slope where they stood.

"That way." He pointed again. "There, at the upper end of the valley, where the left fork of the road comes to an end, is El Serrat; a dozen buildings or so between meadow and trees, if your eyes are good. Above El Serrat there are two ways to go; an easy climb northeast, a harder climb northwest. I would aim the escape northeast, the way I often send my own men. The pass is well known, and many Spaniards reached France through it at the end of the Civil War. They were political refugees, given asylum by the French government, and did not need papers."

"I remember."

"Certain other political refugees, who were not Spaniards nor welcome in France but who preferred France's jails to the alternative of a Spanish firing squad, crossed by way of the more difficult northwest pass. Below the northeast pass are several small villages—Marc, Auzat, Vicdessos—where my men are known and welcome. Below the northwest pass there is only forest and a river valley that goes down to a motor road beyond Marc and the buildings of an abandoned mine sometimes used as a shelter by hunters and vagabonds, by my own men as a drop when Marc and Auzat is inconvenient for them. It is called the mine of the Rancié, and it can be found on any good road map of the region without the need of a blueprint to point it out."

"Rancié," Holland said. "I'll remember. Thanks."

"For nothing," the baron said politely.

Rancié was one of several names marked as reference points on the map he drew for them at the dining table that night, pointing the way over the northeast pass to Marc. Magill was at the table for the first time since his illness; thinner than before, a little sallower, his eyes more deeply set behind the lenses of his glasses. He was inexplicably in a bad mood after a long telephone call to Cannes. Candelas had gone with him and the chauffeur to Andorra la Vella as a safety measure, and was dead set against any further visits to the French post office, to telephone or for any other purpose. The baron's effective local intelligence service had reported the departure of the big Mercedes Benz from the valley, but Carlos, in leaving, had not cut himself off from his lines of communication.

"Those two mierdas of his are still hanging around," Candelas told Holland. "I saw ashtray-head in the plaza. We're only about fifteen kilometers from the Spanish border by road here. He wouldn't have a chance if they took it into their hands to bag him and run."

"They're not going to bag me in broad daylight with you and a chauffeur keeping me company," Magill said.

"Maybe. Maybe not. Why take chances when you don't have to? You'll be back with your women in a few days now, patrón. You can tell them all about it when you see them. Listen to me just this once—"

"Oh, shut up!" Magill snapped. "I'm tired of listening to you! Croak, croak, croak!"

"Listen to me, then," Holland said. "I agree with him. There's no point in taking unnecessary chances. If you have anything important to say on the telephone, I can say it for you. If it isn't important, it needn't be said before we reach France."

"I promised I'd call tomorrow," Magill said sullenly.

"Call, then. We'll go with you. But make it the last call."

"Are you giving me orders?" Magill's temper flared.

"If necessary to save your neck, yes," Holland said. "You don't have to like it. Your man is on my side."

That same evening they drew up plans for their departure; two sets of plans, of which Candelas knew only one but held out strongly for the other. It was his view that they should leave as soon as possible, which meant as soon as Magill's strength was up to it. The longer they stayed in Andorra, he argued, the more time Vilasar's hunting dogs would have to plan some scheme of getting Magill back to Spain.

"They aren't hanging around here for the mountain air," he said. "Besides, the moon is down until after midnight now, and the weather is clearing. You can't take another wet night like the last one, patrón. I say, let's pick up and go as soon as you've had a day or two to get your legs back."

His arguments, sound ones, were beaten down by the baron, who planned to send a group of his own men with them and could not, or said he could not, have them ready to go before the weekend, and by Holland, who argued the importance of relating Magill's crossing of the frontier to his earliest possible call thereafter on the consul-general in Marseille. The planning was done on a Tuesday. Since the consulate would not be open on Saturday or Sunday, Thursday night was the latest they could safely leave that week, as Sunday night was the earliest they could go afterward. In time they arrived at an agreement, Candelas reluctantly, on a departure Sunday night, then moved it up to Thursday as soon as Paquita's irresistible lure had drawn Candelas from the dinner table into the kitchen.

"We'll go by way of the northwest pass and Rancié," Holland said, and pointed out their route to Magill on the map the baron had drawn. "If you're sure you'll be up to the climb by then."

"I'll be as well up to it then as ever," Magill said. "What comes after Rancié?"

"Somebody will have to meet us with a car."

"I'll tell Marsha, when I talk to her."

Holland shook his head, prepared for Magill's answering bristle.

"Not on the phone. It would be stupid to risk even a remote chance that Carlos has it tapped. Write her a note tonight to tell her we'll be there Friday morning at—when?"

"Between midnight and dawn," the baron said. "Don't pin

yourself down any more tightly. The passes are never predictable."

"As you seem to be sure Candelas is," Magill said.

"A Catalan is always a businessman, even in love. He will argue to Paquita that she must yield to him before Sunday, because that is all the time they have left."

"I would rather have trusted him with the truth."

"So would I," the baron agreed. "But I do not know that Paquita's is the only ear in the kitchen, and if there is more than one the stories must coincide. Candelas is not subtle enough to carry the truth on one shoulder and a lie on the other. He would be the first to say so himself."

"You are equally certain that Paquita will talk?"

"Oh, absolutely." The baron smiled. "She has already accepted a bribe from one of the watchdogs. I told her to."

During the next forty-eight hours there was increased activety in the courtyard and wine cellar. Trucks brought cases of absinthe and American cigarettes, the baron's two most profitable exports to France. Four dozen cartons of cigarettes made up into a bulky but manageable pack; a smaller, heavier load was a dozen liters of absinthe packed in straw and canvas. On either load there was a profit to be had in excess of four hundred francs, divided equally between the baron and the carrier, and two hundred francs was two weeks' wages on the northern slope of the Pyrenees, more to the south. The baron had all the manpower he could use, from both sides of the mountains.

If Candelas had not been absorbed by other interests he could have thought it odd that the simple operation of making up a dozen or so loads of contraband should delay them so long. But the pursuit of Paquita preoccupied him most of the time, and the continuing presence of the marqués' watchdogs the rest.

He and Holland both went with Magill to Andorra la Vella for the agreed final telephone call. It was delayed by another call placed ahead of it on the single line to France. The guardia with the brawler's nose was waiting for the first call to go through; alone, it seemed, until Candelas, reconnoitering, found the other one unobtrusively under cover in the doorway of the Spanish post office across the plaza. He reported back with a grin.

"The ashtray has a pair of shiners on him like eggplants, and he lost at least a couple of teeth the last time he tried to chew. If you're smart, Dutchman, don't let the guardia civil hear about it the next time you go back to Spain. They remember things like a knee in the face."

He lost his grin when Magill explained that they would have to wait for the telephone, and why.

"I don't like it," he growled. "What business has a mierda like that one with the froggies?"

"Obviously Vilasar is in France and getting daily reports on us," Holland said.

"I don't like that, either. What's he doing in France, eh?"

"Rolling out a red carpet," Magill said impatiently. "Stop trying to think. You'll strain something."

He wandered restlessly off to peer into shop windows. The guardias watched him, one from the doorway of each post office. Candelas watched the guardias, scowling.

"I don't like it," he said again. "Mother of Mary, I'd feel happier if they started something. It isn't normal for them not to be pushing their weight around. I've got a feeling, Dutchman."

"Save it," Holland said shortly. Magill's restless irritability was catching.

The guardias disappeared from the plaza as soon as their call had gone through. Magill, in his turn, stayed at the telephone a full fifteen minutes, andHolland's jealousy came back to gnaw him more sharply than before. He tried to build a defense against it by submerging himself in the stale news of a five-day-old Paris newspaper he found on a bench in the plaza, but had not succeeded when Magill came to the door of the post office and motioned to him.

"She wants to talk to you."

"What about?"

"She'll tell you."

Magill pushed by without further explanation, his mouth tight.

Holland took up the telephone. Marsha's faraway voice said, "I had to talk to you once more before you leave there, Andy. It's going to be dangerous, isn't it?"

"For me, no. For him, only if he gets caught and sent back to Spain before we can get him a passport and in a position to run from extradition if he doesn't choose to fight it."

"You can't let him be caught."

"I'm doing everything possible to see that he won't be. You know that."

The line buzzed emptily.

He said, "Or do you? Is that what you wanted to talk to me about?"

"I have to have assurance, Andy. I need assurance terribly. I know in my heart that you're doing everything you can, but I want to be told. Say you'll bring him, without fail. Please."

"I'm not God."

"I know you're not God. But say it for me." A long pause. "Please, Andy."

"I'll bring him."

She said something in reply that he did not catch. It might have been thanks, it might have been an expression of faith. He said, "What have you told him to upset him?"

"Upset him?"

"He's been edgy and irritable since he first talked to you the other day."

The line hummed in his ear for moments before she answered wearily, "I suppose it might be upsetting, in a way, to learn that your wife is a liar and a cheat."

"Nothing more?"

"Nothing more."

"That's all, then. We won't call you again. Tell Micaela her father sends her his love."

"I will. And—Andy."

"Yes."

"Please, please, please—be careful. Of both her fathers."

"We'll be careful."

He hung up. He and Magill had nothing to say to each other during the drive back to Ordino, nor for some time afterward.

In the afternoon a quick heavy rainstorm soaked the valley. Afterward the streams that came down from the peaks above it were roiled and muddy, and the baron took Holland net-fishing for trout. The nets, effective only in dirty water, were a backbreaking exercise of throw and recovery with little reward, but he was glad of a chance to work off some of his restlessness. In the space of two hours he netted one trout to the baron's three. He was wet, tired and muddy when they got back to the castle, and rang for a bath.

Paquita and the other maid brought in the tub and filled it, leaving him to soak until it was time for Paquita's return with the first installment of reheating water. She brought it in just as it was becoming necessary.

"You're a good maid," he told her.

"Thank you, señor."

"I have a handful of pesetas that will be of no use to me after we leave here. You'll find them on the table when we go. They're for all of you, from all of us, with many thanks for the way you've treated us."

"Many thanks to you, señor. To all of you, from all of us."

"Do you know when we go?"

"Yes, señor."

"Does Candelas?"

"No, señor. He still thinks it will be Sunday."

"He isn't as observant as he might be."

The girl laughed.

"He's been too busy thinking up piropos." She imitated the musical growl as best she could: "Little flower, your eyes are bigger than your feet. Trample my heart," and laughed again. "What a tongue! Like a bear for honey."

"Does he offend you?"

"Offend me, señor? A girl does not take offense at a piropo. If they were not said to her, she would know she was not pretty enough to invite them."

"It doesn't matter who says them, then?"

"A piropo from a guapo is more pleasing than a piropo from an ugly man, certainly."

"Or a bear?"

"No, señor." She shook her neat Catalan head without hesitation. "I know what you are asking me, and I tell you honestly, I would have him. He is all man, and if he lacks brains, as he boasts—I do not entirely believe it—he has enough heart to make up the lack. If he also wanted a wife—"

She sighed, interrupting her own thought. "But he does not want a wife, only a girl, and I am no slut to be picked up and tossed down again afterward. Not for the price of a few pretty words."

"Yet you invite the pretty words."

"And why should I not? They cost him nothing."

She was wrong, as it turned out.

In the morning, Candelas could no longer be kept from learning of the trick that had been worked on him. They had to dress for the heights of the cordillera they would cross that night, and when the baron sent woolen climbing clothes to their rooms the secret was no longer a secret. Holland came upon him sulking in a corner and tried to salve his wounded feelings.

"It was the simplest way to do it," he explained. "The baron knew already that Paquita had been approached. If we hadn't given them wrong information through her, they could have got better information through someone else. It might have been done without having her get the lie from you, but–"

"The devil with that! It's not that you and his Excellency and the patrón tricked me that hurts! I know I'm too dumb for subtleties."

"What does hurt, then?"

"That she tricked me, too."

"It was all part of the same trick."

"No, no, Dutchman!" Candelas beat his fists together in the gesture of furious frustration that was his. "You don't understand! She cheated me with a promise! It was to be tomorrow or the next day, when she knew we would be already gone, and I was stupid enough to believe that a woman who says no for today could at the same time say yes for tomorrow. She tricked me, to laugh behind my donkey's back. God's curse on her and all her whore sisters. If she were not of his Excellency's house, I'd beat her!"

Holland could say nothing more. Candelas' pride was too deeply wounded to be treated with words. He spent most of the day in the wine cellar packing and unnecessarily repacking knapsacks, and when meals were served he ate with the other men who gathered inconspicuously under the baron's floor during the course of the day. Paquita was quiet and unsmiling. When no food went down to the wine cellar the other maid took it, or the cook.

There were sixteen men in the wine cellar by nightfall, besides Candelas. Magill, Holland and the baron had an early dinner, then a final coffee and brandy together in the medieval dining hall while the baron went over details of the operation that would take them through the mountains.

"You will each carry a pack for me, of course," he said. "Business is business, and besides it will make you less easily distinguishable from my other men. I *think* we have outmaneuvered Vilasar, but one does not prosper as a contrabandist by taking avoidable risks."

"Do we all go together?" Holland said.

"No. More than four or five men in a group make it conspicuous, fewer than three are inadequate in case of a fall and injury. My thought was to send five groups through five different passes. That way, in the event that we have not been too clever for the watchdogs, they will have to divide themselves into five to follow, or not at all. We will all be dressed alike, and I have chosen men for the odd sizes, like your own. What else?"

"The telephone."

"Inaccessible before morning. There is a remote possibility that the watchdogs, if alerted, would have the equipment and skill to tap the line for themselves, but it will do them no good. I have temporarily interrupted wire communication with Europe. What else?"

"You said 'we' would be all dressed alike. Are you coming with us?"

"Part of the way. I want to see you off to a good start."

"When do we go?"

"Any time you're ready."

"I'm ready now," Magill said.

He had taken off his glasses and was polishing them unnecessarily. There was a tight nervousness about his movements that Holland did not like. If Magill was not as fully recovered from his illness as he believed himself to be, they could be in for trouble on the cordillera. One way or another, they were committed to it.

He said, "I'll be ready in a few minutes," and went to his room.

The hard-used suit would still serve another wearer who did not mind cinder burns. He left it on a chair. All that he had of importance to transfer to the pockets of his climbing clothes were his passport, a toothbrush and the necklace for Micaela. He buttoned the necklace into a shirt pocket. The flask of perfume for Marsha and the doll for Odile were too big for pockets. They would have to go in one of the packs. He left his remaining pesetas in a pile on the bedside table, went methodically over the room to make sure he had forgotten nothing with the money belt strapped around his middle he had nothing to forget, but method was a habit after so many hundreds of other rooms in which he had passed a night, two nights, a couple of years—and left.

He found Magill and the baron in the courtyard, where two trucks waited in darkness. Someone with a flashlight was directing the loading of the packs into the carriers that would take them over the first leg of the smuggling operation. Both trucks had box bodies inside which a bench ran along either side wall. The packs were stacked between the benches, leaving room for the men to take their places afterward. All were dressed alike, as were Holland, Magill and the baron, in drab cotton coveralls over the wool of their mountain clothing, Basque berets and short boots. Climbing into the trucks, they made Holland think of a platoon of troops loading up for mock warfare. There was no seriousness about them. It was a lark they were embarking on; a lark for which they would be rewarded, in which they might experience a thrill or two but would harm no one and would not be harmed. The banter and low-voiced jokes that passed among them as they climbed into the trucks were in Catalan, Candelas' mother tongue, but he among them was the only one who did not joke or participate in the horseplay of loading up. He was the first man to climb into his seat, and chose it well forward in the truck, out of sight.

At Holland's request the baron had one of the packs swung down to the flagging of the courtyard and robbed of enough of its contents, cigarettes, to make room for the flask of perfume and the doll. One of the trucks had switched on yellow dimmers. Kneeling in the dim glow of illumination, he was refastening the straps of the knapsack when Paquita spoke to him from the shadow. He could not see her until she put her hand into the light and beckoned. He followed her into darkness.

"Thank you for the pesetas, señor," she said. "You were more than generous."

"It was nothing."

"Then may I ask you for something?"

The truck had started its motor, and her voice was low. He had to bend his head to hear her. He said, "Of course. What can I do?"

"He has not said good-by to me, nor will he. He thinks it was I who abused him, because I did what his Excellency asked me to do. Will you explain that the trick was not mine?"

"It was the trick of your own that abused him, Paquita."

"Mine?"

"Yes."

"What have I done to him that he spits on the ground at my feet and turns his back to me?"

He told her; bluntly, because she was Catalan, and Catalans never expected delicacy when they spoke of the relationship between a man and a woman. Softly, angrily and, he thought from her voice, close to tears, she said, "Sainted Mary, he is even more stupid than he thinks he is! What kind of a woman does a man want to leave behind him when he has business beyond the mountains; one who says yes easily or one who says no with difficulty? Ask him that, señor; not from me, because I am only a woman, but for yourself, as a man of the world. Make him use his thick head, if he can—"

He lost the next part of it in the grind of the second truck's starter. When the motor caught and he could hear her again, she was saying, in the same tone, "—back, or to the devil! It is all the same to me. Tell him that, but say also that no woman laughs at a man because he wants her, in whatever way he wants her. Sometimes she may even cry for him, even when—even when—"

All at once, she ran out of anger to sustain her. Both of the truck motors were going by then, filling the courtyard with muffled clatter. Bending his head further to hear her words, he discovered that there were no more words to hear. She had gone.

He picked up the knapsack and swung it into the truck that waited for him. The other truck was already pulling out of the courtyard. His began to move as he was finding his seat in the black obscurity of its interior.

VIII

THERE WERE EIGHT MEN in the back of the truck—the baron, Magill, Candelas, Holland and four others. They did not again see the other truck, which took a way of its own. Theirs turned northward from Ordino, climbing toward El Serrat and the dead-end road in the valley's uppermost thrust at the barrier of the cordillera.

The truck did not get as far as the road-head. An avalanche of earth, boulders and broken trees, brought down by the heavy rain of the day before, blocked their way a kilometer short of El Serrat. The men took up their packs at the blockade and climbed around it to the hamlet, where they were to divide into two bands and separate. There was nothing to indicate that they had been followed.

Holland gave Paquita's message to Candelas at the first moment that came for talk, between the avalanche and the hamlet. He repeated it verbatim, as nearly as he remembered it, because he did not believe that his own qualifications as a man of the world came up to those of the baron's housemaid as a woman. Candelas heard him out in silence, without comment when he was done. But afterward he lost some of his bear's surliness of manner, and offered Holland a cigarette when he lit one of his own. Still later he made a joke about the fiesta they could celebrate with the load of cigarettes and alcohol they carried between them. He had taken one of the packs of absinthe "—because with absinthe you can burn whatever part of the evidence you don't drink, whereas who can smoke up four dozen cartons of cigarettes at a sitting. Eh, Dutchman? Am I so dumb?"

"Paquita would say, at times less so than at others."

Candelas laughed and was surly no longer.

The baron carried Magill's knapsack of cigarettes, against Magill's objections, to El Serrat and for an hour's climb beyond.

"You're only a few days out of a sickbed," he said in justification of the help. "You might need all the strength you've got before you're finished. It would be poor business for me to tire you before you had delivered my merchandise."

Magill said, "Business aside—"

"Never," the baron interrupted quickly. They had reached the beginning of the high climb, at timber line, where the forests lay below and their way went up over grass and bare rock to the pass. He was leaving them there. He said, "With us Catalans, business is like breathing."

"Then as one businessman to another, I'll say something for all of us," Holland said. "It's going to be hard to repay what we owe you—"

"Please, do not speak of owing. It is bad luck. You have been my guests, my house is your house. Come back to it when you can. That is all that need be said."

"Excellency—" Candelas began for himself, but got no further. The baron shut him off with a spate of final instructions for the climb. The instructions did not seem to be wholly necessary; Candelas pointed out, or tried to point out against the baron's vocal opposition, that he had been through the northwest pass more often than the baron himself. But the baron, refusing interruption, managed to escape any further expressions of thanks, and in the end to put himself in the position of asking a small favor of them rather than of having done them a large one.

"I'll have the telephone line working again before the post

office opens in the morning, and I'll be there when it does," he said. "You can leave the packs at Rancié, but give me a call to let me know that they got through all right, as soon as you reach a telephone." He added stiffly, in embarrassment at his own concern, "A man worries about twelve hundred francs." After that he shook hands formally with each of them, warned them unnecessarily against making a noise or showing a light or otherwise inviting attention to their presence on the exposed mountainside, and when he could think of nothing more to say turned abruptly back into the darkness that shielded him from gratitude. For more than a thousand years his people had been giving aid and comfort to strangers in their mountains, without having learned to accept thanks gracefully for what they gave.

The climb to the pass was moderately tiring, but difficult in one place only. They took their time, resting often, saving their breath except as was necessary to communicate. In the moonless night neither a drab coverall nor the trail, if it was a trail they followed, was visible, and they had to speak to each other now and then to stay together. They came without incident to the difficult part, half an hour's climb beyond the point where they had left the baron.

Candelas stopped them to explain what lay ahead. In the thin chill mountain air his breath was warm in their faces when he spoke, although they could see him only as a vague dark bulk in the darkness.

"There's a cliff face to cross. I won't fool you. Anybody who went at it with his hands in his pockets would have plenty of time for a couple of Hail Mary's on the way down. But it's not dangerous when you're careful, and I'll take the packs across myself after I explore it. There's nothing to worry about."

"How far?" Magill asked. His voice was without inflection.

"Down?"

"Across."

"About eight meters. Not as much as nine."

"How wide?"

"Wide enough for me to walk on, most of the way, and I make two of either of you through the beam. It's a corniche; flat, good solid rock, a little seepage from the cliff face but no mud." He breathed twice before he went on. "There's only one tricky spot, in the middle. A traverse. You've got to suck in your belly and hug your way around a bulge in the cliff, but there's nothing more to it than getting the front of your coverall wet. Snap out of your pack now, patrón, while I'm trying the footing, and I'll take you over the way we crossed the Ramblas when you lost your peepers."

"Take the packs across first."

"It will be easier—"

"Shut up and do as you're told."

Magill's voice was still under the same tight control. Holland could guess nothing from it. But while they sat together on a rock in the dark, waiting for Candelas to carry out his orders, Magill began to shiver, suddenly and uncontrollably.

A cold wind blew on the mountainside, a downhill wind that came off snow somewhere above them and poured like falling water into the unseen dark depth above which they had to cross. But the wind was only cold, not bitter, and they wore good wool under their coveralls. Holland said, "Afraid?"

"Deathly."

"Think about something else."

"I can't." A full minute later, still shivering, Magill said, "I'm acrophobic."

"Candelas wouldn't expose you to it if it were dangerous."

"I know that, rationally. Phobias aren't rational."

Magill retched.

Holland said, "Would absinthe help?"

"No."

"You could try it."

"I'd throw up."

He retched again, and then again. They were anguished, comical sounds, like the squeak of a toy mouse. In the same controlled unemotional voice he said, "Excuse me," and went on shivering. The heel plate of one of his climbing boots ticked against rock in time with the trembling of his leg.

Holland said, "You should have gone with him right away, before you had time to think about it."

"I know."

"Was that why you wouldn't go first up the gangplank of the *Montserrat?*"

"Yes."

"You couldn't have fallen more than a few feet there, into water."

"I was only uncomfortable. Not sick to my stomach, the way I am now."

"How bad was it in the nightmare?"

The boot heel ticked metallically for seconds before Magill said, "What nightmare?"

"When you had the fever. You talked."

"About what?"

"Falling, and other things."

"What other things?"

"A poor dog, for one."

Holland was working to keep the conversation going; if possible to force Magill's mind to rationalize its irrational terror. He was not himself particularly fearful of heights, but he knew how the phobia could affect other people. Nausea and vertigo were genuine ailments, not imaginary ones. If Magill went out on the corniche suffering from either, he would create a danger where one did not exist.

He said, "You know your own man. If he says there's nothing to be afraid of, you can stop worrying."

"Quite." The heel plate continued its delicate mechanical ticking.

"Have you ever fallen?"

"All my life." Magill was doing a superb job of holding his voice under control, in spite of his body's weakness. "My nightmares always begin like this, in the dark, above an enormous silent howling endless bottomless—emptiness—"

He retched again.

Holland said, "You're a thinking being. This is not a nightmare."

"I'm not convinced."

"Would it be any better to wait for daylight?"

"Worse. I could see the drop in daylight."

"Do you want to turn back?"

For the first time, a spark of emotion flared faintly in Magill's controlled voice. He said, "Of course I want to turn back! Don't be a damn fool!" Then, hearing, or sensing, Candelas' approach in the dark, he asked, "Are the packs across?"

"Yes, patrón."

"Then let's go, while I can still do it. I'm not going to last much longer."

He did not speak again, but his ragged breathing spoke for him when they followed Candelas out onto the blustery blackness of the corniche. Candelas kept up a reassuring flow of conversational encouragement as they went: "—nothing to it here, patrón, you're as safe as the ham in a bocadillo, I'm keeping you between me and the mountain, just make sure of your footing and move as I do," stringing a lifeline of words between Magill and panic until they came to the bulge of cliff that narrowed the corniche. At that point there was no longer room for a man to stand as safe as the ham in a bocadillo between his man and the mountain. There it became necessary to stand alone, exposed, spread-eagled around and across a smooth swell of stone. It was not truly dangerous; the rock, although slick with seepage, was inclined inward above the corniche, sloping well back from the vertical. To make the traverse in security a man had only to face the cliff, lay his body on the stone and slide his feet sideways until the corniche widened again. But it was no place to stand in fear and dizziness above a too clearly imagined void, and Holland felt his own nerves tighten for Magill as Candelas explained what they had come to.

"We've got to pass him hand to hand here, Dutchman," he said, as if Magill were not there to listen. "He needs something to hang on to. Anchor on to the rock there and give him your fist. I'll go on across and take a hold on the other side. When I say so, give him to me quick and easy."

"I've got it. I've got him. Take your time."

"Good. When I say come, patrón, come. I'll have my hand out for you. There's nothing to be scared of."

Magill made a sound. It was not speech.

His hand, gripping Holland's so tightly as to be painful, was hot and damp with sweat, and Holland could feel the wild flutter of pulse under his fingers. Magill's breathing was harsh with terror above the rushing fall of air down the cliff. Holland thought, wondering, What kind of effort of will has it taken to carry you this far? He felt an immense pity for Magill, trapped and helpless in his nightmare. On impulse he said, "For what it's worth to you, if it happens it will happen to both of us together," and heard, immediately, as if on cue, Candelas' call: "Now."

During what might have been four or five seconds Magill made no move. Holland, gripped and gripping, his feet braced, his arms and legs set to extend through the tie of his body the security of the spur of rock that was their anchorage, thought that he had not heard. But then he moved, in what was very nearly, frighteningly, a lunge, and was on the traverse. His movements, interpreted through the bond of their hands, were jerky; a tug, a pause, another tug, another pause as he sidled his way, foot by sliding foot. Taut between grip and anchorage, Holland paid himself out like a stretching spring; first the bend of his arm that reached to the traverse, then through the loosening muscles of his back to the reserve of flexion still in his anchor arm; careful not to allow too much slack, careful not to give less than enough, feeding security to Magill through the lock of their grip until Candelas' hand could reach out and offer him security on the other side. Inch by inch, muscle by muscle, he let himself extend until the unexpected moment came when there was no further extension left in him. He stood stretched in his own place as Magill would be stretched on the windy exposure of the traverse; still gripped, still gripping, still without having reached far enough.

Afterward he could not remember making a conscious decision. There was no time for the kind of choice that could be reasoned. Between one small movement when he had slack to give and the next, when he had not, in the interval it took Magill to shift his weight from foot to foot and reach the end of their joint tether, there was only time to release what he was free to release, the anchorage, and shift his own balance to continue the illusion of security that held Magill from his illusion of danger. He did not know how much farther he could carry the illusion. Part of another foot of Magill's progress, perhaps. He would have to follow him out on the traverse then, or be overbalanced. After that it would depend on Magill; forward, backward or down, according to his reaction to the consciousness of insecurity.

Palm and cheek pressed to the cold dampness of the cliff, clinging to it and vanishing balance with the pores of his skin, he thought, Am I afraid? He decided that he was not. In the faith of insha'Allah, fear was pointless. It was all decided for you ahead of time. Take care of both her fathers.

Another tug pulled him a little closer to the ultimate moment. He felt moisture, he thought at first seepage from the rock against which his face was pressed, roll down his cheek and drip off his chin as Magill's sweat-slick gripping fingers released themselves from his and the reaction took him in their place. Sick with the sudden shock of adrenalin in his blood stream, near nausea from the animal protest of his own glands, he stood as he was for another minute; limp, still with his cheek pressed against the rock, his eyes closed, dry-mouthed in cold abysmal fear of the void at his back. He could not have moved then to save his own life.

Afterward he felt drained and sluggish, in reaction to the reaction. Even when the fear had left him he was depressed by the thought of having to make the traverse himself, and reluctant to begin it. Part of his brain said dispassionately, Lack of oxygen. In the Andes they called it soroche, altitude sickness. He went back to the widest part of the corniche and did deep-breathing exercises until his mind cleared and his muscles were responsive again.

When he returned to the traverse Candelas was calling to him, anxiously, "Eh, Dutchman! Dutchman! Are you with us?" He called back that he was on his way, then made the crossing without any feeling of fear at all, even experiencing an exhilaration in the consciousness of height and danger overcome. Part of his mind said, dispassionately, *Too much deep breathing*, but another part denied it. It had been an accomplishment. Without him, even Candelas could not have got Magill across the traverse. The fact that he could not have got Magill across without Candelas did not spoil it at all. They had both been necessary.

Beyond the traverse the corniche was wide and easy once again. At its far end, Magill and the packs were outlines of darkness against a lesser darkness of rock, with Candelas standing over them. The wind kept a faint odor of sickness in the air from being more than noticeable.

"How does it go now, patrón?" Candelas said. "With the stomach empty, you'll feel better."

Magill answered something weakly irritable. Candelas, kneeling, opened one of the packs. They heard the pop of a withdrawn cork.

"Wash your mouth out with this," he said. "Swallow a

mouthful or two, no more. At this altitude it goes to the head."

"I don't want any."

"Take it just the same."

"I don't want any!" Magill said again, more snappishly. "It will make me sick."

"You've already been sick. This will settle the stomach. Just listen once to somebody who knows the mountains."

Magill made a noise of impatience, but took the bottle. They heard him drink, spit, drink again. He gave the bottle back with a testy grunt that could have been interpreted as thanks or a criticism of the taste of the absinthe. Candelas chuckled.

"He'll live," he said to Holland. "As sour as ever. Here, take a swig yourself. Sometimes the mouth gets a little dry on a traverse like that one. It's nothing to be ashamed of."

"Mine did," Holland said.

He had a couple of swallows of the strong sweet-anise-bitter spirit. The slow spreading warmth of the alcohol in his stomach was welcome. Giving the bottle back, he said, "How far now?"

"To the pass, about forty minutes." Candelas took a gulp of absinthe, smacked the cork back into the bottle with the palm of his hand and buckled the bottle again into his knapsack. "Straight up to where you see the tail of the Bear sticking over the ridge. After that, fifteen kilometers of easy going downhill to Rancié, and it's all over but the abrazos. You'll be eating breakfast with your women in the morning, patrón."

Magill grunted.

They went on and up; slowly, carefully. The way was steeper than it had been, rising to the backbone of the cordillera, and there were patches of snow where the sun had not been able to reach behind some outcrop of rock or earth; rotten snow, honeycombed with melting. They had no trouble avoiding the danger of its bad footing. In starlight the snow patches were faintly luminescent, and the stars themselves seemed bigger and more radiant than normal, like lamps.

Between starlight and snow reflection Holland found that he could see his climbing companions, dimly. Candelas no longer led the way, but followed at the rear to backstop with his body either of the others who might lose footing on the steep stony slope. They climbed, rested, climbed, rested and climbed, to come in time, breathing more quickly than usual in the thin atmosphere of the mountaintop but still with unused reserves of strength, to a ledge of rock from which they could see more than just the tail of the Bear hanging above them; the Bear himself, spangled and bright in the northern heaven. They were looking through the gun sight of the pass at the sky over France.

“Smack on target,” Candelas said. “Not bad for a dumbhead in the dark, eh, Dutchman?”

“You’d be less of a dumbhead if you kept your voice down,” Magill said.

Candelas laughed aloud. He was feeling the exhilaration of a mountain climber at his goal.

“You could dance a sardana up here for all the notice it would win you,” he said. “Nobody has used this pass in five years.”

Holland said, “What’s on the other side?”

“France.”

“What more? How does the land fall? Which way do we go from the pass?”

“You can see how the land falls by walking through the pass and looking at it.” Candelas was still agreeable. “As for which way to go, you follow me. What more do you want, a blueprint?”

There was no barb on the gibe. Holland took it without offense. But he said, “A blueprint could lead us out of trouble.”

“What kind of trouble are we in?” Magill asked bluntly.

“None, now. Maybe none to come. I hope none. But once

we go through the pass, we're committed. On this side, we're not. We can stop as we like, we can figure ahead, we can talk things over. Nobody is pressing us. On the other side, it may be that we'll be pressed. It's at least a possibility that we could be separated. Each of us ought to know where we're going and how to get there if anything does happen."

"Of course," Magill said. "You're right."

Candelas' pack straps squeaked as he shrugged his shoulders in good-natured acceptance of the majority vote.

"In two words, you go downhill until you get there. But look, then. Can you make out the patch of snow where I stand?"

"Well enough."

"The pass is here, between my feet. In front and below, four or five hundred meters down, there at the stone, the mountain breaks two ways; left, right. Both breaks shape into valleys, with woods and water. Timber line is at the stone, where the valleys begin. Above that there'll be snowpack, because the sun doesn't get over on that side. Below timber line—"

"Back up," Holland said. "That's four or five hundred meters of open mountainside covered with snow. What will the footing be like?"

"At this temperature, good for tobogganing." A note of beginning impatience had come into Candelas' voice. "Why not wait to try the footing when you get to it? It will be sunup before we see Rancié if we stop to nose over every five hundred meters between here and there."

"Just so long as we get there, no harm. Go on. Below timber line?"

Candelas went on, increasingly grumpy at each question raised. It offended him that his guidance was in challenge, and he did not try to hide his feeling that Holland's meticulous tracing of their route down fifteen kilometers of mountain slope was a waste of time. At one point Magill said sharply, “Answer the questions you’re asked and stop grumbling.” After that Candelas gave surly short answers, and when the questioning was done swung his pack to the ground. They heard the slip of straps through buckles, a clink, the sound of the cork coming out of the bottle. He swallowed loudly; once, twice, three times.

“Anybody else?” he asked. It was a bald rudeness to have drunk first from the bottle without offering it.

“No,” Holland said.

“No,” Magill said. “This is no time to be getting drunk.”

“I’m not getting drunk. I’m warming my cold feet. Am I the only one of us not to be permitted cold feet?”

He drank again, defiantly, then recorked the bottle. They did not hear him put it back in the pack before he swung the pack to his shoulders again and led the way toward the pass.

He’s going to give us trouble now, Holland thought. With the bottle in his pocket and injured feelings to brood on, Candelas would be surly drunk before long. It had been a mistake for them to have allied themselves, or to have appeared to ally themselves, against him. The mistake needed correction rather than compounding, yet Holland’s every instinct, all his training, all his engineer’s margin-of-safety caution impelled him to compound it by urging the further need to scout the pass before they, or in any event Magill, went through it.

He knew that Magill would stand with him again. It was not enough that Candelas was certain of their security, that the baron’s strategy worked for them, that the pass had been long unused. The risk of walking into a possible trap, however remote, was avoidable, therefore to be avoided. If a trap had been set he could himself spring it at no great cost to any of them simply by laying down his load of cigarettes, not yet contraband, and crossing the frontier alone. If the trap closed, he had a passport, and the irregularity of entering France without submitting it for inspection first was a minor one. He could think of a dozen sound reasons why he and Magill should not be following trustingly on Candelas' heels as they moved into the steep slot of the pass, only one reason why they should—Candelas' injured feelings. But the one outweighed the dozen in his mind, and he did not balk as he should have balked before they came to solid snowpack and the mountain sloped down under their feet instead of up.

The wind did not blow in the pass. But the air lying on the snow was icy, cold enough to condense their breath, and Magill's glasses fogged immediately. He took them off several times to wipe them before they had gone a hundred meters from the mouth of the pass, kicking their heels for footing into the firm crust of the faintly luminescent snow. The last time he said crossly, "Oh, damn! Wait! I've dropped them!" and crouched awkwardly under the burden of his pack to feel the surface of the snow with his hands. In that position he was brought instantaneously into visual existence like a projection on a screen, pinned there under their eyes by a glare of bright white light that held them all in its scope. An authoritative French voice called loudly, "Stand as you are, messieurs!" in the same moment that Candelas roared, "Scatter!"

Holland's eyes, adjusted to the dark, were blinded by the sudden dazzle of light on snow. He could see only outlines and movement; Candelas' quick break out of the trap of the searchlight beam, Magill's clumsiness in coming to his feet to run. But sound carried clearly in the cold air, and there was no mistaking the metallic double slap-and-click of a breech mechanism, nor the equally sharp warning in the shout of the repeated order, "Stand!" He threw himself bodily at Magill while Magill was still coming erect, knocking him off his feet, sliding with him on the frozen crust of snow but pinning him. A rifle began cracking flatly while they were still down, then two rifles, spacing each other; aimed rather than hurried shooting, from the intervals between the shots, and within a range that made continued misses by both shooters improbable.

To risk himself or Magill under fire had never been a part of his consideration. Candelas' promise that French customs guards did not shoot had been one of the specifications. But the bright glare of light was no longer on them, and Candelas, whom it followed, was still lucky, still running. The careful shooting continued. He dragged Magill to his feet in the shelter of the restored dark and urged him, aided at first by the descent of the steepening slope and then impelled by it, toward the wall of dark shadow beyond snow that meant forest and escape into cover.

It did not occur to him to slip the straps of his knapsack and drop it, as he would have done if he had been obliged to run uphill with it, or on level ground. Running downhill the extra weight was less of a hindrance than an aid, part of the impelling force; at first within control, then, as the smooth declivity of the snowpack increased, beyond control. They would have had to throw themselves flat and skidded to have stopped. Pushed on by gravity and their loads, they had run more than half the distance to the dark line of trees when the shooting stopped.

Poor dog, Holland thought fleetingly. In a moment the light swung over and past them, searching, then quickly back; not so glaring or so sharply focused at the greater distance but bright enough to send their long shadows leaping ahead of them into the cover of the trees. The paced, unhurried firing began instantly, without further warning.

It angered him, this time, instead of making him cautious. There was no feeling behind those carefully squeezed-off shots; not even enmity. They were like an exercise in rifle fire; medium range, medium elevation, windage zero, target in motion. He hated the two riflemen as much for the calculation of their shooting as he did for Candelas; not because they wished their targets ill but because they did not, and could yet be trying to hit them.

Magill still ran at his side, too close. He shouted, “Run left!” and ran to his own right, almost but not quite losing balance in the change of direction. The first trees were very near. Magill shouted, “Can’t—see!” in appeal; for what, he could not tell. He was without breath to answer. The glare of the searchlight was still on the trees ahead of him, but his shadow had disappeared among the first spindling outposts of the forest. Then he was among them himself and quickly into deeper growth; unhit, unhurt, safe.

The shooting stopped as it had begun; first one rifle, then the other. There was no other sound. The searchlight held its steady beam on the forest for another moment, swept back and forth along the line of trees twice, then either went out or was turned somewhere else.

He moved away from the light while he could still see by it, instinctively, a beetle scuttling for a dark corner. As the forest deepened, the snow on its floor became softer and patchier; soon he walked on pine needles instead of snow. Safe in the dark, no longer scuttling, thinking again rather than instinctive, he turned left in the direction Magill had been running and went back up through the trees as he had come down, from pine needles to patchy snow to snowpack. He was not worried about leaving tracks. It would take an army of men to beat the forest, even in daylight, and an army would have had more than two rifles. He tried not to think of Candelas. It was important that he think first of Magill and himself.

The fact that the searchlight was no longer focused in their direction was a reasonable guarantee that both of them had arrived unhurt in the cover of the forest, unless Magill had been hit in the last few steps that took him to shelter. It did not necessarily mean that they were no longer hunted; only that, in the literal sense, they were not being looked for. An incautious sound could still give them away. The forest was very quiet, with only an occasional plop of snow from a branch to break the silence. In its shelter, without starlight to see by, he had to feel his way from tree to tree, taking direction from the slope of the ground and judging his approach to the thinning upper edge of the forest by the size of the tree trunks and their distance from each other. It would not do to be exposed in inadequate cover if the searchlight came back again. On the other hand, he reasoned, Magill couldn't have come far without his glasses, and did not realize the absurdity of the thought until his groping hands passed on either side of a too slender trunk and he banged heavily into it with his nose. When his nose began to bleed he stuffed it with snow, and found that he could make out the whiteness of the snow in his hand. He looked up to see the Bear again, sparkling through scant foliage.

He was back in the upper fringe of trees. Magill should be somewhere in the neighborhood, unless Magill had been feeling his way down into the cover of the forest while he himself was feeling his way back up out of it. Logically Magill should have done just that, insuring his own escape by beetle instinct, in which case they were probably separated beyond conjunction. But he remembered the appeal in Magill's shout, and could not meet it with a reliance on logic alone.

Holding snow to his nose, he considered the possibilities. If Magill were within hearing distance, they could communicate only at the chance of being overheard, and for him to find out if Magill was or was not within hearing distance would be to take that chance possibly to no purpose. A clear case of calculated risk, as Larry would have defined it; something to be considered and accepted or declined after thought. On the corniche, without time for thought, it had been much easier. He considered the choice for the time it took his nose to stop bleeding. Then, still without having decided, stooping to clean his hand of blood and snow in fresh snow, he moved his foot a scant inch or two, put his weight on a deadfall branch that broke soggily beneath him and somehow managed to trap his boot, so that, falling, pulled off balance by the weight of his pack in an awkward position, he heard or felt or experienced a clean snap of bone in his foot accompanied by a searing flash of pain, and either fainted from it or hit his head against a tree in falling. He was never sure of anything except that he blanked out for an interval that seemed to be no more than a wink but had to be longer. When he came out of it, his ears ringing with pain and his foot a coal of fire, Magill was there; Magill kneeling beside him shutting off his wind with a hand over his mouth, whispering, "Wake up! Wake up! Wake up!" until he woke up and discovered that the moans he had been listening to with black disapproval for the unmanly weakness of the moaner were his own. He closed his mouth under Magill's pressing hand.

Magill said anxiously, "What happened? Are you all right?"

"I broke my foot." Pain was making him sweat. It would have been a relief to go on moaning. "How did you get here?"

"I heard you go down. It sounded like another fall of snow at first, but then you began groaning and I had to find you to shut you up. They're within earshot. I heard them talking."

"Candelas?"

"I don't know. I couldn't make out what they were talking about."

He listened to the ringing in his ears. The pain had to be pretty bad, to make his ears sing like that. It screamed at him from both ends of his body.

Magill said, "Can you walk?"

"Help me get free of these pack straps and I'll find out."

Getting to his feet, even without the pack and with help, was unpleasant. Putting tentative weight on the foot was moderate torture; bearable, but not for long.

"I won't get far on it. You'll have to write me off."

"What do you mean by that?"

"Every man for himself. Go on alone."

"I won't do it."

"It's only sensible. You've got to get to Marseille, I don't. I've got a passport and money to meet any fine they want to lay on me for not using it. The most they'll give me for smuggling is another fine. The moon will be up in another few hours. As soon as we can see—"

"I can't see. I lost my glasses. How far do you think I'd get stumbling through a forest by moonlight?"

"How far would you get stumbling through a forest with me on your back?"

"I don't have to carry you. I can skid you."

"On what?"

"A pack. A tree branch. Anything. It's all downhill. We can at least get far enough to be able to wait up for daylight, and after that we'll know more about what to do next." Magill sounded old and very tired. "I can't do it alone. Without him—or you, one of you—somebody—I don't know. I don't know what it is I want to say. Only that I couldn't ever do it alone. I've never been any good alone."

"There's a good chance that he got away," Holland lied. "Don't give him up yet."

"I haven't given him up. I haven't given myself up. I'm just telling you what I need to keep going. I can't do it alone."

Holland shivered, although not from cold. Fifteen kilometers of rough mountainside to go with the coal burning in his foot was not going to leave him much in the way of nerve tissue. Still, a contract was a contract. You had to accept the penalties along with the reward.

"Strap the two packs together, then," he said. "They ought to make a fair kind of sledge as long as the canvas lasts."

They waited for the sliver of waning moon to rise before they set out. It gave very little light when they could see it, none when they got into the forest's deeper shadow. But Magill had a near-blind man's instinct, or practice, whatever it was, at feeling his way in the dark, and scouted ahead at short intervals before coming back to drag Holland after him on the packs. The knapsacks were stiffened by light aluminum frames that substituted fairly well, with the inner bracing of the cigarette cartons they contained, for the framework and runners of a sled, and they skidded even better on packed pine needles than over snow. Holland rode one pack with his good leg resting on the other, his bad foot crossed on top.

The jostlings didn't greatly matter. There was little variation in the pain. The foot had swollen inside his boot, whose strings Magill had loosened but which Holland declined to let him remove. He knew he would never be able to get it on again, and the boot, painful as it was, served as a protection. If the time ever came when he had to hobble, the foot was going to need all the protection he could arrange for it.

They did not go far or quickly; two or three hundred meters in an hour. By that time the sides of the beginning valley they were descending had steepened to such an extent that the knapsacks developed a tendency to slide off down the slope toward the stream they could hear running below them. Magill had to spend more time dragging the packs back on course than in the direction he wanted them to go, and Holland's bad foot, instead of safely trailing, twice swung into obstructions. Both times he was unable to keep himself from cursing. Magill, contrite, would not risk a third accident. He arranged the knapsacks against the bole of a tree to make a kind of seat and leg support, into which he got Holland settled on a springy duff of pine needles to wait for dawn.

At their altitude, only meters below timber line and the snowpack, the night air was very cold. But Holland found that the pine duff made a good heat insulator when stuffed inside his coveralls, in the manner of a straw mattress. He passed the discovery on to Magill, who in minutes of patient finger-scraping got together enough dry pine needles to stuff both their coveralls full, from boot top to neck and wristbands, then piled another drift of them over Holland and made a second drift for himself to burrow into. Afterwards they were reasonably warm, except for the nip of chill on their ears and noses. Holland could even have done with less warmth, in spots. His swollen foot throbbed feverishly inside the tight confinement of the boot, and his head was hot. He wished he had a drink, or half a dozen drinks. He thought of the bottle of absinthe, and turned his thoughts deliberately from it because he could not think of absinthe without thinking of Candelas.

By an accident of position, their squirrel nests against the tree bole looked out through a break in the forest cover over the expanse of valley to which the smaller valley they were descending was a tributary. Holland, visualizing the baron's sketch map, could identify the irregular groupings of light that were French villages. From an elevation of a thousand meters or more above the valley floor they were almost in the same perspective as they had been on the map on the baron's dinner table. Marc, to which the false blueprint had pointed, was invisible behind a spur of mountain, but Vicdessos and Auzat were small neighboring light clusters like distant constellations, with a vague tailing below of individual star points which were farmhouses marking the valley's descent, and a creeping yellow twin-cone comet of French headlights on a lonely late car or bus or truck coming up the road from the lowlands. It might even be the car that was to meet them at the rendezvous. The time was about right. He hoped that the driver of the car, whoever it might be, did not suffer from impatience. The halt and the blind were going to take a long time to skid those fifteen kilometers.

Magill said, "How's the foot?"

"Hot."

"Anything I can do for it?"

"Not unless you brought a bottle of something to drink in your pack."

"I'm sorry. Mine is all cigarettes."

"So is mine."

Not so dumb, Candelas had said of himself, choosing the load of absinthe. But he had been dumb to run with it. He had been dumb to think the French would not shoot. He had been dumb to go through the pass without scouting it. He had been colossally dumb because they had combined against him to hurt his feelings, and nothing was to be gained by thinking of spilled spark plugs.

He said, "We're at quite an elevation here. Doesn't it bother you?"

"In what way?"

"The phobia."

"I can't see anything. It's a visual thing. If I can't see it, I'm not afraid of it."

"You couldn't see anything on the corniche."

"The trouble was, I could: I'd been there many times before. In nightmares." Magill had to hunt for words. "It's hard to explain an irrationality rationally. If I hadn't been able to see the drop in my mind, it wouldn't have bothered me. Or if we'd been at a height without any visual connection with a depth, real or imaginary—in an airplane, say—I'd have been all right. Airplanes don't bother me. Looking out of the window of a plane in flight, as long as I keep my eyes and imagination off the danger of the wing, is like looking at a television screen. It's all contained in a safe flat plane, without depth perspective. In a tethered balloon, on the other hand, where I could see or imagine the drop of the cable to earth—ugh!" His shudder rustled the drift of pine needles in which he was buried. "I'm queasy just from talking about it."

"You don't have to talk about it."

"It's all right. We're still at the rational level. If you're interested."

"I'm interested."

"It has something to do with the attraction of the eye by descending lines; not the height itself so much as the plunge.

Elevators don't bother me much; I'm in a box with a solid floor, and normally I don't have to look or think beneath it unless the crack between the box and the landing traps my eye or mind. Here on the mountain I'm *on* something. I'm supported, not suspended. I might fall and roll, even hurt myself, as I did jumping from the train, but I can't picture myself tumbling into space. From a cliff or the top of a high building, on the other hand, I can see the drop, straight down. It reaches up for me. I've got to hold onto something, or be held, to keep from going over." Magill laughed uncomfortably. "That's the terrifying thing about it, the dominating urge to jump. Can you understand that? To be horribly afraid of something and yet impelled toward it, hypnotized by it?"

"I think so. Yes."

"I daren't go near a drop-off. It makes me dizzy to think of one. I can't look out of a high window unless there are bars across it to hold on to, and I'm uncomfortable then. In my nightmares—"

He stopped talking, abruptly.

"What about the nightmares?"

"That would take it to the irrational level."

"You mean you don't want to talk about it."

"I mean I could use a drink myself, now."

It was the thought of the absinthe again, intruding, with his rejection of the thought for something else, that made him remember what he carried in his pack besides cigarettes. Feeling for it, behind his back and then beneath his throbbing foot, he found the doll first, the package of perfume under it. He broke a fingernail before he got the hard plastic covering off the glass stopper of the flask and could ease the stopper out. Marsha's flowery fragrance rose out of the bottle like the bouquet of a good wine.

Magill said sharply, "What's that?"

"Perfume. Hold out your hand." Holland reached for it, clamping Magill's fingers around the flask. "You'll smell a little sweet afterward, but it's got alcohol in it. Go ahead."

"How do you know it's safe?"

"If it stays down, it's drinkable. If it comes up, no harm done. I'll try it first, if you like."

Magill drank.

He breathed with difficulty after he got it down. Holland, in his turn, felt his throat close at the bite of the raw spirit. But the drink did not sicken them immediately, and the warming stomach glow that followed it more than made up for the burn. He had a second drink, which Magill declined. The throbbing foot began to hurt less.

Some time later Magill said, "You bought it for Marsha, of course."

"We weren't going to talk about Marsha."

"I'm talking about the perfume."

"All right." The warmth of the alcohol was relaxing in more ways than one. "Talk."

"You bought it for her."

"Of course."

"Why?"

"That's an inane question."

"I'm sorry. What I meant to say was, why did you buy her that particular fragrance?"

"It's what she wears. It's her perfume."

"Did she tell you that?"

"She wore it when I married her. She wears it now. She's never changed."

"Did she say that?"

"As a matter of fact, yes. She did."

Magill made no comment.

"What's behind the question?" Holland asked, and drank again. "Since we've decided to talk. Have another?"

"I'd prefer a cigarette. Do you think it would be safe to light a match?"

"No. Have a drink instead."

"One is enough for me, thanks."

More minutes passed. They were cold, dragging minutes but fragrant, scented with Marsha's scent. He had another drink, a big one; fiery, throat-searing, stomach-warming, pain-killing. The aftertaste, when the burn died, was the flavor of Marsha's mouth as it had tasted when he kissed her in the garden—or had it been toothpaste? No, the toothpaste was Micaela's. He was too tired to remember clearly. The anodyne was working in his brain as well as in his foot. He could no longer picture either one of them clearly on his mental screen, only Marsha-Micaela, blurred. Had she kissed him back or had she fought him? He couldn't remember. But he could smell her fragrance clearly enough. There was no confusion about her scent.

"About Marsha," he said, with an effort. "Why shouldn't she have told me about the perfume?"

"She lied."

"How lied?"

"She hasn't worn that scent since she left you."

"You're lying."

"I have no reason to lie."

"Neither had—"

He didn't finish it. Magill said, "You see?"

"No. I don't see."

He was on the verge of drunkenness, and welcomed it. He had a feeling that he might be sick within a few minutes, but vomiting wouldn't take the alcohol out of his blood stream. He had another drink, a quick one.

"I don't see," he said again. "Tell me."

"You're not going to like it."

"I don't like a lot of things. Tell me."

"All right, then. She let you think what you wanted to think. I made her own up to it when I talked to her on the phone in Andorra la Vella. All this time you've been able to convince yourself that you could take her away from me, that all you had to do was bring me safely out of Spain and the loyalty that held her to me while I was in trouble would be overwhelmed by a revival of her dormant love for you. She wanted you to think that, even while she was telling you it wasn't so. She hasn't given you a thought for years. You mean nothing at all to her. You could no more go back to what you once were together than you can take eighteen years off your age, or turn Micaela back into an egg in her mother's womb. Marsha is my wife, just as Micaela is my daughter. You'll never have either of them."

"That remains to be seen."

"No! Listen to me! I'm not fighting you now! I'm trying to save you hurt, if you can believe me. Can you believe that, that I'm telling you the truth?"

"I believe that you're honest in what you believe to be true."

"In what I know to be true! I tell you, Marsha and I had it out on the phone! I made her confess to it, but even if she hadn't I *know* her. I've been her husband for eighteen years, Micaela's father for as long. You had one of them for a few weeks, the other never. Do you think you can know them better than I—or that the great disclosure that Micaela carries your blood instead of mine can make any difference to her, between us?"

Holland had another drink. He knew he was going to be sick soon, but the haven of drunkenness was close. The pain in his foot was detached, something belonging to someone else.

Magill said, "Let me tell you what Micaela wrote about you in the letter you brought, as well as I can remember. She said—"

"I don't want to hear what she said."

"—'I danced with your friend Mr. Holland the other night. He likes me, quite a lot I'm pretty sure, although he must be at least forty. I feel kind of sorry for him—' "

“That’s enough. Thanks for the revelation.”

“No, listen. ‘I feel kind of sorry for him. He seems to have so little. I don’t mean money or anything like that, Mama says he’s rolling in it, but no family or ties or attachments or anything at all if you don’t count the kind of girl who asks about m’sieur’s bank account before she’ll go to bed with him—’ ”

“That’s all.”

“—‘If it weren’t for Carlos I think I’d like to be nice to him. He’s starved for love—and we have so much of it, you and I and Mama, dearest, dearest Dad—’ ”

“Shut up!” Holland said thickly, feeling the nausea rise and burst in his throat. He rolled sideways off the knapsack and was sick, his gullet burning, the sweet-sour stench of rotted flowers in his nose. Afterward he lay inert, his head swimming, the pain in his foot a distant irritant that kept him from sliding off into unconsciousness, semiconscious until Magill came to him, much later, with the perfume flask. He tried to push it away until he found that it was full of fresh ice-cold water. The welcome chill of it in his foul mouth and on his face revived him. Magill helped him back to the knapsacks, then covered him again with pine duff against the chill that was making him shiver.

“Sorry to be so long about it, but I had to feel my way down to the stream and back,” Magill said. “You’ll be all right when you warm up a bit. How’s the foot?”

“No change.”

“We’ll have enough light to see by in another hour or so. I’ll take a look at it.”

“There’s no point in looking at it.”

“It’s your foot. Can I tell you something more?”

“I don’t seem to be able to stop you.” Holland’s head ached, his foot throbbed, the foul sweet-sour taste was strong in his mouth. He was still drunk, and not pleasantly.

“You’ve got your defenses up again, so this may not penetrate, but I’ll try. When I talked to Marsha, she told me how she'd started out to trick you but hadn't been able to go through with it. She told me what you wanted of her, what you'd suggested, and I wasn't jealous because I was absolutely sure of her. That's important for you to understand, because I'd always been jealous of you, my predecessor, her first love, her inseminator. We never had any children of our own. I don't know why. Something missing in me, certainly. It made me even more jealous, that you had been able to get her with child where I could not. I hated you and was jealous of you and afraid of you, tormented by your image, for eighteen years. In nightmares, when I fell, it was always you who dropped me, or pushed me over the edge, or pried my fingers loose one by one while I sweated and begged and pleaded for mercy. When you came along in the flesh, Andy Holland the three-dimensional man, you did me a favor. You stopped being a thing of my imagination and became real. You diminished from nightmare to ordinary man, and then at last to a lesser man even than I, not a better one; you had lost the wife and daughter I had won from you. Instead of hating and fearing you, I could feel sorry for you. Do you know what I dreamed in the nightmare I had during the fever?"

"That I pried your fingers loose one by one and dropped you over a cliff, I hope."

"That you fell. That for once it was not I who dropped forever into an endless empty echoing void of nothingness, but you. And I, because I had fallen so many times myself, and knew how horrible it was, could feel pity. I no longer hated or was afraid of you, only sorry for you. That's all I wanted to say."

"Good. Now we can both shut up."

"I already said I didn't expect it to penetrate."

"Then give up drilling at me! What do you have to prove?"

"Nothing," Magill said. "Not anymore."

They did not talk again. In time Magill slept, peacefully, his breathing regular and gentle.

Holland sat and watched the stars, not thinking. He was still drunk. He clung to drunkenness as a blanket between himself and thought, substituting it for the sleep denied him by the pain in his foot. When the blanket wore too thin he did slide-rule problems in his head while the thin moon moved from right to left across the darkness of the sky and the spangled Bear wheeled slowly on its tether. Birds began to stir and twitter in the trees as the sky grayed in the east. Magill woke, yawned, stretched and reached instinctively to the side of what had been his bed for the glasses that were not there. Another day had begun for the halt and the blind.

They moved out as soon as the light was strong enough to show the way. The knapsack-sledge left no visible track on the forest's smooth carpet of pine needles, and Holland rode it in a position to watch for dislodged stones and conspicuously broken twigs in the wake of their sliding. The chances that an attempt would be made to track them through the forest were still remote, but whenever anything showed too clearly where they had passed he spoke to Magill about it, directing him back toward the stone or twig or whatever it was until Magill was close enough to see it for himself. The stops gave Magill minutes of rest from the dragging burden of the sledge which he would not have taken otherwise. He was driving himself close to the limit of his strength.

They had to stop at other intervals for Holland to survey a route that would take them down the mountainside without taking them too steeply down, or off the safe highway of a declining ridge into the trap of a watercourse, or into some other pocket from which Magill would have to drag the sledge uphill. It happened from time to time, inevitably. Holland could not watch the trail ahead while he rode the knapsacks with his bad foot trailing, the only safe position for it, and Magill could not even distinguish outlines more than a few meters in front of him. When they did wander into trouble, Holland got off the sledge and hopped. He no longer dared touch the foot to the ground. His leg throbbed all the way to the knee, his head had a pulse of its own. He felt dull, dispirited, incapable. His mind would reach ahead only as far as the rendezvous and a cessation of movement, if they ever got that far. It seemed improbable that Magill's reserves of strength would serve for it.

As they descended, their cover of pine trees grew less. The lower slopes of the mountains had been lumbered, selectively in some places, less so in other places. Patches of open pasture and meadowland began to penetrate the forest. They made the surveying of the descent more difficult for Holland and the descent itself more demanding on Magill, both by reason of the decrease in the slope of the mountain and the increasing raggedness of the carpet of pine needles on which they skidded. Holland had to hop more and more often as Magill came to patches of bare earth or rock outcrop, and the canvas of the sledge began to show bad signs of wear. The knapsacks would not last much longer. Neither would their rider, as he was beginning to realize. He had broken a primitive crutch from a tree branch, but he did not have the knack of letting it take his weight, and his movement was still pretty much of a labored hop. Their progress had slowed to that pace before the sun came up. Holland estimated that they had come at most five kilometers, over the easiest part of the descent.

He said, "We're never going to make it this way."

They had stopped at a small stream for rest and a drink. Magill had brought along the perfume flask, which he refilled and carried to Holland before himself drinking, face down in the stream. Wiping his wet face afterward, he said, "How much do you weigh?"

"Eighty-five kilos. Ninety, in what I'm wearing."

"Candelas used to carry a hundred."

"You're not Candelas."

It was the first time they had spoken of him since the

mountaintop. Holland felt a dull stab of resentment at being forced to think again of what he had managed not to think about.

"I've been mulling over the shooting," Magill said. "I don't think they were trying to hit us."

"They put up a good imitation of it."

"I wonder if that isn't what it was. I've never been shot at before, but don't bullets make a noise when they go by your ear?"

"Ricochets make an ugly sound. An unscarred bullet zips."

"I didn't hear any zips. Did you?"

"We weren't listening for zips."

"It seems to me we'd have heard them without listening for them, if there'd been any."

"All right. Let's say we heard no zips. What follows?"

"Well, Candelas said the French don't shoot; more exactly, he said that the French are too civilized to put a bullet in a man's back for a little untaxed alcohol or tobacco." Magill felt his way carefully along the line of his reasoning, testing it. "Maybe he was wrong, but I don't think so. I don't think he'd have survived as a smuggler for ten years if he'd been wrong about anything so vital to survival, and I think the lack of zips proves it. They were either shooting blanks, or over our heads."

"You want him to be alive. So do I, but we can't cheat him alive. A trap like that, at that pass, on that night, in those circumstances, was more than just a coincidence. Carlos outfigured us, and Carlos wants you taken alive and whole. Maybe he doesn't want me shot, either, although I wouldn't count on it. But the same protection doesn't automatically extend to Candelas."

Magill shook his head.

"Try it for weakness before you trust it," he said. "I know. It may be good engineering, but it's bad reasoning. Those were Frenchmen shooting and a Frenchman giving the orders.

All the Vilasar money couldn't buy official witnessed murder on this side of the mountains even if Carlos wanted it, and he's no purchaser of murder in cold blood. He could kill, but not that way. I know him too well."

"You're talking nonsense. You don't even know yourself that well. Could you have pictured yourself as a murderer before you became one?"

Magill considered it for a moment, only for a moment, before he said, "I don't think of myself as a murderer now. I'm not a murderer, any more than you are."

"You didn't pick a good comparison. I killed a man."

"I know you did. That's why I used you for comparison. You killed in unreasoning panic where I killed in unreasoning fury. Neither one of us consciously planned to kill, or even thought of the act of killing as a possibility if the idea of taking life is as repugnant to you as it is to me; even more so now than it was before I did it. A man can't be a murderer without premeditation. It's part of the definition. You have to make the election. You have to choose to kill, rationally."

"The Spanish courts would disagree with you."

"Oh, I don't argue that they couldn't garrote me, or send me to prison." Magill might have been discussing imports and exports. "I don't contend that I should rightly escape punishment. I'll even go so far as to admit that any society I choose to live in has a right to punish me as it sees fit for breaking its rules. That's not the point. In my mind, in my conscious, sane, thinking mind that would have to devise and order killing by its own will, its own volition, I am not a murderer. Neither is Carlos, for all his other faults. Neither, I believe, is a French customs guard in the performance of his duty. Therefore no one was trying to shoot us last night, and Candelas is as safe as we are. Probably safer."

"He could have been taken without being shot."

"I thought of it. I don't believe it. Not when we got away."

"How do you propose that we take advantage of the situation?"

"Sit down and wait."

"For what?"

"Him. He'll have made for Rancié as soon as he lost touch with us. When he gets there and finds we haven't arrived, he'll backtrack to find us."

"It's no more than a gamble."

"We gambled on him before this. What's the alternative, if what we're doing now is an impossibility?"

"Offhand, I can't think of any," Holland said.

They waited; Holland with his back against a tree, dozing, his foot elevated on one of the knapsacks to ease the pressure of the throbbing blood, Magill restlessly pacing. In time the exercise tired him. He came to sit against Holland's tree and toss twigs into the blur that was his visual world.

"How's the foot?"

"No change."

"If you'd let me take the boot off, you could bathe it in the creek."

"I'm not sure that the boot off would be an improvement over the boot on. Don't worry about it. I'll live."

"You don't take much help from anyone, do you?"

"Let's talk about something else besides me, if you have to talk."

"I don't have to talk."

"Good."

He dozed; not fully asleep, not fully awake, suspended between the throb of his foot and the ache of his head. He heard a church bell somewhere far off striking the hour, the ripple of the creek over pebbles, a squirrel chattering, a pair of jays bickering with each other, the church bell again, surprisingly striking the next hour, seeming minutes later. He had slept, in spite of the throbbing.

Magill said, "Do you know what the date is?"

"No."

"The fourth. Micaela's birthday."

"I thought we weren't going to talk."

"We have to discuss her future, if you're still planning to inject yourself into it."

"I am."

"To what extent?"

"None of your god-damn business to what extent!"

Holland's mind was working well enough now; forced open, violated and resentful of the intrusion. Magill had challenged too many of the fundamentals of his being. His whole reason for existence would cease to have meaning if he did not defend it where it touched Micaela. He said furiously, "I'm not Carlos, or some college boy asking your permission to take her to the movies! I'm her father! She's going to know that much to begin with, and if you've got all the rest of the answers, all right; they're yours. They don't bind me. I don't have to tell you where we're going for lunch, or that I'll bring her home at eleven o'clock!"

"I suggested a discussion, not an outburst of temper."

"You wanted to know to what extent I intend to inject myself into her future. Now you do!"

"Do you expect to contribute to her happiness by making a pointless effort to wean her away from the family ties she's known all her life?"

"Pointless? Why oppose it, then? If you're not afraid of me, why try to talk me out of it?"

"I'm thinking of her!"

"*I'm* thinking of her! She's my daughter!"

"Nonsense. All you did was fertilize an egg. In any real sense, you're less even than a stranger to her. You're an interloper!"

"How would you like to go to court about it, find out once and for all who has legal parentage, who is married to whom, settle the whole thing?"

"You couldn't arrange a better way to humiliate them

both! If that's what you want to do, take it to court by all means—sue for their love and affection! See what it wins you! Are you concerned for their happiness? Or your own self-esteem!"

They were bickering as noisily as the jays in the pines over their heads when Candelas found them.

He came up through the trees, staying under cover all the way and moving quietly. Holland might have seen him coming if he had not been so hotly preoccupied by the argument, but he had no attention for anything else and did not look up until Candelas said, "Hola," from the far side of the creek. Magill stopped shouting in the middle of a sentence, turning his head sharply in the direction of the greeting.

"It's me, patrón."

Candelas showed his strong yellow teeth in a grin. A ragged tear, scabbed by dried blood, marked the middle of his forehead, and he no longer carried the knapsack. Otherwise he was as they had seen him last, although in better temper.

"A good morning to you both, caballeros," he said. "What happened to you, Dutchman?"

"I broke my foot."

Holland was unprepared for the surge of feeling that washed through him. To reason with Magill that Candelas must have lived because it was logical for him to have lived was one thing; to see him alive and whole, grinning, was another thing altogether, and not only because his survival assured their own. Magill felt much the same emotion, from his more than usually sour response to Candelas' greeting.

"You took your time getting here," he grumbled. "What did you do, stop to finish off the absinthe bottle before you could find time for us?"

"Stopped to pick pieces of it out of my hide before they chewed me," Candelas said amiably. "You remember what I told you about the snowpack being good for tobogganing? Mother of Mary, I covered a good half of it on my face and the shards of the bottle! All the time I was running I couldn't decide whether the froggies had gone crazy and I'd better give up while I was still whole, or those two mierdas of the marqués had caught up with us and I'd better keep running while I was ahead of the game. Then the booze tripped me, and—cataplungún! I did the rest of it lying down, no trouble at all until I brought up against a tree with my head, as you see, and had to do a little crawling to get out of the light. By then I knew it was the froggies instead of the mierdas, so—"

"How did you know?" Holland was unable to resist the interruption.

"They didn't shoot while I was down and sprawling. So they were froggies, and when I heard them popping at you I knew you were off and running, too. All I had to do after that was pick broken glass out of my belly and open a new bottle to quiet my nerves."

"You could have tried to find us," Magill said.

"Patrón, what do you think of me?" Candelas was hurt. "I scouted the woods for an hour before I set out for Rancié. There was nothing else for me to do. You and the Dutchman had your blueprints. When I got there and found that you had not yet come, I stopped for no more than five minutes to talk with your señora, then—"

"Wait. My señora, at Rancié?"

"Yes, señor. Also the señorita. Also another American, a tall one. Also—also—"

The jays in the pines were unusually noisy. Candelas interrupted himself to curse them, unexpectedly and at length. But there was no heat in the cursing, only a recital of obscenities of diminishing filthiness, as if he were deflating a pressure built up too long. When he had exhausted himself he said, in good humor, "Also the marqués, who is now your señorita's novio. I am to tell you this for her, in case you have fear of him; that you need not fear him, because they are to be married as soon as marriage can be arranged. She knows the truth of the stain upon her mother, and how you erased it, and why it was that you had to leave Spain. She knows more than I do, now, because I am perhaps too stupid to understand how a man can be a friend, then an enemy, in the end a son-in-law. But for the love of God and his holy mercies, in simple words, patrón: From what have we been running all this time?"

Magill did not answer.

The jays screamed, the squirrel chattered, the creek made its small noises. Somewhere in the valley below them a church bell rang the hour. Holland's foot throbbed dully. He thought, It's a good question. From what have we been running all this time?

He lowered the foot carefully from the knapsack and began working off the boot.

IX

CANDELAS MADE a good mount; short-coupled, strong, sure-footed. He carried Holland without any apparent effort, towing the knapsack-sledge behind him by the belt of his coverall until the canvas of one of the packs wore through at last and loose cartons of cigarettes began to dot their back trail. When that happened he set his rider down on a fallen tree trunk while he went back to recover what had been lost, refusing to listen to a suggestion that the packs had served their purpose and might be abandoned without any great injury to the baron.

"A good businessman does not dump merchandise worth ten thousand pesetas by the roadside for the first peasant who stumbles on it to profit by," he said. "We have brought the stuff this far, we can move it a little farther. I'll shove the packs behind a bush until I get you off my back and can carry something worthwhile, Dutchman."

He was in great good humor, either because he had proved that they were inadequate without him or because the flight was done and he had no more need to worry about his patrón. He came back from hiding the knapsacks with the doll in his hand, grinning.

"Something of yours, señorito?" he asked Holland, heavily coy.

Holland took the doll without comment, stuffing it inside his shirt. The foot pained him less since he had got rid of the tight boot, but his head still ached and the jog of Candelas' steady downhill gait had not helped it. He was not in a mood for broad humor.

"Eh, patrón, have you smelled how sweetly the señorito stinks this morning?" Candelas rolled his eyes. "What have we been traveling with? These Dutch tulips—"

"Shut up!" Magill snapped. "You're not funny."

"I try. I try." Candelas still grinned, unabashed. "With two tongueless mourners like you for company, a man has to make his own humor. Come on, señorito. Up in the saddle again with your dolly. Two kilometers more and it's all over but sawing off the leg."

They were, as he had said, tongueless. They had not exchanged a word since hearing the news he had brought from Rancié. The silence between them was less a refusal to talk than an inability, on Holland's part at least. He was both defeated and indifferent to defeat. A part of his mind recognized the drugging effect of extreme fatigue and nerve strain for what it was, but even that part of his mind was indifferent. In an inert way he was glad that he didn't have to exert himself further, and that was all. He couldn't even care that he didn't care.

Two more kilometers, he thought emptily. His dull brain made the computation without instruction; two thousand meters times three point two eight equals six five six ought in feet; at two feet to the jog, three two eight ought jogs. He began to count Candelas' steps.

The count had passed three thousand before they stopped to look down from the brow of a hill into a clearing surrounding the ancient workings of Rancié. Half a dozen buildings, weathered gray and sagging, waiting for final ruin at the end of an overgrown trace of road that came into the clearing from the forest beyond it and ended in a rutted loop of turnaround at the foot of the hill where they stood. The old mine shaft ran into the hillside beneath them, and the tailing dumps that pointed to it were so old that grass had sodded them back into the configuration of the hillside. Two cars, Larry's scruffy Fiat and the big Mercedes with the Barcelona plates, were parked in the clearing. Larry stood by the Fiat morosely kicking at one of its tires. Nobody else was in sight until Micaela stepped quickly out of the Mercedes and came running up the hill slope to meet them.

Magill heard and recognized her coming before he could see her. He stopped, his arms held out to catch her, not faced in quite the proper direction, squinting to find her in his field of vision before she ran into his arms and caught him in her own hug. Neither of them spoke at first, until he said, angrily, "I lost my darn glasses again," and she, only half articulate, whispered, "Dad, dearest Dad, dearest, dearest Dad!" Holland did not have to listen to any more, or watch it. Candelas took him on down the hill, pacing off the last few jogs to the Mercedes and Marsha, who stood now by the car, waiting.

Larry and Carlos waited with her, to help him from Candelas' back to the seat of the Mercedes. He did not need help and tried to decline it, relieving the constraint of an impossibly difficult moment by asking them to let him manage for himself. Marsha poured him a welcome cup of hot coffee from a thermos.

"How bad is it, Andy?" she asked.

"I broke a bone in my foot. Nothing serious."

"We'd better get you to Montpellier. Unless there's a hospital nearer."

"It's not an emergency. Don't worry about it."

Still indifferent, he watched Magill and Micaela come down the hill, their arms around each other. His only feeling was a mild surprise at his own lack of jealousy. It failed to sting him, then or when Magill and Marsha came together in an embrace that spoke for their years of marriage. There was no passion in it, none of the show of ardor Marsha had made for his benefit in the airport at Nice, not much even of affecttion openly displayed. But they held each other closely for a moment—Larry's simile of the two halves of a broken plate came immediately to Holland's mind—and some kind of wordless communication passed between them before they stepped apart. Candelas, who had stopped to watch the embrace with more than passing interest, went on back up the hill to recover the cache of contraband. They had at least half an hour to wait for his return.

From the first moments of the half hour Holland was conscious of the same feeling that had come to him at Marsha's table during the evening of the gala; that he was watching her manipulate actors responsive to her direction in a scene of her choosing. The illusion of a stage performance was heightened by the fact that he among them was the only one not free to move about on the stage, so that he became the play's immobilized audience as well as one of its principals, and the lines were of necessity delivered for his benefit. He was lightheaded with fatigue and nerve strain. The illusion grew as Larry was brought forward to be introduced to Magill as an otherwise unclassified friend of Micaela's, then retired backstage to make way for Carlos in his new role as Micaela's fiancé. Larry's presence at the rendezvous, like Carlos', remained unexplained and undiscussed until Micaela refused to accept further the part assigned to her.

"I'm sorry, Mother," she said. "We have to talk. We can't just pretend that nothing has happened."

"I think we might talk on another occasion," Marsha said. "Mr. Holland's foot needs attention."

"Mr. Holland's foot will have to wait for Candelas in any event. We're all here together now, and we may never be all together like this again. I think it's important to—all of us—to know where we stand." Micaela looked uncertainly to Carlos for support. "Don't you?"

"I know where I stand with you," Carlos said. "Nothing else matters."

He and Holland had avoided looking at each other until then. Now their eyes met, and there was no triumph in Carlos' look. It held only hostility. Holland was puzzled by hostility after victory. Surely it was the right of the loser to hate the winner, not the other way around.

Micaela, still uncertain, said, "I know it's impertinent of me to—to make you all listen to me like this, but a lot of things have happened lately, some of them because of me, on my account, and it seems to me if I explain how I—feel about those things, you—we'd be honest with each other. I'm not being very clear about what I mean, I know." She took a deep determined breath. "I'm not going to talk about what happened to my mother, or what my father did about it, any of that, because it isn't my right. What is my right, I think—I hope—is to ask you a very personal question, Mr. Holland, and if it isn't important to you it's terribly important to me, so please don't just laugh instead of saying yes or no, which is all I want you to say. Are you in love with me?"

They all looked at him, waiting for his reply; Magill squinting, Marsha level-eyed, Carlos hostile, Larry curious, Micaela still uncertain of herself, embarrassed but determined to have her answer. Yes or no; a simple response to a simple, uncomplicated question, with five pairs of eyes on him each ready to read its own interpretation into whatever he said and no way back from it if he said the wrong thing. Yes or no.

"I can't answer quite that simply," he said. "My feelings for you require analysis and explanation."

"Are you in love with my mother?"

He looked at Marsha; undefeated, inviolate, invincible Marsha. No man would ever truly conquer her against her will. Not he, not her rapist, not even Magill. Martia Victoria, damn her, was as unbeatable as Kismet. Even when the lines weren't being read as she wanted them read.

He said, "As nearly as I can express it, I'm in love with a

part of both of you; something your mother once was to me, something you are going to be to somebody, some day. I wish I could put it more clearly, but I can't."

"Then for my part, I—I'm flattered, and I like you very much, at least I'm sure I would if I—if we knew each other better, but I don't love you, Mr. Holland. I couldn't ever love you. I'm sorry. I love Carlos. I'm going to marry him."

"I hope not," Holland said.

His own eyes looked back at him; his eyes in Marsha's face, now with the same open hostility in them that he had seen in Carlos'. He said, "It was your insistence that we be honest," then, to Marsha, "Haven't you had a chance to reason with her?"

"All last night. About differences in age, differences in religion, differences of interest, differences of social background. It made no impression. I couldn't penetrate beyond the fact that they think they're in love."

"We *are* in love!" Micaela turned to throw the challenge directly at her mother. "When you married my father, did you stop to think about differences of age, of religion, of interests, of social background? Or did you go ahead and marry him because you loved him?"

"You'd do better to ask me that question," Magill said. "I loved her. She took me as a matter of good judgment. She was in love with Andy Holland."

"That's not fair to any of us," Marsha said.

"We're being honest. And it proves the point I want to make for Mike. It's possible to begin without love, if you've got the other things that are necessary. Love can come into it afterward, as it did with your mother and me. By itself, without the rest, love is not enough. It doesn't leave you anything to fall back on when the novelty wears off."

"How begin without love?" It was a denial, not a question. "How can a man and a woman mean anything at all to each other without some kind of love between them?" Micaela turned to Larry, who stood looking somberly down at her from his height. "Has it really been nothing but big brother and little sister and good pals with us all along? Have we gone swimming and held hands in the movies and kissed good night without *any* feeling for each other, all these weeks?"

"I don't know," Larry said slowly. "That's as honest as I can say it. I just don't know. I thought I did until now, but I don't."

"You might consider an honest answer to a question for yourself," Holland said. "Are you going to marry a man who's been gambling with your father's life to win you?"

"You lie," Carlos said stonily. "I will shoot you for the lie as soon as you are fit to stand and face me."

"Shooting me won't answer the question, or take back the five hundred thousand pesetas you put up for his arrest."

"I told her why I did it. She will not be misled by you, as he was. She knows that he would never have come to harm through me. Arrest was a protection for him, not a danger. You were his danger."

"How much protection would arrest have given him against the garrote if you had not been there to stand between it and him?"

"I was there to stand between it and him."

"And if you had turned over on one of those blind curves that challenge you so irresistibly, caved in your skull instead of only a couple of ribs, what then?"

"My family—"

Carlos bit it off short. His lips were beginning to tremble as Holland had seen them tremble once before; not in weakness but in fury. He was incapable of justifying himself. Conciliation, excuse, explanation were beneath an hidalgo. To Micaela he said, not in appeal but in command, "Don't listen to them! They are trying to come between us with words! Listen to your heart!"

"Listen to me for another minute, first," Holland said.

"You may be able to hear your heart better afterward."

The hostility in her eyes was deeper than before. In the face of it, pausing from moment to moment to make certain of the words he would never be able to withdraw, he said, "A friend of the family can go only so far without becoming an enemy. It's a chance I have to take. Your father can't tell you this, nor your mother. You'd discount it from them, because you know they love you and love makes people distort the truth even when they don't mean to. I don't love you; not as you understand the word. I'm not jealous of Carlos. I only dislike and fear him. He's managed to convince you, somehow, that he would never have exposed your father to any real danger, because if he hadn't been able to convince you of that you wouldn't be speaking of him and love in the same breath. Maybe he even believes it himself, but it isn't true. Carlos has got to win, at all costs. You know that of him. You know the kind of man he is. He doesn't mean to run over the people who are in his way when his racer skids out of control, but they're dead just the same when it happens. As dead as he will be when he turns a car over for the last time, not meaning to. As dead as your father could have been if the trap set for him in Spain had got out of Carlos' control. He doesn't have to intend to sacrifice your father, or bystanders, or himself, or you, or your children, or anybody else who may stand between him and whatever goal he sets for himself. He just has to be Carlos." Holland closed his eyes, in fatigue and to escape what was, in her face, more than hostility, before he finished. "Now I'd like to go to Montpellier, if you don't mind driving me there, Larry. Candelas is coming down the hill. Please have him move me to your car as soon as he's done with the knapsacks."

He did not open his eyes until the transfer had been made. The headache was more easily bearable behind closed eyes, and by withdrawing in that way he had chosen his own moment to see the last of them. Or the last of all of them except Magill, who came over alone from the Mercedes, peering to find his footing in the ruts of the clearing.

In need of a shave, his thin hair uncombed, his wrinkled coverall still bristling with the pine needles in which he had slept, he looked rather like a badly put together scarecrow. To Candelas he said, "Better stay with him until he reaches a doctor. He may need an animal under him again," and, to Holland, awkwardly, "Should we wait for you in Marseille?"

"There's no point in it. They may keep me for a while at the hospital, and you won't need my help at the consulate. Everything is set up for you."

"Cannes, then."

"Of course."

"We'll want to talk, you and I and Marsha."

"About what?"

"Mike."

"If you're thinking about my views on the subject of her future, you needn't worry about those any more. I've changed my mind."

"I wasn't worried. Her future is what I wanted to talk to you about." A faint pink came into Magill's sallow cheeks. He looked quickly at Larry, waiting for orders behind the wheel of the Fiat, and was careful not to look at Candelas when he switched from English into rapid Spanish. "After all, you're her father."

He walked away.

It was minutes later before Candelas said thoughtfully, "So now I know."

The Mercedes had left the clearing. One hand, unidentifiable, had waved a good-by from it. Holland had raised his own hand in salute before the car disappeared into the forest.

"Now you know," he said. "If you respect him, don't repeat what you heard. You could make him sorry that he gave you his confidence."

"Eh, I'll not be around to provide him with reminders

that he did." Candelas kicked at a loose pine cone. "I'm going back up the mountain, Dutchman."

"He expects you to stay with him."

"I would, if he needed me. But now I have seen that he does not, and I think Paquita will have me back if I go humbly."

"How have you seen that he does not need you?"

"It's in the way a man embraces his woman." Candelas kicked again at the pine cone. "You understand, there are men who do not want a woman again when she has been possessed by another man. Not because it is the woman's fault, but because she is soiled. I saw them come together, and she is not soiled for him; neither by you nor by her violator. So I have no worry for him now, and can think of a woman of my own instead."

"Tell her for me that the animal is beginning to show signs of intelligence."

Candelas laughed, indicating Larry with a movement of his head. "How much would this one understand of castellano?"

"Enough," Larry said. "If you want to talk without me, I'll go for a walk."

"Not that. Only to explain that I made him a promise once, to show him a trick with the fingers that would be a surprise, and what is about to happen to him is only the promise being kept. Nothing personal." Grinning, Candelas held out his broad right hand. "Risk yours in that, Dutchman. Take a good grip."

Holland took a good grip; palm flat to palm, thumb well forward, his fingers closed on Candelas' before they could close on his. His own grip was a good one, and while he did not expect to be able to match strengths in a bone-crushing contest, neither did he intend to have a mangled hand to take to the hospital with a broken foot. He could be hurt, but not damaged.

Candelas still grinned. He said, "All set?"

"All set."

"Then we close the fingers, so, not too quickly, a little bit at a time, until the grip is met and equalized; then, still gripping, we move the hands together up and down, once, twice, three times, and the surprise is complete, true?" Candelas burst into a shout of melodious laughter at Holland's expression. "Holy Mother, if only you had been in shape for an abrazo, how I would have had you sweating for your ribs! So go with God, Dutchman, but remember that I kept my promises, and laughed last."

"Not quite," Holland said. He reached inside the coverall and his shirt for the buckle of the money belt, holding the doll that was with it from falling into his lap as he pulled the belt free. "Carry this back up the mountain with you. It's too heavy for me."

The amusement faded out of Candelas' face. He said roughly, "A joke is a joke. Don't mock me."

"I'm not mocking you. Take it."

"Then you're crazy."

"Nor crazy. Take it."

It was the same impulse that had come to him once before, but more than an impulse this time. He had a sudden pressing need to make his money important to someone. It meant nothing to him; it was too easy to come by, too hard to spend, valueless in a belt worn round the waist. It hadn't served as a weapon to beat Carlos, or help Magill, or win himself a wife and daughter, any of the things he had set out to do. He said, "If you don't want it, give it to Paquita for your children," and dropped the belt on the ground. As Candelas, still unbelieving, stooped to retrieve it, Holland motioned quickly to Larry. The Fiat's starter ground, the noisy motor thundered, they were bumping off across the ancient ruts of the clearing into the shadow of the forest. He did not turn his head to look back.

Some time later Larry said, "It's still none of my business,

I suppose."

"I don't know. It depends. Are you in love with her?"

"I answered that."

"Try again."

Larry sighed.

"I guess maybe I am. At least, when I think of her marrying Carlos, it grinds my guts. If that's love."

"Give her this, then." Holland took the necklace from his shirt pocket. "Today's her birthday. You needn't tell her where it came from."

"Isn't it a pretty valuable trinket to give a girl who has just become engaged to another man?"

"Valuable enough to show her you mean business. She may want to fall back on that when she breaks the engagement."

"You sound pretty confident that she will."

"I am."

"Since we agree that I'm an interested party, why? I'd like to believe that you're right, but I could use a little more evidence to go on."

"She can't do any less. What I told her was the truth, and she's wise enough even at her age to recognize the truth when it's made inescapable. It's not in her nature to continue to love a man whose ego is more important to him than her father's existence. Her own is less important."

"By 'father,' in this case, you mean Harry Magill."

"It's time we both began thinking of him that way."

"Women have managed before now to divide themselves between a lover and a father, even where there's a conflict."

"I doubt if it has ever been true when the conflict is irreconcilable. Either Carlos has got to stop being Carlos, an impossibility for him, or she's got to stop being Harry Magill's daughter, an impossibility for her. The break may take a few days, but it will come. Be sure you're around when it happens. There's nothing like catching them on the rebound."

"Carlos could still have Magill extradited."

"Perhaps. But that would destroy any remaining hope he might have of winning Mike, and long before he gets around to thinking of extradition again, even as a revenge, Magill will be in a position to protect himself from it. Carlos has lost the race without learning that it's over."

Ten or fifteen kilometers rolled by under the Fiat's wheels. The interval carried them down off the mountain slope and out of the forestland, into rolling open country where enormous vineyards stretched for miles between foothills and flatland. The road ran straight and wide through the rows of vines, and at that early hour there was little traffic. Driving required a minimum of thought from Larry, and no concentration.

"When did you change your mind?" he asked. "About telling her, I mean."

"I may tell her yet, some day. When it's safe."

"Safe?"

"Right now a direct emotional tug-of-war between Magill and Carlos is essential. Injecting myself into it would only serve to split her loyalties on the side that ought to be reinforced. Was it she who told Carlos we were coming over the mountains last night?"

"You do your daughter an injustice."

"It's a fair question. The French border patrol wasn't waiting for us in the pass only by accident."

"The Spanish ambassador to Paris asked for French cooperation against Andorran smuggling almost a week ago. Enough pressure was put on to get action within a few days. All the passes have been blocked and guarded since."

"It seems that I did the Vilasars an injustice, too."

"Mike sent you, or I should say she tried to send Magill, a telegram last night, telling you that Carlos had you bottled and not to try it. The only way it could go up the mountain was by telephone, and the line was out."

"It doesn't sound like Carlos to tell her he had us bottled."

"He told her all there was to tell, as far as he knew it. To force a showdown. About the rape, the killing, all of it, including what you had said to him about her father being against him. She asked her mother to deny that it was so, and her mother couldn't, or wouldn't. I wasn't there when it happened, but I heard about it afterward. The rugs got pretty well beaten out."

"How did you become involved?"

"Mike asked Carlos to bring her to meet Magill. I guess Mrs. Magill didn't feel like accepting any more favors from him after she had told him the truth of her own feelings about him as a husband for Mike, so she asked me. That's all."

They did not talk again before Montpellier. Holland dozed, off and on, although the pain in his foot still kept him from sliding over the edge into real sleep. Marsha's perfume was strong on his clothes where he had spilled some of it, but the odor that had always been enough to conjure up her picture, bright and clear on the screen of his mind, had lost its effect. The screen would not come to life. His only reaction to the fragrance was a faint nausea at the memory of the taste of rotting roses.

At Montpellier a hospital attendant gave him coffee and brought him an extension telephone while X-ray films were being developed. It was by then nearly the middle of the day. If the baron still waited for his call, it could only be that he had not received a report of the French blockade from some other source, an improbability. But the promise had been asked for and given; Holland could do no less than make an attempt to keep it. He was surprised to have the call go quickly through. "Oh, you haven't kept me waiting," the baron said cheerfully, when he had listened to an explanation and apology. "I've been on the phone all morning negotiating to buy my men back from the French police. Your party was the only one that got through."

"Anybody hurt?"

"Except for yourself, no, fortunately. It appears that the French have taken over the Spanish technique of firing warning shots in the air, and all the carriers who went out last night had had experience on the Spanish side of the mountains. They gave themselves up like real caballeros."

"The French still aren't shooting to do damage, if the information is of any value."

"That they might do so is a risk I can't ask my men to take. No, the contraband industry will have to be reorganized." The baron laughed. "But it has happened before this, and to tell the truth I welcome the challenge. Things were getting dull up here."

"Candelas is on his way back to make them less dull."

"Thanks to God. Paquita has been raining teardrops to muddy trout streams. When will you be coming back?"

"It's hard to say. Not in the immediate future."

"It's still your house, whenever you want it."

"Thanks. I'll remember. Until then."

"Until then," the baron said.

The X-rays showed a clean small crack in the bone of the instep. The doctor who examined the films saw no need for hospitalization. He fitted Holland with a cast and crutches which, he said, could be replaced by a cast and walking-iron within a few days. He charged nothing for the medical treatment, a reasonable bill for X-rays and crutches that Holland was unable to pay. He had only a few francs in his clothes; no dollars, no pesetas, nothing even of possible trading value except a wrist watch and the doll inside his shirt. Larry volunteered a loan, and bought the good lunch they had before setting out for Cannes.

They ordered only a single bottle of wine with the lunch, but Larry declined to take more than a small glass on the grounds that more would make him sleepy. Holland drank the rest of it, for the same reason. It cured what remained of his hangover, and with the good food and the action of the sedative that had been injected into his foot at the hospital brought on such a strong euphoria that he suspected the nature of the sedative. He felt well, relaxed, content, unencumbered, free of concern; like a good Moslem in the bosom of Allah, he thought, although good Moslems didn't find the bosom of Allah in the best part of a bottle of wine for lunch, with the possible exception of his Turkish friend at La Belle Poitrine. Settled once again behind the Fiat's monotonously roaring motor, drowsily watching the towns and farms of the neat French countryside slide by, he considered the Turk's offer, and Anatolia.

There was a good job to be done there; a big job, an important job. There would be important money in it, too, although money was not an incentive. Part of the euphoria stemmed from having got rid of the money belt. It had cramped him, like a too tight corset. A lot of things had been cramping him that cramped him no more. In his state of peaceful, slightly drunken drowsiness, he felt not a twinge of regret, no sense of defeat or loss. Looking back was profitless, looking forward pleasant.

Who had it been who said a man's needs could be boiled down to three essentials: something to do, something to look forward to, someone to love? He had two of them; no, all three. Magill had Marsha and Micaela, but he still had his own creation, Marsha-Micaela. She was neither one nor the other. He considered Marsha-Micaela, trying to bring her into focus, but the effort was too much. Comfortably, peacefully, he slept.

Cessation of movement and motor noise woke him, hours later. It was early evening. They had arrived in Cannes, where La Belle Poitrine's doorman was doing his best to give proper reception to a guest arriving with no luggage except a pair of crutches and the doll that had worked its way out of his shirt while he slept. The doorman held doll and car door while Holland found his balance on the unfamiliar crutches.

"Anything more I can do?" Larry asked.

"Two things. Let Mike know that you've seen the light, and book me a seat on a plane for Istanbul. The first when it seems appropriate, the second as soon as possible."

"Tomorrow?"

"A little too soon. The day after."

"It will have to be the day after that. We don't have a daily flight."

"Good enough. Send the ticket to me here. I'll mail you a check."

"Round trip?"

"One way."

"That's pretty definitive, isn't it?" Larry said, and added quickly, clumsily, "Not that it's any of Pan American's business. We just like to sell those round trips, when we can."

"I'd stay if I thought I could help you with Mike, but it's up to you, now. You needn't let her or the Magills know that I'm leaving quite so soon."

They shook hands. Larry said, "It's nice having her father on my side, anyway. I'll give it everything I've got, Mr. Holland, and if she'll have me I'll make her glad she did or break my neck trying. And I don't mean in the Mille Miglia."

He drove away in a roar of controlled power.

Barot was at his desk in the lobby, barricaded behind the protective photographs of his wife and children. He said, "But mon cher! What have you been doing with yourself? You look like a fugitive from the film festival," and sniffed, delicately. "The scent is perhaps a bit overdone."

"I'm about to take care of it." Holland swung toward the elevator that waited for him. "Did my bag arrive from Barcelona?"

"It's in your room. Also a magnum of champagne, with the compliments of your friend in the tarboosh."

"Why champagne?"

"He did not confide in me."

"Is that discretion, or don't you know?"

"I could hazard a guess."

"Please do."

"You are perhaps about to enter into some kind of an arrangement that calls for a toast to its success?"

"We have been talking contract, yes. But it hasn't reached the toasting stage yet."

"Voilà," Barot said, and shrugged. "I could be mistaken. Occasionally I am."

The champagne remained a puzzle, more puzzling because of the card that was with it. The Turk had written, in his bad French, *Congratulation and all best successes*. The wine was a good vintage, good enough to toast the signing of any contract. But they had not yet signed anything; in fact, he had not even committed himself to signing, as far as the Turk knew. He rang for a bucket of ice, but changed his mind before the sommelier arrived. A magnum was too much wine to open without company. He ordered coffee instead, then called the Turk's room. There was no answer.

The floor valet helped him off with his clothes. He gave himself a careful sponge bath, washed his hair, and scrubbed his hands and nails with more than ordinary care. Afterward he shaved, rang for another coffee and smoked a cigar while he composed a note to Marsha.

It took him three false starts to discover that he had only one thing of consequence to say to her. On a piece of notepaper from which he first tore the hotel's letterhead he wrote, in Spanish: *This is my permission, in accordance with the laws of Peru, for my wife, Marsha Holland, to leave Peru as and when she wishes, for as long as she wishes, for whatever purpose she wishes,* and signed it. Then, calculating backward eighteen years and the duration of a pregnancy, he predated it from Iquitos. It could be challenged, but nobody would ever challenge it. To himself he repeated the Arabic formula three times—I divorce thee, I divorce thee, I divorce thee—that was all a Moslem needed to cast off a wife.

Much could be said for Mohammedanism, he thought, in good humor and peace of mind, and telephoned the Turk's room. There was still no answer.

He called the valet again to give him the clothes he had worn since Andorra; everything, down to socks and underwear. He told the man to burn them or salvage them as he saw fit, but in no event to bring them back. When that was done he had freed himself of everything to connect him with what had taken place since his discovery of Micaela's existence, except for the cast on his foot and the doll. The cast, for the moment, was beyond his control. The doll was not.

He asked the telephone operator to put him through to Mademoiselle Solière's suite, and occupied himself while he waited for the call in reshaping the doll's stuffed body where it had been distorted by its travels inside the knapsack and his shirt. It was remarkable how much it resembled Odile, even to pink fingernails and the golden tint of its skin. He thought, *Maybe I should have given it to Carlos instead, as a consolation prize,* but thinking of Carlos spoiled his mood. He closed his mind to Carlos except as it was necessary to think about him in connection with Odile.

Odile herself, not the maid, was on the phone when it rang back. Her soft voice was unmistakable. He said, "Andy Holland. May I see you for a few minutes? I brought you something from Andorra."

"Of course. Where shall we meet, and when?"

"If you don't mind the inconvenience, here, in my room." He gave her the number and explained about the foot. "I'm not very good with the crutches yet. In half an hour, if you're free?"

"I'm free," the soft voice said. "In half an hour."

He put on a robe and made himself presentable. The crutches were a nuisance, but he could get around on them. Ringing again for the sommelier, he ordered ice and glasses, and when the wine was chilling in its silver bucket, placed the doll where Odile would have to see it the moment she entered the room.

She was, as always, immediately sensitive to his mood. She laughed in delight at the gift, and took it to a mirror to try to copy its expression, ruffling her own wine-pale hair to match the doll's ruffled mop.

"It's prettier than I am, but thank you for seeing the resemblance," she said. "Thank you, also, for your roses."

"Was Carlos properly jealous of the note?"

He thought the laughter went out of her face for a moment, but he was seeing it in the mirror and could not be sure. She was smiling when she turned away from the mirror. He decided that it had been no more than a trick of light.

"Very jealous," she said.

"Good. I'm not going to be around for long to keep him that way, but I think you'll have a clear field with him from now on. At least I hope so."

"Would you like to tell me the reason for your hope, m'sieur?"

He had not meant to confide in her. But she was such a good listener once he had begun to talk, so expressive of interest with eyes and lashes and pretty mobile mouth, asking the right questions at the right moment to lead him, not probing, that in the end he told her the whole story. The Turk's champagne might have helped to loosen his tongue, but he did not believe it. He did not drink enough of it to affect him while he talked, and drunk or sober, he had not exposed the bare nerve of a personal confidence in more years than he could remember. It took him an hour of almost uninterrupted narrative to tell it all.

"So you see," he ended, "she isn't going to marry Carlos, but the affair as it stands may drag on longer than it should. For her to find out that he was keeping a mistress, had in fact acquired a mistress almost under her nose at the same time he was courting her, would hurry the break between them. It will also eliminate her as competition for you. Will you help yourself and me by making my daughter aware of your existence?"

She was holding a glass of champagne in one petal-tipped hand, the doll in her lap with the other. At the question she looked down at the wine, as if uncertain whether to drink or not. Then, almost inaudibly, she said, "I would help if I could, m'sieur. But I am not the marqués' mistress. I have never been his mistress."

He did not know what to say. The denial was so stunning, so completely contradictory of all he knew to be true, that he could not find words before she went on, still low-voiced, "He wanted me to be. I would have accepted him, if you had not sent me the roses with your message. The day they arrived, the same hour, I wrote to tell him that I had changed my mind; that I was going to—wait."

"Oh, my God!" he said.

She sat quite still watching him, waiting, the untouched wine in one hand, the doll under the other. He got awkwardly to his feet, reaching for the crutches. The room had a small exterior balcony overlooking esplanade, beach and sea where the night breeze always blew, and he felt the need for fresh air. The champagne had been more potent than he thought.

He felt exhilarated and reckless, as he had felt on the corniche after the shock of fear had worn off. He was conscious of another kind of vulnerability, something he had almost forgotten he knew. From the sheltering darkness of the balcony he said, "And the suite? The maid?"

"I moved out of the suite and told the maid to go."

"Didn't you realize the purpose of the note?"

"I thought it might have meant what it said."

"And if it did not?"

"Then you owe me nothing, m'sieur. I have made mistakes before now."

She put down the wine glass, still without having drunk from it, and stood up. He could not see her expression as she bent to place the doll in the chair where she had been sitting, but there was no reproach in her face when she looked toward the balcony afterward; slim, pretty, poised, desirable, the golden kitten who would always land on her feet, always find a lap open to her; if not his, somebody's. As she had said, he owed her nothing.

"Thank you for the champagne," she said politely. "Please don't come to the door with me."

"Sit down. I have to think. I wasn't prepared for this."

"I thought you might prefer to be left alone."

"I don't, at this point. How old are you?"

"Twenty-one."

"You told him—" she could not see his gesture toward the champagne, but it was not necessary— "that you were too young for the gambling rooms. If you tell me one lie, they can all be lies."

"That was two weeks ago. Your daughter is not the only one to have birthdays."

"Have you gone to the casino with him?"

"I have gone nowhere with him, m'sieur. Although he has invited me to Anatolia, and other places."

"What reason did you give him for refusing?"

"The same reason I gave the marqués."

"Either one of them has more money than I'll ever have."

"If you had no money, I would not have waited. That is the truth, because you have asked me for truth. But if you had much less than I know you have, I would still have said no to both of them until you had told me that the note did not mean what it said."

"What would you expect of me besides money?"

She had not sat down when he told her to. Now, standing, under cross-examination, she lost some of her poise. For the first time since he had known her she seemed to be in need of something more than her own resources when she said, slowly, "He talked to me about Anatolia, what it is like. He told me of the color of the water in the bay at Antalya, and camel trains, and dancing bears with flowers behind their ears. It sounded like a wonderful place to go, to be, with someone. Not just anyone, but someone. He said—"

"I'm an engineer. I go down into holes in the ground and come up with mud in my hair. There's more of that in my life than dancing bears with flowers behind their ears."

"—he said that he would offer you a contract, perhaps for a year, perhaps for two years, however you wanted it, and at the end of that time he would hope to be able to hold you because the work you were doing would hold you; that it was the kind of work a man like you could not leave for another man to finish. He said it was the only kind of contract you would sign, so you could withdraw from it when you wished, but that he did not think you would want to withdraw from it." She looked down at her hands, which she held clasped together in front of her, then up again at the darkness that protected him on the balcony. "I would not ask better terms for myself, if I were going to Anatolia."

He cursed the broken foot, silently. It was damnable to be crippled when contracts were under discussion. It left no approach but the straightforward. A man couldn't maneuver. On crutches, he couldn't even walk out on the negotiations.

"The Turk is going to regret it," he said. "He's made me a sharper bargainer than I thought I knew how to be. Come out here on the balcony."

She came to stand at his elbow. A crutch leaned against the parapet between them, but he was strongly aware of her nearness and his own new vulnerability. His feeling of recklessness and exhilaration grew.

Below the balcony a bright double strand of lights outlining the esplanade swung in a long swoop between casino and casino around the curve of beach where he had first seen her and Micaela. The loop of lights was like a necklace against the darkness of the Mediterranean. It made him think of the necklace he had bought in Andorra, but even then, with the gleam of it in his eyes, he could not visualize the throat it would clasp, the face above it, anything of her. He could no longer look back even when he made the effort. Looking ahead—

He did not want to look ahead. Not then; not for a while. He had only just caught up with the present, and the pleasure of the moment, of living in it and for it, was too good to give up. He needed more time. He needed much more time. Temporizing, he said, "What would you like for your birthday?"

"You have already given me the doll, m'sieur."

"It's hardly appropriate. Something more in keeping with the occasion. What does a woman grown want most for a birthday gift?"

"Whatever it pleases a man to give her, m'sieur."

She was not helping him. She waited for the answer he had given her the right to expect: Yes or No. She would accept either gracefully, he knew. But Yes and No were fetters, and once you had chosen one of them, rightly or wrongly, you were locked to it beyond escape. Marsha had taught him that, by forcing the choice upon him when he had not meant to choose. Micaela had asked him for Yes or No, and believed it an equivocation when he had been unable to choose. Magill had convinced him of the need for thought before choosing. Candelas had shown him how and where hard choice between Yes and No became inescapable, Paquita the reward for a correct choice, Carlos the dangers of wrong choice, Larry the penalty for hesitating to choose. On the corniche, for one moment, he had known what it was like not to be faced with Yes or No. Given no choice, it had been the one moment of his life in which he could not have made a mistake.

He said, "Bring the champagne, then. I'll give you a birthday toast."

She went obediently to bring the wine glasses; her own still untouched, his refilled for the third or fourth time. He could not remember ever before finding so much exhilaration in a few glasses of champagne. It was like standing on the corniche all over again, after the fear and depression had left him. Watching her turn from the table to come back to him, the glasses sparkling in her careful hands, he had no faint ghost of an idea what the toast would be when he gave it. But he knew it would come to him right, and at the right moment. He thought, expectantly: *Insha'Allah*.

CPSIA information can be obtained
at www.ICGtesting.com
Printed in the USA
LVOW11s0745290517
536140LV00007B/655/P

9 780988 306288